LAST GIRL

LIED TO

L.E. FLYNN

【Imprint】
MAKE YOUR MARK

NEW YORK

[Imprint]
MAKE YOUR MARK

A part of Macmillan Publishing Group, LLC
175 Fifth Avenue, New York, NY 10010

ISBN 978-1-250-15813-0 (hardcover) / ISBN 978-1-25015812-3 (ebook)

Our books may be purchased in bulk for promotional, educational, or business use.
Please contact your local bookseller or the Macmillan Corporate and
Premium Sales Department at (800) 221-7945 ext. 5442 or by email at
MacmillanSpecialMarkets@macmillan.com.

Book design by Elynn Cohen

Imprint logo designed by Amanda Spielman

First edition, 2019

1   3   5   7   9   10   8   6   4   2

fiercereads.com

Some things aren't meant to be stolen.
Boys.
Hearts.
Secrets.
Books.
If you borrow this book, return it to its rightful owner.
Or else something of yours might just go missing too . . .

For my mom, the best woman I know.
I want to be you when I grow up.
(How am I doing?)

WHEN I FIRST met you, that stupid-hot day last September when you jumped into my car and slid down in the passenger seat and told me to drive, you were bleached blond. You had a pixie cut with dark roots, the kind of hair that was less a hairstyle and more a lifestyle. You were wearing too much eyeliner and had a ring in your lip and I never said it out loud, but I thought you were beautiful. Not in the regular way, but in your own way. And that was so much better.

You looked the exact same, day after day. You used to bleach your head every two weeks in your tiny bathroom at home. You asked me to trim your ends for you because you sucked at getting them even.

"My hair has to be short," you told me. "It's too damaged to grow out. I wish I had long hair like yours, but some things aren't meant to be."

"You can have mine," I said. "It's too thick. I hate it." Really, I would have given you anything of mine you wanted.

Then, right after you graduated, just days after I watched you walk across the stage with your diploma and away from me, you showed up at my house with a stubby ponytail. A stubby, mouse-brown ponytail. I could tell by your smudged hairline that you had just done it on your own.

I barely recognized you.

"I never pictured you as a brunette," I said.

"I wanted to try it," you said. "Haven't you ever just been so sick of yourself that you had to do something about it?"

The next week, your hair was copper, with choppy bangs that you must have cut yourself. You didn't ask for my help, but I tried not to feel hurt. "It was a spontaneous thing," you explained. "I saw the dye and just went for it."

Two weeks later, it was black, with long extensions you said you bought on the internet. "I'm trying new things," you told me when I finally asked why. "It's time for a change."

After that, I didn't think much about it when you had a new look. Purple hair and streaked hair and bangs and bobs and curls and clip-in pieces. Then you started playing with makeup too, ditching your beloved, sooty eyeliner for false eyelashes and color contacts, and your lip ring for bright red lipstick that got on your teeth. I lost track of which version of you I would see, even though I saw you every single day that summer.

But I didn't think much about it, because lots of girls do things like that.

I didn't think much about it.

But I should have.

Because when you disappeared after the party, the police asked me for a description of you. They needed a description because they didn't have a recent photo. They didn't have a recent photo because no recent photos of you existed. You stayed out of pictures. You didn't think you were photogenic.

"I always look weird in front of the camera," you'd said.

"Besides, I'd rather just live in the moment. Why do people feel the need to document everything?"

I should have known you better than anyone.

But when they asked me, I squeezed my eyes shut and tried to stop the room from spinning long enough to picture what you looked like, and I realized I had no idea.

2

WHAT I REMEMBER about that night: everything that matters.

What I tell them I remember about that night: everything that doesn't matter.

I know lying is wrong, but isn't breaking your promises worse? There's something about a promise that's more important. A permanent tie to somebody else. A signature scrawled in the air, pinpricked thumbs pressed together. Swallowing someone else's desperation. Hiding someone's biggest mistake. Speaking the three most important words in the English language:

I'll never tell.

So, as bad as I feel about lying to the cops about the night Trixie disappeared, it feels more natural than the alternative. And that's the thing about choices: When you put them on either side of a scale, they never weigh the same.

One is bound to be heavier.

3

YOU WERE THE one who insisted we go to Alison's party, which was out of character, since you didn't even like Alison. You didn't like any of the people we went to school with.

Trixie had graduated in June and couldn't wait to get away from them, from everything. I still had another year to go, and the thought of not having her there was something I was dancing around, even weeks before school started.

"It'll be fun," she insisted, dropping her backpack on my comforter and yanking her shirt over her head. "Plus, it'll be open bar. Let's just drink our faces off and celebrate."

Celebrate what? I wanted to ask. But I didn't.

I watched her open her backpack and pull another shirt out, a brown tank top. She stood in front of my mirror and shrugged it on. Trixie would have looked good in anything, so I wondered why she was wearing that to the party—an oversized top the color of shit with JERSEY GIRL across the front in blocky white lettering. Her skinny arms poked out of the too-big armholes and I could see her bra underneath. It wasn't even a cute bra, just one of those nude ones you buy to wear under white shirts.

"What are you going to wear?" she asked, straddling my desk chair.

"I don't know. I hate everything in my closet. It's all so ugly."

"What are you talking about? Your clothes are the best."

The truth was, I was afraid to try on most of my clothes. I had always hated something about my body—my thighs, my hips, my broad shoulders—more because girls are predisposed to be at war with their bodies than for any real reason. But over the summer, I knew I had put on weight and I was too scared to stand on the scale and find out how much. As long as I didn't know the number, I could convince myself it was all in my head.

"I'll find you something," she said, standing up and putting her hands on her hips. "Do you trust me?"

"Of course," I mumbled. "Just something boring though, okay? I don't want to dress up."

Trixie opened my closet and started rifling through my clothes. I felt a pang when I saw everything on hangers, ironed and color-coded and neglected. Bright yellow sundresses. Tank tops with skinny straps. Jeans that used to hug me in all the right places. Denim miniskirts. My cheerleading uniform, the one I never returned like I was supposed to. I stared at the clothes like they were old friends I didn't know anymore. I used to love getting dressed up, even if I wasn't going anywhere. I'd buy fabric and try to make my own clothes that I imagined people would stop me on the street and ask about. But nobody ever did, except Trixie.

"You have such good stuff in here," she said, twisting around to look at me. "Why don't you ever wear it?"

"I don't know. I just feel like nothing suits me." *Or fits me.*

"You could always make something new. Go buy another sewing machine. Right? You're so freaking talented."

"Maybe," I said, staring down at my legs, which had barely seen the sun all summer.

I didn't try to make clothes anymore because I didn't know how to dress this girl, the pale one who looked back at me in the mirror, the one with a sloppy auburn bun on top of her head who felt doughy and stretched out in her own skin. My summer uniform was made up of forgiving long skirts and baggy T-shirts. Fashion had become an afterthought.

"This one," Trixie said, pulling out the one item of clothing I was avoiding the most. The red dress I was supposed to wear to Alison's party last summer, almost a full year ago. "You should wear this one."

"Isn't it kind of fancy? You're not dressed up."

"Maybe I'll change later. You should definitely wear it, though. Who knows, right? You might meet the love of your life tonight."

I already have, and he doesn't care, I wanted to say, but instead I just grabbed the hanger, my face flaming, and made my way to the bathroom. I tried to step into the dress, but it wouldn't fit over my butt. I tried pulling it over my head and my heart leaped when it managed to go over my shoulders. I had this thought, this one, confident thought. *Maybe I worried for nothing.* I tugged it down around my stomach, ignoring the film of sweat on my skin.

Then I felt the back rip.

Tears stung my eyes. I bit my lip and counted backward from ten. I didn't want to cry. Not with Trixie in the next room. Not when she had never cried, not about anything, not ever.

"It doesn't fit," I said, trying to keep my voice from wavering. "I'll find something else."

"Just wait a sec. I'm coming in."

She never knocked. Which was ironic, because the one time I snuck up behind her when she was hunched over her computer, she flipped out. It was the only time I ever saw her angry. "You have to respect people's space," she had muttered. But she inhabited my space.

I took the beer she offered as she barged in and drank it while she fastened the back of the dress from the inside with a hidden safety pin and fixed my hair so the rip wouldn't be noticeable. I marveled over the power she had. The power to turn everything around, to make me feel like the most beautiful girl in the world. I hadn't just grown bigger since I met her. I had grown out of everything that used to be important to me, everything I used to think mattered. My old life didn't fit anymore. I had grown into somebody Trixie called a best friend.

"See, it fits just fine. You look hot. I wish I was a redhead so I could look this good in red. You'll be fighting guys off tonight." She slid her feet into her well-worn flip-flops.

"You could pull off red hair," I said. "You've tried pretty much every other color. I can help you dye it."

"No," she said. "It's more your thing. Let's go."

I drank another beer on the way to the party as we walked to Alison's house, Trixie's backpack bumping against the small of her back with each step she took. Her shoulders sagged under the weight. I wondered why she was bringing a backpack to the party at all.

"I can carry that for a while if you want," I said. "It looks heavy. What's in there?"

"I've got it," she said. "And it's just a bunch of extra beers. In case this party has a shortage and we need some entertainment."

But whatever was in there wasn't clanking around like beers would. *Why would she lie about that?* Still, I dropped it.

Later, the police asked me about the backpack.

It was black. It had white trim. It was the same one she brought to school. She said it was full of beer.

But what I remember most was the red dents it left in her shoulders.

Of course, I didn't tell the police about the red dents. I told them that Trixie and I left the party around the same time and went our separate ways because she told me she had plans with her dad in the morning and couldn't sleep over at my place.

I didn't tell them how my vision was blurry when Trixie shoved an ice cube down my back. I was holding a drink in my hand and the shock of the ice cube on my skin made me fling my cup. Red liquid spraying in the air—something sweet and strong—misting over Trixie's shirt before coming to land on cream-colored carpet and blooming like crimson inkblots.

I'm sure it wasn't funny. It wouldn't be funny when Alison saw it, or when her parents came home and found evidence that their daughter threw a party big enough for a spill like that to go unnoticed.

It wasn't funny, but Trixie laughed. She shook her head and put her hands on my shoulders.

"Oh, Fiona," she said with this long, drawn-out sigh. "What am I going to do with you?"

Those were the last words Trixie said to me, and they didn't sound like a goodbye. I had said goodbye to Trixie a hundred times, in a hundred different places. Her goodbye was always the same. A peace sign, hand tossed over her head. A promise to call me later.

She really did tell me she had plans with her dad in the morning.

But I didn't leave the party with her.

Two days after the party, when the police talked to that guy on the beach and found what Trixie left behind, I realized what she really meant. I finally heard what I should have heard that night.

She said: "What am I going to do with you?"

But she meant: "What am I going to do without you?"

MOM MAKES ME eat breakfast on the first day of school, even though I feel sick. She plops a bowl of something that looks like birdfeed in front of me and tells me to finish it.

"I know the last three weeks have been rough," she says. "But this is a fresh start. Your senior year. I want you to go in with a clean slate and take every opportunity you can. You only get to have one senior year."

This is the part where her eyes get all misty, the part where I'm the elephant in the room because it's my fault Mom never had a proper senior year. It's my fault she had to finish high school from home. Because she got pregnant with me when she was sixteen and my grandma pulled her out of school. When I first became a cheerleader, Mom was so excited. She came to all the basketball games in the smelly gym and sat on the hard bleachers during football season just to watch me sing stupid Robson game chants and throw girls in the air. Mom hated Trixie because she thinks Trixie took me away from all that. Although that's not the way she phrased it. When she brought it up, she was "worried I was impressionable." Like I was a wad of clay, not a girl.

I force myself to swallow a mouthful of the seedy substance in my bowl. It's sandpaper scratching the back of my throat.

"Remember, we're seeing Dr. Rosenthal after school." Mom stands up. "I'm supposed to have a meeting at four, but I'll cut it short and meet you there."

I don't want to see Dr. Rosenthal. He's a psychologist who specializes in teen issues, which makes me wonder if he never outgrew his. I'm not sure if Mom wants me to talk to him so badly because I put on weight or because I have a dead best friend or maybe both.

"You've been through a lot of emotional trauma," she said before she called to book the appointment. "Talking to someone will help you get back on track."

All I heard was *You're disgusting. You're not good enough anymore. You let yourself go.*

She opens her mouth to say something else, but her cell phone rings and she answers it right away. When I was little, Mom stayed home with me, in a tiny one-bedroom apartment my grandma paid for. But when I got a bit older, just being a mom and working at the grocery store part-time wasn't enough for her, so she went to college and got a business degree and a job at a marketing firm. Now she travels all the time for work. It used to be just a random day here or there, but now it's sometimes weeks. And two months in Tokyo in the summer. She wanted my aunt Leslie to come and stay with me, but I protested, told her seventeen was old enough to be home by myself. I reminded her that in a year, I'd be in a whole different city, maybe even state, on my own anyway.

Trixie helped me convince her. "Tell her you'll call her to check in all the time. Tell her it'll be a lesson in independence. Use those exact words. Parents eat that shit up."

Trixie was a good liar. Now I am too. I wonder if lying works like that—if it's contagious, a disease. I never used to lie to Mom about anything, but after I met Trixie, I became a liar by association. I told myself they were just fibs and that Mom didn't need to know everything about my life. But it was more than that.

"You know, I can drive myself after school," I say, letting my spoon fall into my bowl with a clatter. "You should just go to your meeting."

Mom's forehead creases. "You sure, honey?"

I nod. "I'm sure."

I dread seeing Dr. Rosenthal. I know he's just going to ask all the wrong questions. He'll want to probe my brain and try to find the scientific cause for why I'm unraveling, which should be a relief. But he thinks this is all happening because of what I put inside my body, who I chose to let inside my life.

And maybe the problem isn't who I let in, but who was already there.

5

I DON'T KNOW how long it took us to become best friends. Two weeks, maybe. Two hours. Or maybe it was in the first two minutes after you hopped into my car, when all I felt was this rush of possibility.

The funny thing is, I never should have met Trixie Heller.

I should have been at cheerleading practice, on the bottom of the pyramid. Coach Hogan liked to call me her powerhouse. "Look at those strong legs," she used to say. She meant it as a compliment. But all I wanted was to be like my best friend, Jenny. The kind of girl who fit perfectly under any guy's arm. The kind of girl who could date any guy she wanted.

The kind of girl who wanted to date the one guy I told her I loved.

Ten minutes before I met Trixie, Jenny and I were heading for the gym. I was walking. Jenny was doing that annoying bounce-walk thing she did, as if life was so great that she couldn't bear to walk normally. Later, when Trixie said that walk made Jenny resemble a demented duck, I could have kissed her.

I was already pissed off at Jenny. Not because of her loud

voice or little snub nose or perky butt or the fact that she barely ever let me get a word in edgewise. I was irritated because we couldn't even have a conversation anymore without Toby Hunter's name coming up. But that day, she said another name that made my breath catch in my throat—Beau Hunter.

"He asked me out," she said, her words rushed. "It's not like I could say no. I mean, the guy's brother just—well, you know. Offed himself."

I knew. Of course I knew. Everyone in Morrison Beach knew what Toby Hunter had done, and half of them had their own theories about it. But Jenny knew my truth. I thought about that night, which was long before I knew Trixie, when Jenny and I drank wine coolers outside on Alison's deck and I told her I loved Beau Hunter. She had hugged me and told me to ask him out, because he was too shy to ask me.

Eight minutes before I met Trixie, I wanted to wring Jenny's neck.

I waited for Jenny to say something, anything, to acknowledge that night, the way we were close enough for me to smell her bubble gum–flavored lip gloss when I told her my biggest secret.

But she didn't. I could have almost convinced myself that she didn't remember, but then I saw her lips curl up, ever so slightly. She knew. She moved on, started talking about the football game on Friday and some party after. I lagged behind, digging my fingernails into my palms so hard my hands hurt. Then I stopped walking altogether.

"I forgot my uniform in my car," I said, my voice flat. "I'll catch up with you."

She was my best friend and should have known it was a lie. I never forgot anything. But she just flipped me this dumb little wave and kept bounce-walking away.

Tears blurred my vision as I turned and walked back down the hallway, breaking into a run in the parking lot. When I got to my car, I opened the door and collapsed inside, the leather burning my thighs from the heat. I wrapped my hands around the steering wheel, even though it set my palms on fire. I balled my hands into fists and pounded the wheel. I opened my mouth to scream.

Then my passenger door opened, and Trixie was in my car.

"Can you do me a favor," she said, sliding down the seat, her skin making a *smuck* sound as it stuck to the leather. "Can you give me a ride? I just need you to drive. I just need to disappear for a while."

It wasn't a question. She told me to drive and slunk down farther, until her legs were bent under the dashboard. I noticed the scrapes on her knees, like a little kid who kept falling down. She kept her hands in her lap and her nails were badly chewed, and she looked at me out of the side of her eye as if to say, *What are you waiting for?*

And for no reason other than that, I listened to her. I didn't ask who she was or tell her to find her own ride or tell her to go to hell.

I drove.

I drove away from cheerleading practice, away from Jenny. I drove away from Robson High. I waited to feel guilty, but I never did.

She put her head down as we left the parking lot, and I wanted to ask her who she was hiding from, who she was running away from. Where we were supposed to be going.

But it didn't seem to matter. She hummed and tapped her fingers softly against her bare thigh, and I stared at the back of her head, at her dark roots and the peak of hair on the nape of her neck, and I wanted to go where a girl like that was going.

I drove past the beach, past downtown. I kept driving until she sat up and wiped her forehead with the back of her hand.

"Hey, do you want to get something to eat?" she said.

No *thank you*. No explanation. After all that, she was the one who had the question.

"Sure," I said, even though I wasn't hungry.

"Turn left at the intersection. There's a place that has the best cheeseburgers. Sorry, but I'm starving. I skipped lunch today." She stretched her arms over her head like a cat. I noticed the raised pink lines on her left wrist, under a throng of bracelets, but pretended I didn't. "I really owe you one. Let me buy you lunch."

I didn't tell her that I had eaten lunch hours ago, or that I didn't eat meat. That I hadn't eaten a cheeseburger since I turned twelve and Mom watched a documentary about how eating meat was evil. I thought about my cheerleading uniform waiting in my locker, how a cheeseburger would make it that much harder to squeeze into.

"Sure," I said. Trixie had reduced me to one-syllable answers.

"Seriously," she said. "Whatever you like, I'll buy it for you. What's your favorite food?"

I realized nobody had asked me that in years. "Salad," I said instinctively, because that's what Jenny and Alison would say.

The corners of her mouth turned up. "Come on. Salad sucks. What's your real favorite food?"

I stared down at my patchwork jeans, the ones I had deconstructed and put back together myself. Jenny thought they were ugly, but suddenly I didn't care what she thought.

"Chocolate," I said, the very word filling me up. "Chocolate anything."

She broke out in a huge grin. "They have the best chocolate milkshakes at this place. See, it's perfect." She paused. "I'm Trixie, by the way."

"I'm—"

"Fiona, right? I've seen you around."

I stifled a smile. She had seen me, and that seemed important somehow. Maybe because nobody else did.

"Yeah. I'm Fiona."

I was Trixie's getaway car that day, and I never told her so, but she was mine too.

6

WHEN I GET to school, I park my car in the student lot and make myself get out and walk through Robson's red double doors. I mostly keep my eyes fixed on the ground, because the ground is the safest place. If I keep staring down, I can pretend he's not here, beating heart and all, walking the same halls. And I can pretend that she is here, and that her heart really is still beating.

I bump into a bunch of people going the other way. I hear them mutter *Watch where you're going* and *Get out of the way* and then *Oh, that's the girl whose friend died.* Because that's how I'll now be remembered at Robson. The girl with the dead best friend.

Beau is around every corner, behind every open locker door, in front of every classroom. He's everywhere and nowhere. Then, without warning, he's actually right in front of me.

I don't expect him to say anything. He stares at me like a deer caught in the headlights. I stare back, my brain flooding with all the stuff that never happened: drooping white roses and broken glass and cold tile and the sound of confessions slipping out just to be sucked back in.

"Hey," he says. "I'm sorry."

I'm numb, too numb to think of something to say. What

does that mean, *I'm sorry*? What does it mean, coming from Beau Hunter? How many times has he said those two words in his lifetime, and how many people has he said them to?

Anger bubbles up so fast that it takes me by surprise, so hard that I want to punch him in the face to see if he bleeds. But I don't, because his voice is so fragile and he's still the Beau who took poetry books out of the library and got shy in big crowds, the Beau who brought me snow in Southern California, the Beau who offered me rides on his bike before any of us could drive, the Beau who gave me his chocolate milk at lunch. I don't want to hurt that Beau, because he wouldn't hurt me.

"I know what it's like," he says, "when someone just goes away." Then he clears his throat, jams his hands in his pockets, and walks in the other direction, all crumpled over, like he's trying to fold himself in half. I wait for him to turn around, and the fact that he does—only for a second, with his hair covering most of his face—is enough proof that I do still know him, at least a little bit.

Pressure builds behind my eyes and I count backward from ten, telling myself I'm not going to cry, not right here in the middle of the hallway, like a pathetic loser.

The next time I see him, he's opening a classroom door for Jenny, just like a perfect gentleman. I wonder if he'll go home with her after school, if he's taking her out on a date, or worse, if they're staying in and they'll be alone together. I told myself I could handle this but now I feel like I could shatter at any minute.

He looks around before entering the classroom after Jenny, but he doesn't see me. Or he does a really convincing job of pretending he doesn't.

Then again, he's good at that now.

7

I WAS MAD at you the night of Alison's party. I was mad because things had changed between us. You had been lying to me, and I wanted to ask you a thousand questions about why.

Why she really quit her job at the restaurant, and why she didn't think she could tell me. Why she was always messaging Jasper on her phone when she claimed they were just friends with benefits and nothing more.

I was mad at her, but I still clung to her like a pathetic piece of Saran Wrap. I used her as a shield, dogged her like a shadow, hoping she'd give me the power to remain invisible.

"What are you drinking tonight?" she said. "I'll get you something."

"Anything alcoholic," I said, because it didn't matter. I just wanted to be out of my body. When I slunk through the crowd, the whispers and stares started. I couldn't actually see or hear them, and maybe it was all in my head, but it didn't feel that way. I tried to read their lips, imagined what they were saying.

Oh my god, she's so big.

How'd she let herself get like that?

How does anyone let themselves get like that?

My eyes darted around the room. I was even angrier with

Trixie because she had made me wear the red dress and I knew I must have looked like an overstuffed sausage. She had picked this outfit and dragged me here and stuck me inside a nightmare. It was like she knew I wanted to talk to her and she kept slipping around it, dodging the sharp edges of my questions, taking me to the one place we couldn't be alone. Pushing me away and pulling me back, like seaweed caught in the tide.

I knew the bathroom was upstairs, first door on the left. I ran up the stairs. I was breathing hard when I got to the top, and I opened the bathroom door without knocking to make sure it was empty.

I should have knocked, because it wasn't empty.

The lights were on and Jenny was sitting on the counter, with her legs wrapped around Beau's waist. I saw Jenny's eyes fly open, watched her expression go from shock to annoyance and back to shock again. Then I made the mistake of making eye contact with Beau in the mirror.

I saw the one thing there that could break me: softness. He was still in there, the old Beau, the one I fell in love with, the one who looked for the quietest room at a party because he couldn't stand the noise.

I turned around and ran back down the stairs. And I hated Trixie the whole time. It was easy to blame it all on her. Because if she hadn't jumped in my car that day, I would have screamed and pounded the steering wheel and went back to cheerleading practice and lived my old life. Maybe it would have been me in there with my skinny jeans–clad legs wrapped around Beau Hunter. I would have been invited to Alison's party instead of just showing up. Maybe listening to

Trixie when she told me to drive was the biggest mistake of my life.

But when I got to the bottom of the stairs, she was waiting with two plastic cups. She thrust one out toward me and told me to drink it, and then raised her cup up to mine.

"Cheers," she said, and my drink was so strong that I sputtered. "Hey, is something wrong? You look upset."

"It's fine." I took another gulp of my drink. "Seriously."

"Okay," she said, dragging out the word. "You know you don't have to lie to me, right?"

"I know. Everything's fine."

By the third drink, I could barely taste the alcohol. My head was spinning, but in the best possible way. I felt light, airy, uncomplicated.

Trixie was beside me, matching me drink for drink.

But when I think about it, she didn't seem drunk at all.

8

THE WORST PART of starting senior year with no best friend isn't feeling alone. I was prepared to start the year without seeing Trixie in the halls, but that was in a world where I'd see her after school and tell her how horrible it was without her. But this new world is all phantom pain. It's the morbid sensation that she's still here, that any minute she'll spring out from behind an open locker door and ask me what I think of her purple lipstick, and I'll tell her it looks great on her, because it does, because somehow she can pull off everything that I never have the courage to try.

It's watching people move on, people who didn't know her and read the news about a missing girl—which she was, for forty-eight hours—then read the news about her suicide and got the Talk from their parents about being open and honest. I'm sharing the hallways with people who will never question the idea that Trixie Heller walked into the ocean and drowned, because Trixie Heller was wallpaper to them, a girl who didn't smile much and kept to herself. Trixie Heller was a cautionary tale, a tragedy. By the time they start college, they'll forget all about her because other tragedies will be layered on top—a bad haircut or a bad breakup. I want to grab them by the shoulders, leap on their backs, and tell them who she was. That she was wickedly funny. That she was just plain wicked sometimes. That she had great taste in clothes. That the ugly JERSEY GIRL tank top she left behind on the beach, folded neatly on top of her flip-flops, was not really her at all. That the fact she wore it that night feels like a message.

The locker we shared is mine now. We cleared it out together at the end of last year because the school makes all the students dump their locker contents before summer starts. As a joke, we left a picture of us inside a magnetic frame. Except, when I open the locker door now, the frame is all that remains. The picture, one of the only photos existing of the two of us together—taken by Trixie's dad on her last birthday—is gone. Somebody must have taken it, but I can't think who would want it.

I turn around like I'm being watched, and I am being watched. Jasper is lurking by the door to the art room—okay, he's only standing there, but everything about Jasper's posture is creepy. He hunches, like his shoulders have given up on trying and decided to just cave in. Plus, his face is etched in a permanent scowl, like he has never had a happy thought. Maybe he hasn't. Maybe his whole life has been one long series of disappointments.

Maybe we have that in common.

I feel like I should say something to him, that we should try to find some shared ground. Because he's the only other person in this school who actually knew Trixie—who knew her laugh lost its sound when she thought something was really funny, who knew she had zero patience for slow walkers and slow talkers and, most of all, slow drivers, even though she was always the passenger because she never got her license.

He's the only other person in this school who might not

believe she actually walked into the ocean on purpose and let the tide carry her away, because she wouldn't have had the patience for that either.

But when I open my mouth, hoping the right words are there, it doesn't matter. He's already gone.

9

*YOU KNEW MY mom didn't like you, and you didn't care.
You were used to the judgment, wore it as easily as your clothes.*

Trixie wasn't anything like Jenny, who was forever trying to suck up to my mom. Always complimenting her on how young she looked and asking for her vegetarian lasagna recipe and inviting her to watch movies with us. *Hi, Ms. Fontaine. You look nice today, Ms. Fontaine.* That just wasn't Trixie.

Trixie came back to my house with me after we ate cheeseburgers on that first day. I didn't invite her—she just got back into my car, like we had already made plans.

"Can we stop at that convenience store quickly? I just want to get some snacks. I know we just ate, but I'm always hungry." She patted her flat stomach, and before she went into the store, pulled a blue baseball cap out of her purse and jammed it on her head, a clumsy disguise. It was too big for her, as if it belonged to a boy.

I could tell Mom disapproved the second her eyes skirted over Trixie. She saw the bag of potato chips in Trixie's hand and the ring in her lip, and then she looked right at me and asked why I wasn't at practice.

"It was canceled," I said. I was surprised at how easily the lie slid out. It had been waiting to escape the whole time.

Trixie never asked what kind of practice I was supposed to be at. She never asked me why I wasn't there. The way I saw it, she didn't need to.

"You look like your mom," she said matter-of-factly when we were upstairs in my room, sitting cross-legged on the floor.

"I guess," I said. "I've never even seen a picture of my dad. He split before I was born."

I don't know why I told her that. I never told anyone that. Jenny and Alison both had parents who were still together, who wanted them home to eat dinner as a family. I felt embarrassed that I was different, and I waited for Trixie to judge me.

"People suck sometimes," she said, staring up at the ceiling.

"How about you? Do you look like your mom or your dad?"

"I don't know." She shoveled a handful of chips into her mouth and wiped her hand on her shorts. "I'm adopted. My birth mom got rid of me."

I felt like an idiot, but maybe we were alike. We had both been abandoned by somebody.

"Is this what you're all about?" she said, touching my jeans with her fingers and pointing to the sewing machine in the corner. "You make clothes?"

I'd never heard it put like that before. *Is this what you're all about?* But I just nodded, hoping she didn't think it was lame. I could tell Jenny didn't get it. She liked to shop at the mall, where everything looked the same.

"Cool," Trixie said, running her fingers over one of the patches. "Maybe you could make me a pair."

My cheeks burned with something that felt an awful lot like pride. I wanted to be alone with that emotion, wrapped up in that feeling, before it went away.

"Do you have a boyfriend?" Trixie said.

"No," I said too quickly. I thought about Beau, about the day we met, the spark I felt so vividly that it was like I stuck my finger in an electric socket. Our texts and bike rides and one almost-kiss at the end of sophomore year. I thought about Jenny in the hallway, the way she wouldn't quite look at me. *He asked me out. It's not like I could say no.*

"Good," she said. "They're overrated. Once they go and fall in love with you, everything gets ruined."

I didn't know who she was talking about, and she wasn't even looking at me anymore. She was staring at the photo collage on my wall with a quirky little half smile. I had made it the summer before, printed pictures of me and Jenny and Alison and cut letters out of magazines to spell *best friends* and *love* and *laugh*. Suddenly, I was embarrassed by all of it. The collage, my lavender walls, my canopy bed. I had a stuffed rabbit on my pillow and collector Barbies in unopened boxes on my bookshelf. The whole room was so babyish and felt too small with Trixie in it.

"So I take it you don't have a boyfriend either?" I was desperate to say something to make her stop looking around, but it felt like the wrong thing to say.

She rolled her eyes up to the ceiling and sighed, this huge shuddering sound. "I had this thing with my lab partner. But it doesn't matter anymore."

I grabbed a chip out of the bag and popped it in my mouth. The salt stung my tongue and the crunching sound drowned out all the noise in my head. Then I ate another chip, and another. I knew I shouldn't have been eating them, and that made them taste even better somehow.

"This guy I hooked up with, he keeps texting me," she said finally, standing up and leaning against my windowsill. "That's why I needed to get away for a bit. I needed some space. You know?"

I nodded, even though I didn't know. I hadn't ever hooked up with anyone.

"Your lab partner?" I said.

She lit a cigarette and blew the smoke out the window. I knew Mom would smell it and I'd get in trouble later, but I didn't care.

"We should have lunch together more often," she said. "I know a great place we can go next time. You'll love it."

She barely knew me, but it seemed like she knew me better than anyone. Well enough to know what I would love before I did.

IO

TWO ANNOUNCEMENTS ARE made when I'm in homeroom. One is about cheerleading tryouts. The other is about Patricia Heller's memorial service, to be held on Friday. Trixie hated her real name: Patricia. Nobody called her that, not even her dad.

Both of my old lives, back-to-back over a crackling intercom. It's almost comical, the universe conspiring to make this day a wreck. I ask Mr. Hanson for a hall pass, which I use to go to the bathroom and lock myself in a stall and curl up in a ball in front of the toilet.

If it were me—if I were the one who was gone—she would have found the evidence. She would be following my trail, chasing the bread crumbs even as I swept them away, because she would've known where I was hiding. Maybe she left me a trail, and I never knew her well enough to follow it.

I wonder what she would think if she knew I was covering up someone's tracks from the night she disappeared. I wonder what she would think if she knew they weren't hers.

My eyes sting and my hairline is damp with sweat. I lean against the wall, resting my forehead on the toilet paper dispenser. I consider what Mom said this morning when she hugged me before I walked out the door: *It's never too late to start fresh, sweetie.*

I remember how Mom's voice sounded when she got back from Tokyo, when she was on the phone with Aunt Leslie and I overheard her. Maybe she meant for me to.

"She's always hanging around with Trixie," she said as I listened at her bedroom door. "She's a bad influence. All they do is drive around and eat junk food. And I think she's been drinking too."

I had held my breath and imagined what Aunt Leslie must have been saying on the other end. Hopefully something in my defense, but I knew the mention of drinking would shake her up because of her own history with it. Then Mom exhaled deeply. I could almost see her face, the lines deepening on her forehead. "I'm worried about her. She needs to find other friends. She can't just be spending all her time with this one girl."

I had turned around and silently snuck away, my heart pounding. I was sick with worry, sick and angry. She couldn't separate me from my best friend. She couldn't take away the one person who understood me. She wouldn't.

The bathroom door swings open. I wrap my arms around my knees and stay quiet.

"It's emotional eating," a girl's voice says. "It happened to my aunt when she and my uncle split up. She used to be skinny. Now she can barely walk down her driveway."

I cover my mouth with my hand. I'd know that voice anywhere. High-pitched and airy, like wind chimes. Alison James, captain of the cheerleading squad, my former friend. If anyone is an emotional eater, it's her. She's the girl who once cried over the perfect chocolate cake Jenny and I made for her fifteenth birthday.

She's also the girl who threw the last party Trixie ever attended.

"No, it started before her body changed," another voice says. Jenny. "She started acting different last year. It was like she was brainwashed or something."

"Maybe they were lesbians," Alison says in a hushed voice. "They spent basically every minute together."

I dig my fingernails into my palm so hard that they leave little red crescent moons.

"I don't think so," Jenny says. "Trixie was fucking that weird guy in my geography class. Jasper. Remember, the one I told you about? They sat in the back row and, I swear, he had his hand up her skirt during class."

Liar, I want to shout. *Trixie never wore skirts.*

"That's messed up," Alison says, and I can tell by the lilt in her voice that she's tilting her head up, probably applying makeup like she used to before practice, even though she'd just sweat it right off.

"Whatever," Jenny says. "Plus, I saw them in the smoke pit once practically doing it. Just gross."

"I wish we could help her," Alison says, smacking her lips together.

"Yeah, except she's dead now," Jenny says, and the word is a dull thud in the air.

"Not Trixie," Alison says. "Fiona."

"Look, not to sound mean, but she's not our problem either. This is senior year. I'm not getting dragged into some-one else's drama. I have enough drama of my own."

A snapping sound, probably Alison closing her powder compact. "Beau?" she says gently, and the word sounds so tender that I almost want to barge out of the stall and hug her. Alison isn't a mean girl. Alison cares about people. Maybe she even cares about me.

"He's still drinking a lot," Jenny says. "And after your party, I don't even know how to bring it up without him going off on me. He said he was sorry, but I never know which version of him I'm going to get, and it's scary."

Maybe Alison doesn't, but I hear the excitement in her voice, buried under whatever else she's trying to layer on top of it. Jenny hasn't changed a single bit. She just loves the idea of tragedy: the romance of a boy wrestling with a ghost, the drama Beau brings to her stale little life. And I hate her for so many reasons, but that's the biggest one of all.

Alison drops her voice to a whisper. "Is he still involved in, you know, that shady stuff?"

"No," Jenny says, and I bet she's shaking her head adamantly, her bangs flying across her forehead. "No, he gave all that up."

A shoe taps on the floor. "I just don't really get what you see in him. He's not a good boyfriend. He doesn't do anything nice for you and doesn't make an effort around us. And he was psycho at my party. Like, someone-should-have-called-the-cops psycho. That would have been the last straw for me."

"You don't know him like I do," Jenny says, and her words are knives, carving me up. "You don't know what he says to me when we're alone. He loves me. He needs me."

"Maybe that's the problem," Alison says, shuffling toward the door. "He needs you too much. And you're starting to need him just as badly."

When they're gone and the door swings shut behind them, I want to scream. They think they know everything, that they have it all figured out. The whole story, the lie. Just like last year, with Toby Hunter. The rumors, collecting like dust in corners. The air foggy with bullshit, so thick that people were choking on it.

I get up and wash my hands and take my time walking back to class. I pretend to pay attention to Mr. Hanson, but when he asks us to write down our thoughts on some Shakespeare scene he just read out loud, I put something else on my page. Something I need to write down to actually believe. Because Jenny is wrong and Alison is wrong and my mom is wrong and everyone else is wrong. Trixie didn't walk into the water and drown. She wouldn't do that. She might not be here, but she isn't dead, and I'm the only one who can prove it.

The words, scrawled deep and heavy in my notebook, are their own truth:

REASONS WHY TRIXIE DISAPPEARED

THERE'S PROBABLY A *reason why people were so eager to believe that man's story about how you walked into the water. There's probably a reason they gave up so easily. Actually, several reasons. But the first one came from before I ever even met you.*

His name was Toby Hunter. Everyone at Robson High knows that name, and now everyone in Morrison Beach, California, does too. He became the poster child for suicide, the example of how you don't always see the warning signs. I'll never know the whole story of Toby Hunter and why he did it, because I didn't know the real Toby Hunter. I only knew the version everyone else knew. The football star, the captain of the swim team, the guy dating the most beautiful girl in school. The guy who was supposed to go on to become president or something. Clean-cut, nice, smart. Everything a girl wants in a boyfriend. Except, I didn't want Toby. I wanted the other Hunter brother.

Toby Hunter was going places. Until he went to the last place anyone expected: he left a party drunk and jumped off the Morrison Beach Pier.

I wasn't at that party. I was supposed to go, but I had

stayed home with food poisoning, puking like clockwork every five minutes. Later, Jenny told me in hushed tones about the fight Toby had with his brother, Beau, right before he stormed off. He was wild, she said. Probably drunk or high or both. Nobody tried to stop him, because everybody figured he just needed to cool off. Nobody thought he would do what he did.

Three people saw Toby jump off the pier. One went in after him and nearly drowned. The waves were too big, the current too powerful. It was immediately ruled a suicide, a tragedy, a terrible waste, even though Toby's body still hasn't been found.

The rumors started immediately too. Maybe he just fell, lost his balance. Those were the people in denial.

Then there were the other people. The ones who said he wasn't dead at all. The ones who said he was too good a swimmer to drown started circulating theories about why he would stage his own death. Like, he wasn't dead but was working on an oil rig in Canada. Or that he moved into the Ozark Mountains and grew a beard and farmed goats. And while the truth sank, the rumors sputtered to the surface. Completely out of control. All of a sudden, everyone seemed to know someone who knew someone who had spotted Toby somewhere in the world. Nobody wanted to let Toby Hunter rest in peace.

It's different with Trixie. She mostly kept to herself, didn't have a thousand friends. People flung words at her, tried to stick labels on her like tape. *Loner. Weirdo. Trouble.* She'd snuck out of Alison's house like a shadow after everyone else had left, except the ones too drunk to know where they were.

She didn't say goodbye to me. It's easy for everyone to believe she walked into the ocean and drowned. *The signs were all there*, they'd said. *A classic case of somebody who wanted out.*

The signs *were* all there. But not the signs everyone thinks, the ones tossed out like a last-minute life preserver from somebody who planned to die.

Trixie had all the signs of somebody who wanted people to think that.

12

THE LIST IS in my pocket as I drive to Dr. Rosenthal's office. I'm speeding, in a rush. I was late to leave school because Mrs. Moss, Robson's guidance counselor, insisted on cornering me after class and telling me her office was always open if I needed to talk. Like I'd really tell Moss anything. Her eyes would go wide and her jaw would drop if I told her what I did at the party, and who I did it with.

The list is in my pocket but I can hear the words in my head. My blocky handwriting in bullet points like I'm studying for a test. Except, if this is a test, it's the first one I'm failing.

REASONS WHY TRIXIE DISAPPEARED

I'm wondering if the list is total bullshit, if she really did do what that man said he saw, when I slam on my brakes to narrowly avoid hitting someone walking through a red light. My chest tightens and my pulse races and I raise my hand to pound the horn, but then I see who I almost hit. Or rather, who almost hit me. The same person who stared at me across the hall today.

Jasper Hart, the only name currently on my list.

He doesn't even look to see who almost hit him, just raises an arm in the air and waves it, like he's conducting a symphony in traffic. Then I see that he has earbuds in and think that maybe he is.

Somebody behind me honks and I slowly inch forward. Jasper is on the sidewalk now, and when I see him cut the corner down a side street, I make a hasty decision in the form of a sharp right-hand turn. I recognize this street because Alison's house is on it.

I look at the clock on the car radio and know I'll never make it to Dr. Rosenthal's, but suddenly, I couldn't care less. He's just going to tell me to start eating better and maybe give me a lecture, some canned bullshit I already know. None of it matters.

I stay a good distance behind Jasper and watch his lanky figure. He's wearing a long black jacket, despite the heat, and it swings from side to side like a pendulum. He takes giant strides and periodically snaps his fingers, and I chug alongside the curb, hoping I'll figure out a plan as I go.

When he stops suddenly, I do too. I hunch against the back of my seat and slide down as he stops in front of a driveway.

But he doesn't walk up the driveway. He turns around and walks right toward me instead. I stare at my key in the ignition. I should just drive away and avoid him for the rest of the year. For the rest of my life. But I'm paralyzed, either out of fear or curiosity or a thick mixture of both. And it's too late, because he's beside my window, rapping his knuckles against it, motioning for me to roll it down. His face is completely expressionless.

I roll the window down and he rests his forearms there until our faces are inches apart. "Following me?" he says. I can't tell if he's pissed off or amused or both. "I never would have presumed I was interesting enough for a girl to follow."

I suddenly wish the plate of glass were still between our faces. He's too close without it. Close enough for me to see his dark eyes and the fringe of thick black eyelashes casting a shadow on his cheeks. Close enough for me to see the smattering of acne scars, stark against the whiteness of his skin. His mouth is wide and his lips have a reddish tinge, like he has been drinking fruit punch. Trixie told me he was a good kisser, but to me he looks more like a vampire, ready to suck the life out of everything.

"I didn't see you at the funeral," I say when I finally find my voice.

Jasper bites his lip and stares at the ground. I notice the top of his head for the first time, which I never saw before because he's so tall. Blond hair is growing in at the roots, a stark contrast to the black hair hanging down to his shoulders. Blond roots and dark hair, the total opposite of Trixie.

"I don't do well with grief. I'm better at expressing it by myself."

I nod like I understand, but I don't. It's a strange thing to say. Nobody deals well with grief. Nobody knows what to say at funerals. Jasper makes grief sound like an art form.

He looks directly at me, which is unnerving, like he knows all my secrets. "So, I'm intrigued. Why are you following me?" he says slowly, enunciating each word.

I squirm in my seat, wishing I had just gone to see Dr. Rosenthal like I was supposed to. Being prodded and judged couldn't possibly be any worse than this.

"Because I don't think she's dead," I say, my voice coming out in a high-pitched squeak.

He says nothing and I'm sure he's going to say that I'm delusional, that I'm just sad and lonely and making stuff up.

Then he glances around, like he's checking to see if we're being watched, and walks around to the passenger side of my car and hops in. Just like Trixie did that day. Uninvited. He leans over the console and his hair flops in his eyes.

"Well," he says, his voice almost a whisper, his hands pressed together like he's praying. "If she's not dead, where in the world is she?"

13

YOU WEREN'T A part of my life in sophomore year. I had probably walked past you countless times, but I never saw you once.

The first day of sophomore year, before I knew Trixie existed, I wasn't searching for a girl who was presumed dead. I was searching for Jenny and Alison, who were supposed to meet me outside the school's front doors. We weren't eating in the cafeteria that day. We wanted to celebrate the first year of not being freshmen—of being higher up on the high school food chain—by having lunch away from school. None of us could drive, so we planned to walk to some little place near the beach that Jenny claimed had good taco salad.

I waited for them, trying not to feel annoyed by the fact that it was always me doing the waiting, never them, and that I always seemed slightly separate from them, that they were a tighter unit together. But it was fine, because we were sophomores and we were eating lunch off campus and when the wind lifted my hair off my neck, it felt like freedom somehow.

"Are you going home?" Beau came up behind me, putting a hand on my shoulder. He always seemed to find excuses to do that, to touch me in ways I would barely remember when I was home alone later, when I would wonder if it had actually happened. "I was going to sit on the benches over there and eat lunch, if you wanted to join."

Beau always brought his lunch to school, which was endearing somehow. His mom packed him and Toby a brown bag every day with the same turkey sandwich, yogurt, apple, and baggie of pretzels. Sometimes she added a date square if she had baked that weekend. I tried not to think about what it meant that I had memorized Beau's lunch.

"I would," I said. I considered blowing off Jenny and Alison. Would they really care if I didn't show up? As we would wait on our taco salad—I always ended up ordering whatever they ordered—we'd have the same conversation we had the week before and the week before that. Alison would talk about some new diet she was trying or some shampoo she was using and Jenny would talk about whatever boy she was in love with. I'd listen and provide advice, because that was my role.

"Great," he said. "Maybe we can—"

But I never got to hear about what we could maybe do, because Jenny chose that moment to bounce over, Alison trailing behind her, staring at her phone.

"Hey, girl, you ready to go? I can't miss any of fifth period!" Jenny grabbed my hand and practically pulled me along, as if they had been waiting for me, not the other way around.

I should have told them I changed my mind, that I was staying at school and eating lunch on a bench with Beau. But for some reason I didn't. I thought Beau might read too much into it, me ditching my friends for him. I knew Jenny and Alison would read too much into it. I hadn't told them yet how I felt about him, because I had barely admitted it to myself.

"No worries," Beau said. "Another time."

But that other time didn't happen. There was always something else, someone else, some other plan. I still wonder how things would have been different if I had stayed.

14

I WONDER IF they held hands, if behind closed doors Trixie and Jasper acted like a couple. I wonder if he ever got tired of her pretending he didn't exist in public. If they came back to his house during the lunch hours that Trixie didn't show up for. If she got excited to see Jasper the way I used to get excited when I knew Beau was going to be at a party or a game.

It's weird, going into Jasper's house and walking up the stairs to his room. It's my first time ever going upstairs with a boy. It feels wrong that I'm going with this boy, Trixie's boy, like cheating and getting away with it.

Jasper's bedroom barely looks lived in. A twin bed, dark blue walls, plain black curtains. A desk with nothing on it but a laptop. There's nowhere to sit but on his bed, so I stand.

"So, this is interesting," he says, sitting on the edge of his bed. "You don't think she's gone. But someone saw her walk into the water. And there was a funeral."

"With no body," I say so quickly that my words trip over each other. "I think she wants everyone to believe she's dead. But she's not. I know she's not. And you're the only person who really knew her besides me, so I need your help."

He lies back on the bed and folds his hands in his lap.

Trixie must have been in that bed at least a dozen times, but it doesn't look big enough for two people.

"Somebody saw her," he says, tapping the back of his head lightly against the wall. "That man saw her. You can't really argue with that. And I'm sure you know that she couldn't swim."

I bite the inside of my cheek. In my head, I correct him. *Can't swim*, present tense. I do know that. Trixie and I spent so much time at the beach during the summer, but she never once went in the water. I was relieved that she couldn't swim, because it meant I never had to put on a bathing suit and go in either.

"This might sound crazy," I say slowly, rolling the words on my tongue. "But don't you think that his story might have been a little too perfect? Like, he just happened to be there to watch her walk in and didn't try to stop her? And didn't try to call the police?"

"He said he did try to call," Jasper says. "From a pay phone. But it wasn't working, because the line was cut."

Obviously, Jasper had memorized all the articles in the newspaper just like I did. "Exactly. Too perfect."

Jasper stares up at the ceiling. I follow his eyes and notice he has those little plastic glow-in-the-dark stars stuck there, and they seem out of place.

"That doesn't seem like enough of a reason," he says. "I mean, I don't want her to be gone either. I miss her too. But I saw this coming." His voice gets lower. "She had scars. She never talked about them. But I saw them, you know?"

I nod. I do know. I wish I would have asked her about those scars when I had the chance. I wish she would have had the chance to finish what she wanted to tell me that day in her backyard before her dad interrupted.

"Plus, we know that the guy on the beach saw her walk in," Jasper continues. "Because he described her perfectly."

"Too perfectly," I say, before I can stop myself. "Right down to the stitching on her backpack."

"So what?" Jasper says. "He probably had to. You don't just forget about watching somebody die. It becomes one of the defining moments of your life."

I'm starting to hate the way he talks, like he's the human equivalent of a Rubik's cube. Cryptic and hard to put together.

"So, if he really was up on the sand, how could he possibly see the stitching on her backpack? He's close enough to see that, but not to call out to her or grab her?"

Jasper narrows his eyes. "I don't know, Fiona. What are you saying? That he made it all up and secretly kidnapped her or something? Sold her into human trafficking?"

"No. I'm saying that he knew exactly what to say."

Jasper crosses his arms and exhales deeply. "You lost me."

I clear my throat before I can chicken out, before I can take it back.

"He knew exactly what to say. Almost like somebody put the words in his mouth."

15

JASPER WAS NEVER *going to be your boyfriend. But you liked having sex with him.*

"It's a friends with benefits thing," Trixie told me one day at lunch while we shared a greasy pizza in my car. "You get all the good parts and none of the bullshit."

I was confused. This was the same person who was the reason why we met—why she jumped in my car that day. He was the one she had wanted to get away from. Now she was texting him, making plans to meet him.

"Relax," she said, wiping her mouth with a napkin. "It's no big deal. Haven't you had a casual hookup before?"

I thought about the party after the last football game of sophomore year. A cup of beer sweating in my hand and my shirt sticking to my back. Beau's arm on my shoulder while he leaned in. His fingers trailing up my waist, before we got interrupted by the stupid sprinkler turning on. The one minute of my life where everything was perfect and everything had possibility. Back when Beau still had a brother and Jenny and I were like sisters and junior year was going to be the best thing ever.

"No," I said, picking up another piece of pizza and shoveling it into my mouth. The cheese was starting to congeal and the smell of the pepperoni made me queasy, but I ate it anyway. It was better having my mouth full. It was better for Trixie to do the talking.

"Come on," she said. "You're telling me you've never messed around with a guy? You're gorgeous. I bet guys look into those big green eyes and fall madly in love."

I swallowed a giant lump of crust and the pointy part scratched my throat going down. I didn't want to tell her about Beau. Look what happened after I told Jenny about him, after I used the word *love*. Everything fell apart.

"You can tell me," Trixie said, sucking Coke through a chewed-up straw.

And just like that, I did tell her. I stared at the grease spots on my napkin and told her about Beau, even though the words didn't want to come out. They were stuck like the pizza cheese on the roof of my mouth.

When I was finished, I ate another piece of pizza. Because it was there, and because nobody was keeping score. Jenny wasn't obsessively pinching the skin on her stomach and Alison wasn't entering the calories into that stupid app on her phone that told her what to eat and what to avoid. Mom wasn't hovering over me. It was just Trixie, and I knew she wasn't going to judge me.

I waited for her to say something. A *good for you* or *attagirl* or *way to go*. But she just sat there, chewing her straw, completely unfazed by my outpouring of feelings.

Finally, she said something that I didn't expect. "Why do you like him? Why him?"

I didn't know how to answer that. The reasons sounded stupid in my head, but they bubbled onto my lips and I somehow started talking. "Because when he smiles at me, it's like the smile says something nobody else can hear. He has the perfect words for everything and there's this whole other dialogue underneath all that. Like our own language. Like he's trying to tell me so much more." My face flamed. "Haven't you ever felt like that?"

"No."

I stared at my lap, embarrassed beyond belief. Everything I had just told her, all those tissue-thin layers, came apart with that one syllable.

"He's a loser." Her voice was aluminum, flat and steely. "We'll just have to find you someone better."

I wanted to defend him. To tell her that she was wrong. Beau wasn't a loser. Sure, there were rumors about how messed up he was now. Rumors about his drinking. Every time I tried to make eye contact, he looked away. But Toby had only been gone for two months, and what did everyone expect?

Later, it was like the whole conversation never happened. When Trixie met me after school, her words were froth and sweetness, not metallic and hard.

"Let's make a promise," she said as we drove away. "Let's never ditch each other for a guy, okay?"

I nodded. She couldn't have possibly known how badly I needed to hear that promise.

Maybe, at the time, she even planned to keep it.

16

ON THE DRIVE home, I brace myself for a lecture. Dr. Rosenthal probably called mom's cell, and Mom picked up the phone and had to hear about how I missed the special appointment she booked for me. When I check my cell phone, I see one missed call from Mom and one voice mail. I don't want to listen to it, because I know it will either be mad Mom or worried Mom, and I don't know which is worse.

But Mom's car isn't in the driveway, and nobody is in the house. I see a flashing light on the answering machine and push the button.

"Good afternoon, Ms. Fontaine. This is Gloria from Dr. Rosenthal's office. Fiona seems to have missed her three thirty appointment today, and we're just making sure every- thing is okay. Call us back if you want to—"

I hit the ERASE button before she's even done talking, feeling a rush of gratitude that Dr. Rosenthal decided to use our landline number instead of Mom's cell. It's that easy, that simple, to get rid of the evidence. Then I listen to the mes- sage on my cell phone, and it's just Mom telling me that there's some kind of crisis at the office and she won't be home for dinner.

"There's salad in the fridge," she says. "Love you."

But the thought of salad makes me feel sick. I used to eat it for lunch every single day. I choked it down because I was supposed to, because Jenny and Alison ate nothing but salad and I wanted to fit in with them just as badly as I wanted to fit into my cheerleading uniform. They claimed they loved salad, but it left me feeling hungrier than when I started.

By the time I climb the stairs to my room, I'm so exhausted that I just want to collapse in bed and forget today ever happened. Forget about my strange afternoon with Jasper and the fact that he thinks I'm insane. Forget about school, about what Jenny and Alison said about me in the bathroom and the announcements that came on during class. Forget about a thousand eyes on me, on the girl who lost her only friend. I flop back onto my pillow and my head spins. Then my phone vibrates and I crack open an eye and tap the screen.

I bolt upright when I see who the text's from.

> I know you have a lot going on, and I'm sorry to bug you. I just need to know that you haven't told anyone.

A second message comes through before I'm even done reading the first one.

> That you won't tell anyone.

My head throbs. All the details come rushing back, the ones I shouldn't even remember. The cold tile and clammy hands and tequila rising up the back of my throat. All the smells, sweat and pot and spilled beer, rising into an unmistakable party potpourri.

I hesitate before texting back. There's a part of me that likes the power. I have no control over Trixie or my body or my former friends, but I do have control over this one thing. I could flip a switch, blow someone's life apart.

But the brief feeling of power gets outweighed by the soggy mass of reality. It sucks the truth in, like a stain absorbed in a wet paper towel. The truth is in the words I write back.

Who would believe me anyway?

17

THE FIRST THING I did after they said you were missing: I called your cell phone. I waited for you to pick up and sound annoyed with me for interrupting your post-drinking sleep, but you never did.

My fingers felt too big as I hit the screen of my phone, and my fingertips left sweaty marks. The screen was cracked and I wondered if that had happened at the party. I guess a lot of things cracked that night.

It rang and rang and rang. Trixie never had voice mail set up because she figured if someone wanted to reach her that badly, they'd call back. I guess she was right, because I called back. I called back seventeen times that day, and it rang and rang and rang.

Then I had another idea. I remembered how she was glued to her phone, and since she didn't have Facebook or Instagram or any social media anymore, she must still have something. So I texted her and emailed.

> You're scaring me. Please, come home. Seriously. You win, everyone's freaked out. Now, come on. Trixie, where are you?

She never replied. I had stared at that phone every five seconds, and when it finally made a noise, I jumped a mile when I realized it wasn't her, but someone else. Someone who was counting on me.

> **Hey. Did they find her yet?**
> **How are you holding up?**

> **No**

I typed back. Just no. I didn't answer the rest because I couldn't. "How are you holding up" sounds like something you say after someone dies.

> **Do you think anyone knows?**

> **If someone knew, they wouldn't still be looking for her. The police wouldn't be involved.**

The next message made me feel excited and sick and happy and sad and angry, a whole kaleidoscope of colors.

> **No, do you think anyone knows about what we did?**

I hesitated before writing back. I typed *Do you think that would be such a bad thing?* Then I erased it, because I'd never be ready to hear the answer.

> **No**

I wrote back instead. One word, two letters.
And they never will.

18

I WATCH THE cheerleading tryouts from the safety of my car. Jenny and Alison are there, of course, along with a whole throng of would-be cheerleaders. Every girl wants to wear Robson red and be thrown in the air. Every girl wants to be a flyer, because the flyers suck up all the light.

Mom keeps telling me I should try to reconnect with Jenny, that she was a good friend. Mom doesn't understand why we stopped being friends. I never tried to explain it to her because I knew what she'd say. *Boys aren't worth fighting over. Don't let a boy come between you.* And she's wrong, all wrong. Jenny and Alison and I used to make fun of those girls who let boys ruin friendships. Back then, we never thought a boy would be important enough to change anything.

I squirm in my seat when I see the new bases. They're solid, compact. I try to recall myself in that same position a year ago and my legs hurt just thinking about it. There was a time when I thought I was indispensable, the one holding everything up, the one with her feet firmly on the ground. But that was stupid. There are ten other girls on that field just like me, better than me.

A knock on my window makes me whip my head around.

I look up to see Jasper standing outside, cocking his head quizzically. I hesitate before rolling down my window.

"Are you following me this time?" I say, my voice coming out unnaturally high-pitched.

"I changed my mind," he says. "I think you're right. And I want to help you find her."

We blow off the memorial service the school has the next day. It's not like it matters anyway. They had one for Toby Hunter last year and all anyone did during it was cry. All that crying, in the same stuffy gym I'd stood in for a thousand cheerleading practices. It's supposed to be therapeutic or something. I'm sure that's what Principal Shepherd wants us to think. And after the memorial, they'll put a picture of her on the Dead Students Wall. Next to Toby and some other people from before my time.

It's awkward, being alone with Jasper, even more unnatural out in the open than it was the other day in his room. Trixie was always the intermediary, the wall between us. I never had a reason to talk to him, and he never had one to talk to me.

"I think we should go see him," I say as we walk through the parking lot. "The guy from the beach. Maybe he'll tell us something he didn't tell the police."

The guy from the beach. He has a name—Byron St. James, a name that hints at a trust fund and a big mansion in the suburbs. Instead, he looked filthy and disheveled in every interview and was described as a "longtime Morrison Beach resident," which I took as a euphemism for actually living on the beach.

"That's a bad idea," he says. "I was thinking more along the lines of going to the library and doing some research."

"Research on what? That doesn't seem very proactive to me. This isn't a school project."

Jasper says nothing, just makes a grunting sound. When we're in my car, he rubs his eyes with his fists and shakes his head. For the first time, I notice how red his eyes are and wonder if he has been crying. Or not sleeping. Or both.

"I don't know. Reasons people disappear, I guess. Exit strategies. You were there, right? The night of the party? Did she say anything to you? Like, anything strange? You saw her last."

I hear her voice in my head, as loud as if she were here. *What am I going to do with you?*

"No," I say quickly.

"But you left the party with her, right? I mean, she didn't say she was going anywhere except back to her dad's place?"

It's like he already knows I didn't leave the party with her, even though that's impossible. "The police already asked me all this. We left together."

It's a lie I can tell so easily. Maybe I should be horrified by how quickly it leaves my mouth, how true it sounds. If I tell it enough times, I might even start to believe it. I wonder if I could always lie like this but never knew it until now, or if I can only lie this well to protect someone.

"Fine," he says, rubbing his forehead. "I'm just trying to retrace her steps. Like when you lose something and try to figure out all the places you've been with it that day."

"That's what we're about to do." I put the car into reverse and pull out of the parking lot.

When we're leaving the school, I recognize a vehicle parked in the visitor lot out front. A crappy wood-paneled station wagon with LIVE TO SURF and BEACH BUM bumper stickers. Somebody is sitting in the front seat, hunched over the steering wheel. He's sobbing into his arm, and I'm torn between slamming on the brakes and hitting the gas pedal.

It's Trixie's dad.

Jasper notices him too. He flattens himself in his seat, then bows his head into his lap.

"Just drive," he says, his voice pleading. "This isn't the way I imagined myself meeting Trixie's dad."

I just need you to drive. Some of the first words she ever said to me. I do it, just like I did it then.

My hands are shaky as I make a right-hand turn onto the street. "You never met him? Weren't you over at her house all the time?"

Jasper rolls down his window and the breeze blows his hair off his forehead. "She came over to my place, not the other way around. He probably had no idea I existed. It's not like I was picking her up for dates or anything."

"Why didn't you take her out on dates?"

"We were friends who hooked up from time to time. Nothing more. Neither of us wanted anything more than what the other was willing to give." He drums his fingers on his knee.

But I'm not sure he's telling the truth. I know how much he cared—cares—about Trixie. He used to write her little notes and stick them in our locker. That doesn't sound like something a friend with benefits does.

I think about what she said the first time we met. *I had this thing with my lab partner.* I think about Jasper being the one she was trying to escape from. She mentioned that he was in love with her, that he had feelings way stronger than hers would ever be. She made it sound like things got too serious, like he got attached. But maybe she was the one who was afraid of getting attached.

"I'm sure you get it," he says. "You knew her too."

I knew her and I knew my place. Now I suddenly wonder if she liked me because I stayed put, because I only jumped when I was told to jump and sat still on command. Maybe Jasper didn't do as good a job at staying put. Maybe he was spilling all over the edges because he couldn't fit neatly inside his box.

"How did you meet?" I say, desperate to change the subject, because thinking about our friendship like that makes me feel like I gave up everything for nothing at all.

"She never told you? Of course she didn't. Nobody could keep a secret like that girl."

"We just didn't talk about stuff like that." I don't know why I'm defending her when she's not around to hear me lie for her.

"Sure you didn't." He clasps his hands into a ball on his lap. "All girls do. Anyway, we met in class. I was a freshman and she was a year older. I was intrigued by her. She didn't know I existed." He laughs, but it's not a funny laugh. It's a sad one, each syllable thick and dense. "I remember we did a project at my house once and it was obvious she didn't want to be there. She was like some kind of caged bird, looking for a way to escape."

I wait for him to keep going but he stares at his hands instead. His fingernails are painted black, just like his whole outfit. Trixie never painted her nails, not once in the time I knew her. I guess she was too busy changing the rest of herself to care about something as insignificant as her nails.

"But then she came over one night," Jasper finally says. "She snuck in my bedroom window at two in the morning. And you know, my room's on the second floor. So she must have climbed a tree or something to get up there. The ultimate romantic gesture." He lets out a long breath. "Anyway, I should have asked questions. I should have turned her down."

"But you didn't."

He shakes his head. "It kept happening. Mostly, she started it. Somehow, she always knew where to find me."

I think back to those times when Trixie wasn't around during lunch hour, when I'd eat by myself in my car, hoping she'd show up. Those times when I'd leave school late after practice and there she was, sitting beside my car like she'd been waiting for me forever. I never thought we were unbalanced like that for a reason.

"When did it end?" I ask him, because it suddenly seems important. "When was the last time she came over?"

He leans forward, and in my peripheral vision, I can see him trace the edge of his jawline with his thumb. I imagine Trixie doing the same thing, touching his face, outlining his features like a map.

"The last time she came over was the day of her graduation," he says. "She told me she had two tickets and I wouldn't be able to go. Not that I wanted to. That's the kind of gig for a boyfriend." He says the word *boyfriend* like it's toxic.

Two tickets. Her dad and I each got one, sat side by side in the sweltering auditorium.

"Anyway, she came over that night like nothing had happened. But I wasn't in the mood to see her, so we kind of had a fight."

"And what, you never saw her again after that?"

"No, she just stopped texting me back. I saw her only once, when she was on her lunch break at the restaurant. I was standing outside and she wouldn't talk to me, so I figured her days of climbing in windows were in the past."

I grip the steering wheel tighter, panic ripping through me as Jasper's voice grows bitter. "That's impossible," I say, but even as the words come out I know it's completely possible. I was that easy to lie to. That easy to blindfold and lead around.

"It's the truth," he says flatly. "I don't know what else to tell you."

"But she was always on her phone, all summer. She was always messaging somebody."

He leans back into his seat, presses his forehead against the window. "So, what makes you think it was me?"

"Because she said it was you." Suddenly, I feel like a total idiot, like the joke is on me. I had believed every word she said. If she had told me goddamn Santa Claus was real, I would have stayed up on Christmas Eve, waiting to catch a glimpse of him.

"Well, it wasn't. If there's one thing I learned from not being Trixie's boyfriend, it's that she said what she wanted you to hear. And not a single word more."

It's too hot in the car now, too small and confined. There's an extra passenger with us, radiating doubt, unfurling uncertainty in handfuls.

If Trixie hadn't been messaging Jasper, that meant she was writing to someone else. Somebody who made her phone vibrate constantly, an angry beetle in her hand.

Somebody with an awful lot to say.

19

YOU HATED YOUR real name, so you gave it the same treatment as everything else you hated. You got rid of it and gave yourself a new one.

"Do I look like a fucking Tricia?" she said when I asked her where Trixie came from. "Or a Patti? I don't think so. When I was a little kid, my dad always said I had tricks up my sleeve. Tricks, he used to call me. So I turned into Trixie."

"The nickname stuck," I said.

She shook her head. "No, he was pissed. He loved the name Patricia. Named me after his mom, who died when he was little. He refused to let me legally change my name to Trixie. But it didn't matter, because I wouldn't answer to anything else."

"Cool," I said. She was the opposite of me. She answered only to what she wanted to be called. I answered to everything, from everyone.

"You could do it too, you know," she said, tugging on the end of my ponytail. "You could be anybody."

What I really want, I couldn't tell her, *is to be you.*

The question is, when she stopped wanting to be Trixie Heller, who did she turn into?

20

WHEN WE GET to the beach, I'm afraid to get out of the car, even though this was my idea.

"For the record, I still think this is a bad plan," Jasper says, stretching his arms over his head. The bottom of his shirt rides up, exposing a strip of pale white stomach. "These people are dangerous."

I pull the newspaper article out of my pocket, the one I fished out of our recycle bins right before the garbage truck came by. The one with the headline I have memorized:

ROBSON HIGH STUDENT'S
DISAPPEARANCE RULED SUICIDE

"I know. But we have to try. I won't be able to let it go if I don't at least ask someone." Trixie's grainy picture smiles up at me, a crease in the middle of her face. Wherever she is, does she think I'm looking for her?

"Well, at least stay close to me. This is out of my comfort zone too. At least we can be uncomfortable together," Jasper says when we're out of the car, reaching for my hand. His is cold, despite the heat. This is the first time I have ever really held hands with a boy, and I'm pathetic for thinking about it like that.

Morrison Beach is overrun with homeless people. Standing in the pavilion, sitting in the sand, sprawled out under the grove of trees dividing the beach from the road. It used to be a big issue when I was a kid. I remember Mom talking about how we had to clean up our city if we ever wanted tourists to come, and me asking why tourists were so important anyway.

But now, it's like the police just gave up on trying to keep them off the beach. Or else they struck some kind of deal with them. You stay out of our hair, and we'll stay out of yours.

Jasper and I walk onto the sand and my breath catches in my throat. I haven't been down here since before she disappeared, and maybe it's too soon. Maybe it's always going to be too soon. Everything about the beach reminds me of her. The places we spread a blanket out and sat, watching the sky turn yellow and pink and black. The wet sand by the water, where we built a sandcastle with the sun beating down on our backs. The shaded spot behind the fish-and-chip place, where she showed me how to smoke my first joint.

Jasper squeezes my hand, pulses my skin into his. "You know, we can go back to the car and forget about this. There are other ways to find her."

"No. There's something here. I just know there is." I'm lying. I feel nothing besides overwhelming uncertainty.

We walk past the homeless people. Some of them look up at us, some of them make jeering noises. Most of them are in various stages of passed out, some holding bottles. I don't see Byron St. James anywhere.

I know I'll recognize him. He was all over the news, telling the story, talking about how he wanted to help because he knows people who have committed suicide. A lot of people felt sorry for him, but some just figured he was looking for his fifteen minutes of fame. He had this big shock of blond hair and looked younger than most of these guys, and he was always wearing the same lime-green vest, the kind made of that vinyl material that dirt rubs off of.

"I think we should just go home," Jasper mutters, his head down. "Or to the library. It'll be quiet there, so we can think." His hand is getting hot and sweaty against mine, which means he's either nervous or scared. Or both.

"Just give me another minute." I stop to do a sweep of the crowd. But we're almost at the graffiti-sprayed brick wall, the one that leads out to the highway, and he's not here.

My chest starts to hurt as I turn my head slowly. Jasper squints into the sun, still clutching my hand. Part of me wants to drop his, but a stronger part wants to hold on for dear life. Especially when I see a person I was not expecting to find here.

Beau Hunter is under one of the trees, on his knees in the sand, drinking from a bottle. He does some handshake with one of the homeless guys and exchanges something in a manila envelope. I know that at any second, he's going to see me here with Jasper and everything will be ruined.

"Let's go," I say, yanking Jasper toward the brick wall. There's an opening nearby, where the words *YOU'RE REACHING OR PREACHING* are drawn over a spray-painted monster's mouth. Trixie and I used to slip through there instead of taking the long way around.

But when we get to the wall, Jasper just stands there, paralyzed in one spot. The opening is too far away. I glance over at Beau and he's still there, drinking in the sand. He's wearing a blue baseball cap, not the one he wears at school but the same one he had on the night of Alison's party. When he took it off, his hair was flat against his head and the ends curled around the back of his neck.

He'll think I followed him here. He'll wonder where else I followed him, who else I have been talking to. Unless I can make it so that he never knows I was here. His head begins to turn in our direction.

I press my back against the wall and let go of Jasper's hand. His drops to his side and he stares down at it, almost like he's just now realizing it's attached to his body. He doesn't have time to react when I grab the outside of his coat and pull him toward me. Beau will see the back of Jasper's head and the dirty fabric of his jacket and think he's just another homeless guy.

My face is pressed into Jasper's neck. He smells better than I thought he would, like soap and a bit of cologne. For some reason, when I used to see Jasper last year—when Trixie and I would pass him in the halls without so much as a wave—I always assumed he smelled bad, like sweat and wool and cigarettes. But I can tell, up this close, that he doesn't smoke at all.

And I don't know why—maybe because we're close enough to smell each other and our hearts are beating together, or because of the adrenaline rushing through our veins—but Jasper tilts his head down an inch and our lips meet, feather-light. We're both completely still, lips touching, breath halted, and I know I should say something, like *This isn't right*, but when I open my mouth, the only thing I do is press my lips harder against his. Then he sucks my bottom lip into his mouth and I feel a sob build in my throat and I should pull away, but instead I wrap one hand around the back of his neck and push my tongue against his teeth. I forget that he's him and I'm me, and it's like we're just at the beach for the same reason lots of people come here. To make out without getting caught.

I only pull away when he puts his hand on my waist and reality comes crashing down. I'm disgusted with myself. Disgusted for betraying her, even though she made it clear he was never her boyfriend.

"I'm sorry," we both say at the same time. It's too hot for us to be this close, and I let go of my grip on his coat. When I step back and look over his shoulder, Beau is gone.

21

I MET BEAU at a party freshman year. Kind of cliché, I know, which is why I never told you. Then again, you never asked.

I had gone outside for some air and he was standing on the deck, staring straight up at the sky. His Adam's apple poked out and the collar of his polo shirt gaped open to reveal tanned skin underneath. I just stood there, staring at him. I didn't know what it was. Sure, he was handsome, in a floppy-haired, preppy kind of way, but there were better-looking guys. It wasn't his bottomless blue eyes as much as it was the peace on his face, the kind of expression that made me think everything would be okay.

I stared at him for a long time, then craned my neck up to see what he was seeing. I expected something fascinating, a full moon or a shooting star, but there was just dark-blue sky, the indigo color of the skinny jeans Alison was wearing.

"You see him too?" he said.

I shook my head. "Who?"

He took my hand like it was the most natural thing in the world. "Look up again. It's Orion. I'll show you."

I still didn't see it, but eventually I said I did anyway,

because I wanted to feel like we were seeing the same thing. And when I stopped looking up, he was looking at me.

As it turned out, Beau was friends with Brad Colton, the guy Alison would spend freshman and sophomore year obsessed with. Plus, he made the football team, and I was a cheerleader, so I saw him more and more. At games. At parties. In the cafeteria at lunch. A few times, he bought chocolate milk and gave it to me because he knew how much I loved chocolate anything. He remembered things like that, little things, ways to make me smile. Ways to make me light up inside. Ways to touch me without being obvious. He would offer me rides home on his bike, even though I was out of his way, and when I stood on my driveway after, I waited for him to lean over and kiss me, imagining how it would feel. But he never did, and I didn't either.

Jenny and Alison teased me because they knew he liked me and they knew I liked him. But they didn't know I loved him, not until I told Jenny that day on the deck. Love was so much bigger.

He never had a girlfriend. I never had a boyfriend. I was too scared to ask him out, so I waited for him to ask me, but maybe he was waiting for me to do the same thing. I blushed around him and was embarrassed about it at first until I realized his neck turned red when he was near me too.

Our kiss would have happened if the sprinkler system wouldn't have chosen that exact moment to send freezing cold water spraying all over us, soaking our shirts and hair. Maybe he didn't try to kiss me again after because he was thinking the same thing I was. That our first kiss would be the start of something neither of us was ready for. It wouldn't just be a kiss, it would be everything that comes after. It would be like falling after you lose your balance and having no way of ever finding the ledge again.

The summer after sophomore year, he asked me if I was going to Alison's party. Then he asked again. Both times, I told him I was. But at the last minute, I ended up with food poisoning. I didn't worry about staying home, because there would be another night for me and Beau. A thousand other nights.

But that night, Toby disappeared, and whatever part of Beau that might have loved a part of me went with him.

22

WE RIDE BACK to the school in silence, like neither of us wants to make an effort to talk about what happened. And what didn't happen. Or what happens next. I grip the wheel and Jasper stares out the window.

"Maybe that guy's not here anymore," Jasper finally says, and I can tell by the measured tone of his voice that he had been thinking of exactly what to say. It's the total opposite of me, when I spill what's in my head in big inky blobs and regret it afterward. "He could have got his life together and made something of himself."

"It hasn't been that long. But maybe he did leave . . . and maybe he has a reason for not coming back," I say, forcing my lips to form the words, even though I know they sound ridiculous.

"What do you mean?" Jasper shifts in his seat, leans over the console.

"Like, maybe not being here was his plan the whole time."

He presses his hands against the dashboard. "I'm not really sure what you're trying to say. He just decided one day to become a magician and vanish into thin air?"

I let out a breath. "I know this might sound hard to believe, but what if he left on purpose? Like, he did what he was supposed to do. And took off because he didn't want to be found."

"Or maybe he's just a junkie who's on a bender somewhere. We can't go chasing a guy who may or may not be homeless. If he doesn't want to be found, he won't be. People are excellent at hiding when they need to."

We don't talk again until we pull into the Robson parking lot. The sky is darkening over the football field, casting the bleachers in tarry blackness. The grass is spiky and everything looks hard, like it was drawn too sharply.

Jasper undoes his seat belt and clears his throat. "I'm sorry we didn't find him. But we can say that we tried."

I know he must be thinking the same thing I am. That our one lead, our one chance to figure out where she is, has disappeared, and there's no backup plan. No other foothold to grab on to. No other reason for Jasper and me to spend another minute together.

"I can drive you home," I say. "I mean, it's a long walk."

He shakes his head. "Thanks. But I could use the walk. I do my best thinking when I do something else at the same time."

I don't know what I thought would happen. That we were in this strange place together, that we had shared something. I'm torn between the desire to cling to his skinny shoulders and never let him go and the urge to push him out of my car and never see him again.

He makes the choice for me. He gets out and shuts the door gently and doesn't look back. I watch him walk away until he's just another hard shadow in the dark.

I should start the car again and drive home. Mom must be wondering where I am, and I'm sure that if I were to look at my cell phone, I'd have a missed call from her. But I can't bring myself to go back there. Instead, I undo my seat belt and open my car door and walk into the school.

Laughter echoes down the hallway. Most of the class-rooms are dark, but the gym is lit up. The basketball team must be practicing, which makes me wonder if Jenny and Alison are there. I almost want to press my face against the foggy glass door and see what I'm missing, what I gave up. But I don't belong there anymore. Besides, there's something else I need to see.

I walk slowly toward the auditorium, where they held the memorial today. There's a trophy case outside on the right-hand side of the double doors, a whole wall of shiny gold accomplishments. And on the left-hand side, in stark juxta-position, the Dead Students Wall.

Of course, that's not what they call it. They call it *In Memoriam*. Up until last year, all the students were from before my time. People who died of illnesses and in tragic accidents. People who died before I was even born. Then Toby Hunter's picture was put up last year. Toby, with his gold hair and blue eyes and strong jawline. So much like Beau, but so different. I had read the inscription underneath his picture, and even though I didn't know him at all, I couldn't believe he was gone.

TOBIN BARTHOLOMEW HUNTER
April 3, 2000–August 31, 2017

I don't stop in front of Toby today. I stop in front of her. I don't know what I expected to feel. Sad, maybe. Angry.

Alone. But instead, I almost want to burst into laughter because she would hate this picture so much. I recognize it as her yearbook photo when she was a junior, taken the year before we met. She never got a senior yearbook photo taken because she purposely missed it, so in the senior yearbook, she's just a silhouette against a white backdrop.

Trixie in junior year was somebody I never knew. Somebody with shoulder-length brown hair and overplucked eyebrows. Somebody who you'd probably never pick out of a crowd. Plain, you might say. Unremarkable. No wonder I never noticed her at school until the day she jumped into my car and didn't give me a choice.

PATRICIA ELISE HELLER
March 4, 2000–August 13, 2018

I stare at her, into her brown eyes, pleading with her to give me a hint. A clue. Anything. I hate that this is what's left of her, a stupid picture that looks nothing like her and a name she hated. I hate that I'm standing in front of it. I wish that I could go back in time. I wish I had a car with doors that lock automatically, so nobody could just jump in.

I don't know how long I stand there. Long enough for my feet to go numb. Long enough for me to stop feeling my heartbeat, hard in my throat. Finally, when I hear the sound of heels clacking in the hall, I turn away, guilty, like I have been caught stealing.

When I'm at my locker, I spin the combination. I figure I'll fill my backpack with books and make it look like I was at school studying. Maybe I'll tell Mom I joined a club, or that I'm thinking of starting to make clothes again. She would love that. Something normal for her to cleave to, something that shows I'm moving on. It's a lie I'd willingly tell. After all, lies that make other people feel better must be kind of okay.

I'm just pulling the lock open when my fingers freeze over the dial and my fingertips go cold. I clamp the lock shut, then spin my fingers over each number again, lingering for longer than I need to as each one etches itself into my brain:

8-31-17

When the lock opens, I leave it that way and run back down the hall, even though I know what I'm going to find. I have to be sure. I have to be totally sure that this means something, anything.

I stop when I'm standing in front of his picture. This time I don't meet his eyes. I focus on the bronze plate below with the numbers carved in:

April 3, 2000–August 31, 2017

I'm falling even though I'm rooted to the ground. If anyone were to walk by, I would fall down. I want to scream and cry and tell someone, anyone, but what would I say? Who would believe me? Who would even care? Panic washes over me in waves, hammering at my temples, making everything spin.

Mostly, I want to slap myself for not figuring it out sooner. I shared a locker with Trixie for almost a whole year. I opened

that locker multiple times a day, and never once did I think
that the combination was more than just random numbers.
But I was wrong.

8-31-17 isn't just a locker combination. It's a date.

It's the day Toby Hunter died.

23

YOU WERE LIKE *a sister to me, but that was different from actually being sisters. We had less than a year of history. Beau and Toby were brothers, actual brothers. They probably shared a wall growing up, had a lifetime's worth of secrets and inside jokes.*

They were close, not just in age and appearance but in other ways. You could tell they genuinely liked each other. When they played football games together, Toby would watch out for Beau, making sure he was safe, as if he had made a promise to somebody to protect him. Maybe he had.

I saw Toby lose his temper once, when Beau got badly tackled by a giant linebacker from the Tasker Titans. Toby shoved the guy, who was built like a wall of bricks. The guy shoved him back. Toby yelled something I couldn't hear from the sidelines, not with the roar from the stands as loud as it was. In that moment, Toby wasn't a golden boy. He was something more. He was a big brother.

I didn't get it, because I didn't have any siblings. I always hoped for one. When I was little, I wanted Mom to meet someone and get married so I could have a little sister, someone to play dolls with. But it never happened.

I wondered if Beau and Toby got sick of each other. They

played on the same football team, went home to the same two-story every night. I wondered if they ever felt competitive with each other, like they were constantly dueling for one source of light. But it didn't seem that way. There seemed to be plenty of light for both Hunters.

Beau went to all of Toby's swim meets. I went too, with Jenny and Alison. They watched the race, but I watched Beau, on his feet, fists flying, screaming at the top of his lungs. I watched him pummel his arms in the air when Toby touched the wall first. It was his victory too, somehow. Maybe that was what it meant to be a brother

But the last time I ever saw them together was the last day of sophomore year, when Beau was getting into the passenger side of Toby's car. He raised his middle finger at the back of Toby's head, then slammed the door. I wondered what they were arguing about, what Toby had done to piss Beau off. Maybe that was what it meant to be a brother too. Arguments that seemed important, then dissolved like sugar in tea, because obviously they would get over it.

But maybe there were some things that couldn't be forgiven.

24

OUR LOCKER COMBINATION stays in my head the whole next week. A week during which I avoid Jasper on purpose, ducking into bathrooms or turning down halls whenever I see a dark coat coming toward me. I almost want to tell him I'm sorry for kissing him. But then I can't remember if it was the other way around, if he was the one who kissed me. I want to tell him about the locker combination, but I don't know what it means.

I turn the three numbers over in my head, again and again. 8-31-17. I saw Toby's picture in the hall a hundred times and spun the lock a hundred times more last year. How did I not figure it out sooner?

Except, I don't know what I figured out. Or why Trixie would have picked the day Toby Hunter died as our locker combination. As far as I know, she had nothing to do with Toby Hunter. She never mentioned him in all the time I knew her. She certainly wasn't part of his group of friends, the ones that used to hang around after football games and pick him up after practice, squealing into the parking lot with their arms hanging out of their cars. Trixie never so much as made eye contact with them in the hall.

More than once, I convince myself that I made it up.

That the numbers are a coincidence, and there's no point in thinking of them as anything different. I push them into the place in my brain where all the secrets are hidden and bury them there. But they keep breaking through the cracks, shooting up like blades of grass.

My phone vibrates when I'm standing in front of my locker at the end of lunch period, fingering the lock absent-mindedly. I'm about to grab my phone from my purse, but a hand clamps down on my shoulder. I close my eyes, thinking it must be Jasper and feeling both nervous and relieved.

"Hey," Alison says, sidling up next to me.

I gape at her like a fish. She's taller than me and has the same perky blond ponytail she always wears to school on game days. She's wearing a shirt that rides up to her belly button, and I fight a pang of envy for when I used to be able to wear stuff like that.

"Hey," I say.

"Look, I know we haven't talked in a while," Alison says. "But I just wanted to say I'm sorry for what happened to your friend. And I'm here, you know, if you ever want to talk. Or anything."

I force myself to smile and hug my books to my chest. I don't deserve Alison's sympathy. Not after how I pushed her away last year when she tried to pull me back, and not after what I did at her party. If she knew about that, she wouldn't be standing in front of me right now.

"Thanks," I say.

"Maybe if you're not busy sometime, we can . . . ," Alison starts, but she never gets to finish the sentence because Jenny comes up behind her and grabs her elbow.

"We're late for geometry," Jenny says without making eye

contact. My face is on fire. The bell rings and Alison waves, walking in the other direction, arm in arm with Jenny, her ponytail bouncing against the small of her back.

In this moment, I hate Jenny more than ever.

Jenny never tried to stay friends. We drifted further and further apart until we got to that stage where we not only didn't talk, but we each pretended the other didn't exist. At first, I conjured the highlights of our friendship in bits and pieces, like a cheesy movie montage, and missed her a lot. I would remember her fearlessness and her ability to make fun of herself and the fuzzy cat slippers she wore at sleepovers. Then I thought of all the things about her that bugged me, like how controlling she was and how she always had to be the center of attention, and eventually I knew I was better off without her.

Then she purposely started flaunting Beau in front of me. Making out with him in the hallway, where she knew I could see, and draping herself all over him. And I hated her.

I consider skipping my last two classes of the day. English has always been easy for me. It's not like one missed day will mean anything. But then I remember we're supposed to be dissecting a frog during AP biology and that if I don't show up, Brett Fillmore will be stuck doing it on his own. Brett, who ended up with me as a lab partner because of where his last name falls in the alphabet. If he doesn't hate me already, he'll definitely hate me if I don't help him with the frog.

It's not until I sit down behind my desk in the lab that everything hits me. The stench of formaldehyde, the dizzying reality of what I should have figured out days, weeks, months ago.

I had this thing with my lab partner.

I want to get up and run away, but Brett is sitting down beside me, giving me a tight-lipped smile, which I return, grateful he doesn't know what's going on inside my head. Mr. Thorpe clears his throat from the front of the classroom and tells us it's time to pick a frog.

After class, I wait for Jasper in front of the school, knowing he'll walk home with his earbuds in. When I see him barge through the double doors, I jog to keep pace with his long strides. "I have to know something. You said you met Trixie back in freshman year. You had class together. What class was it?"

Jasper's face flashes with an expression I haven't seen him wear before. It's so foreign to me that I can't pinpoint what it is. Annoyance, probably. Frustration.

"French," he says. "It was French class. Why?"

"So, you weren't her lab partner?"

Jasper shakes his head. "I hate science. My brain doesn't do well with facts. I'm better with words."

"She told me she had a thing with her lab partner," I say, picturing the frog's soft belly, the way its skin was swollen and bloated like it had been underwater forever.

"Well, I wasn't her lab partner." Jasper stuffs his hands in his pocket and pulls out his MP3 player. "And what does it matter now?"

"I think I know who was. And I think he had something to do with her disappearance."

25

YOUR FUNERAL WAS the second one I went to where there was no body to bury.

I didn't want to go to Toby's funeral. Not because I knew it would be sad, but because I didn't feel like I deserved to be there. I wasn't at the party. I wasn't there for Beau.

I wrote him so many text messages after I found out what happened, but didn't send a single one. None of them seemed right. None of them were enough. I wasn't his girlfriend. I wasn't around.

Jenny, Alison, and I went to the church together. Beau was a pallbearer, along with five other blond guys who must have been cousins. They all looked somber, serious. I waited for Beau to cry, because I knew he was sensitive like that, and I knew how much he loved Toby.

But he didn't cry. His expression didn't change during the entire service, or at the interment, when Toby's coffin was lowered into the ground. I wondered what was in it, because there was no body.

Later, at the reception, Jenny and I approached Beau together. She put her hand on his arm. He stared at it.

"I'm sorry," I said, choking back a sob. "I'm so sorry."

He wouldn't look at me, but just kept looking at Jenny's

hand on his arm, tiny and white like a little doll's. When he did speak, it was something incoherent. I smelled the alcohol on his breath right away. Beau wasn't a drinker, but his brother had just died. He needed some way of coping.

After that, Beau wasn't Beau anymore. He never biked to school and never offered me rides and his eyes were permanently fixed on the ground, not on the stars, where they used to be. I should have tried harder to get through to him, but I didn't. I was scared of who he was becoming.

I figured he would heal with time, that everyone would. I was right about everyone else, but Beau never did.

26

JASPER FOLLOWS ME back into the school. I'm not sure what I'm going to say to Mr. Thorpe, or if he's even the right person to ask. Robson High has at least three different science teachers, and I don't know which one taught Trixie. I almost turn around when we're in the hall, because I can just imagine how insane it's going to sound.

Hey, Mr. Thorpe, remember Trixie Heller? Yeah, can you tell me who her lab partner was two years ago? Or maybe it was three years ago? Why do I want to know? Funny you should ask . . .

"Hey," Jasper says, trailing behind me. "Let's just go somewhere and talk. We can go back to my place. I have this globe she used to love to spin and put her finger on. Maybe we can see if that means anything."

But I'm on a mission. I'm not letting this go. I know I'm right, even if I don't know exactly what I'm right about. Besides, a globe is the whole world. I need to start smaller.

Mr. Thorpe is leaving the lab when we round the corner. His back is to us and he's pulling the door shut. I start talking before I can listen to the voice in my head telling me to stop. Which sounds an awful lot like Jasper's calm, measured voice.

"Mr. Thorpe," I say to his back. "I have a really random question I was hoping you could help me with."

"Fiona," he says when he turns around, clasping his hands together. "Of course, I'm happy to help. Is it about today's experiment?"

I shake my head. "No, it's something else. I'm just wondering if you ever taught Trixie, uh, Patricia Heller. If she was in one of your classes."

His forehead creases and his beady eyes fill with something that looks a lot like pity. He shakes his head slightly. He doesn't know anything and now he probably thinks I'm depressed; I already know Jasper thinks I'm reading too much into this. Maybe they're both right. Maybe I should have just listened to Mom and seen Dr. Rosenthal and started talking about my feelings.

But Mr. Thorpe scratches his bald head and starts to nod. "I did teach Patricia, back in her junior year. She was excellent at experiments. Had a real brain for the math involved." He stares at me with a furrowed brow. "Is there any special reason why you're asking?"

A million butterflies are beating their wings inside my chest. "Yeah. By any chance, do you remember who her lab partner was?"

Mr. Thorpe stares at the ground. "My classes are always alphabetical. I do it that way to be fair. Don't want anyone to get left out because they're not the most popular."

"So, who was hers?" I stammer.

"Hers was Toby Hunter," he says with a deep sigh. "It's such a terrible tragedy, what happened to both of them. I know you were close to her, Fiona. I'm sorry for your loss."

His words stab me. Not just the ones that clarified my

theory about Toby Hunter being her lab partner, but the last ones he said, the ones still hanging in the air. *I'm sorry for your loss.* Mr. Thorpe is the only person who has said those words to me. At the funeral, everyone said them to Mr. Heller, not me. And I'm surprised by how soft they make me feel, like I'm gauzy cotton that could dissolve if I let myself cry.

"Thanks," I manage. "Thanks for telling me." I turn to leave and almost crash right into Jasper, who is staring at the wall. I forgot he was even there.

"If there's anything else you ever want to talk about, come and see me anytime," Mr. Thorpe says, almost warily. I'm sure he wonders why I wasted his time.

"He could have answered your question too," Mr. Thorpe continues, gesturing behind me with his index finger. "Jasper Hart. He was in the same class. Sat one desk over, with Michelle Green." He jangles his keys and drops them in his lab coat pocket before walking the other way down the hall.

Suddenly, I feel like I did when I was ten years old and fell out of a tree house at summer camp. I had landed on my stomach on the ground and panicked because I couldn't breathe. The wind had been knocked out of me, my camp counselor said. It would come back as long as I held it together.

This time, I'm not so sure.

27

YOU SAID SOMETHING I'll always remember. You told me lies were some people's version of a flower bouquet. Sweet and pretty, and too fragrant for the recipient to smell any bullshit. But then they'd start to wilt and the water in their vase would get filmy and brown, and once the decay set in, so would the truth.

Jenny used to lie in little ways. She was a chronic exaggerator, the type of person whose stories would gain momentum as she told them. I never called her out on the details she added because it never seemed like a big deal.

Alison lied by omission. She would just nod her head and let you think whatever you wanted to think without correcting you one way or another.

Beau lied to me once. He told me, during a party in Brad Colton's basement, that he wasn't ever going to get drunk, because he didn't want to do anything he couldn't remember.

"My dad drinks sometimes," he told me when we were sitting side by side on an ottoman, since all the couches were taken. "He says things, like how he should be living a different life. In the morning he never mentions it. I don't want to turn into him."

"You won't," I said, but maybe I lied too.

28

JASPER WON'T LOOK at me. He peers intently at his shoes, long after Mr. Thorpe has disappeared from view. I try to think of something to say. An accusation, something sharp. But I can't think of anything that fits. The words get caught in my throat, too big to come up such a small pipe.

"Look, I didn't know how to tell you," he finally says, his words cluttered together. "I only took the class because my parents made me, and I went along with it since Trixie was there. Toby was, let's just say, difficult. So cocky, always late, never wanting to do what he was told. Trixie hated sitting there. She and I did our homework together and she complained about him nonstop. Trust me, if there was something going on, I would have known it."

I shake my head. "The first day I met her, she said something about her lab partner. And then she never mentioned it again. Why would she even mention it if it wasn't important?"

Jasper presses his lips together. "I don't know. Maybe she was talking about me. We were supposed to be lab partners. Hart and Heller. Then Michelle Green came in at the last minute and everything got shifted around."

I stare at the bank of lockers behind us, then grab Jasper's hand and start pulling him down the hall. "If that's not enough for you, I'll show you something else."

Jasper's hand is sweaty in mine by the time we arrive at my locker. I'm the first one to let go to pull the lock open, reading out the numbers as the dial hits each one.

"Eight. Thirty-one. Seventeen. That was her locker combination, Jasper. Do you still think all this adds up to nothing?"

He rakes his hand through his hair. The same hand that was just holding mine. His fingers are long and pale, and I imagine them on Trixie's face, the same way he touched mine at the beach.

"I don't know what that even means. I'm sorry. It's just a locker combination."

"Eight. Thirty-one. Seventeen. August thirty-first. The day Toby Hunter died."

Jasper doesn't say anything. It's like he's a machine, processing the new information. When he does speak, it's rushed, not measured like when he usually talks. "Well, maybe I didn't know her as well as I thought. Maybe she wanted it that way. She could've had feelings for him. It's not like I was ever her boyfriend, remember? But he's dead, and she's gone, and we'll never know the truth."

My head swims. Part of me knows he's right. The sensible version of me, the one that never skipped a class or flaked out on plans. The part that would have still been on the surface if I hadn't gone to my car that day instead of cheerleading practice.

But an even bigger part of me—this version, the one who doesn't fit into her old clothes or her old life—knows there is more to the story.

"We might never know the truth," I say slowly. "But I have a theory."

Jasper's eyes widen. "What's your theory?"

I clutch the lock in my hand, the dial digging into my palm. "What if Toby's alive?"

"Three people saw that guy go in the water. There's no way he's not dead, unless he grew gills and turned into a fish. Or grew wings and learned to fly. Anyone who thinks otherwise is in serious denial."

I click the lock into place. "So maybe I'm in denial. But I'm going to find out what happened. I owe her that much." I turn my back on Jasper and start to walk away.

"Why do you owe her anything?" he calls after me, his voice echoing down the hall. "What did she ever do for you?"

She made me feel like I was the only person in the world, I want to yell back. *She liked me for who I was, not who she wanted me to be. She let me be myself.* But as quickly as the thoughts rush through my head, I wonder if they're even true. I'm not sure she ever got a chance to know me, because I didn't even know who I was with her. I shaped myself into whoever she wanted me to be the second I listened when she told me to drive. I had lots of chances along the way to tell her I didn't eat meat, I didn't lie to my mom, I liked cheerleading, I loved Beau Hunter no matter what anyone said. But I never took them. I kept being who I thought she wanted me to be.

"Let's go somewhere," Jasper says, quieter this time. "Let's just go talk. Not about her. We can do something normal. Like, see a movie. Or get food. Whatever you want. We have to move on with our lives."

I guess he has a point. If Trixie is gone, not dead, she took great pains not to leave a mess in her place. So why am I making one, smearing all of our memories and everything she ever told me onto what should just be left a blank canvas?

I want to say all of this to Jasper. My heart is wedged somewhere it doesn't even fit and my head is fuzzy. I want to say so much, but instead I just shake my head.

"I can't move on. I need to figure out the truth. I need to know if she's still alive."

29

YOU WARNED ME about Jenny. "Girls like that won't stab you in the back," you said. "They'll put the knife right in your chest." I didn't want to believe you, even though she had already broken the skin.

They were standing there. Right in front of the locker Jenny and I shared. By the time Jenny and I became best friends, lockers had already been assigned, but she bribed some girl into switching. I couldn't even count the times I had stood there and braided my hair or listened to gossip or bitched about a stupid teacher.

But there she was, with her back pressed against our locker, with her fingers laced around Beau's neck. It was dark, but I could see her hip jutting into his. His head bent.

I expected it to hurt, seeing them together. But I didn't expect it to hurt that much. Part of me hoped they would go on one date and realize they had nothing to talk about. I was realizing they didn't have to talk at all.

I spun around and stormed back to the parking lot. I just wanted to be alone, to cry and pound my steering wheel and scream. But Trixie was there, sitting on the curb.

"Hey." She stood up and dusted off her jeans. "What do

you say we buy some beer with my fake ID and go to the beach?"

I almost told her about Beau and Jenny then. I almost told her everything. Instead, I said something else.

"Hey, do you think we could share a locker?"

Later that night, my head buzzing, I stood on my bed and tore down the collage. The pictures got ripped to pieces and thrown in the trash can beside my desk, along with the swatches of fabric for dresses I didn't want to make. I shredded the stupid smiling photos, the ones of me and Jenny and Alison in a mall photo booth, the team shot from last year's cheer meet. We looked so young, so wholesome, and it was such a lie.

The next day, I purposely left my cheerleading uniform at home. And the day after that.

When Jenny finally cornered me in the bathroom at school, asking why I moved my stuff out of our locker, I told her things had changed. I wanted to give her the same line she had fed me. *It's not like I could say no.*

30

JASPER'S WORDS ARE the soundtrack of my drive home. He talks about moving on with our lives like it's some milestone we can achieve together, and maybe he's right. But I don't want to need someone else that badly. Everyone I've ever needed hasn't needed me back.

When I pull into the driveway, Mom's car is already in the garage. Normally, she works late and I always beat her home, so I'm surprised to see her. I'm even more surprised when she's sitting at the kitchen table, leveling me with a disapproving stare.

"What?" I ask.

"I got an interesting phone call today," she says, crossing her arms. "From Dr. Rosenthal's office. It seems that you missed your appointment. The one you told me went well."

My shoulders go up around my ears. I can't think of a lie to get out of this one. Mom asked me about Dr. Rosenthal and I told her I was glad I went, that I learned a lot about myself.

"What's going on here, Fiona? Did you have something better to do than keep the appointment I booked for you?"

Yes, I want to say. *I was searching for my best friend. The one you disapproved of. The one I know isn't actually dead.*

"I guess I was just scared," I tell her, and her face softens. She takes off her glasses, rubs the bridge of her nose, where they always leave a mark.

"I told you I'd go with you, honey. I just need you to go, at least once. It doesn't make you weak to talk to someone. You know, I talked to Dr. Rosenthal after everything that happened with Leslie. He really helped me. And talking about it helped me and Leslie become close again."

I didn't know that Mom had talked to Dr. Rosenthal too, or to anyone. My aunt Leslie is an alcoholic and Mom likes to refer to whatever she did as "everything that happened," which I'm sure is a euphemism for something really bad. But now Aunt Leslie is sober and has a nice apartment in Costa Mesa and she and Mom talk on the phone almost daily. She's all about yoga and hiking and making her own skin care products out of things in her kitchen. Even if she weren't my only aunt, she would be my favorite one.

"I'll go," I say quickly. "I promise. But I don't want you to go with me."

"I'll be calling the next day to make sure you actually went," she says. "I'll make you another appointment, and this time there will be consequences if you don't keep it."

I don't really want to know what she means by that. Mom has never been very good at being a disciplinarian. She's so much younger than all of my friends' moms and sometimes she treats me more like a friend than a daughter.

"Why do you *really* want me to go?" I say before I can stop myself. "Is it because I've gained so much weight and you're ashamed of me?"

Her face is a mask of shock. "Honey, how could you think that? I could never be ashamed of you. I love you more than anything. And you're beautiful, no matter what. This has nothing to do with what weight you are. It's about what's going on up here." She taps her head.

"But all the health food and everything. I thought—"

"I think what we put into our bodies makes a huge difference in how we feel. All I'm trying to do is set us up to be the best versions of ourselves." She pauses. "I'd love you at any weight. I just want you to be happy. You deserve that."

I try to believe her—that she really doesn't think I'm fat, and that she thinks I deserve to be happy. I help Mom prepare dinner—zucchini pasta made with her new spiralizer—and it feels almost normal, the two of us spending time together. When I go upstairs afterward, I open my desk drawer where I keep my junk food and stare at packages of licorice and bags of chips and rolls of Life Savers and twist-tied bundles of Sour Patch Kids. My myriad of rebellions. But they don't look tempting anymore, just gross. So instead of opening something, I toss the entire stash into the garbage can beside my desk. That's when I see what was buried at the very bottom of the drawer.

My fake ID, the one Trixie got me. The one I brought when she made me go to clubs with her. I was somebody named Beth Winchester. I felt pretty the first night we went because a guy hit on me. He asked what my name was and I told him Fiona. Trixie had jabbed me in the ribs with her bony elbow.

"Don't use your real name," she hissed.

"Why not? I'll never see him again," I said.

"Exactly." And she went right up to the same guy and

introduced herself as Sarah. Sarah Brown, the girl on her fake ID, who didn't really exist.

That's when it hits me.

Maybe I don't need to look for Trixie. Maybe I need to look for someone else.

31

I HATED BETH Winchester. I was offended because I thought she was ugly, with a round face and thin eyebrows that made her look scared. I was afraid her face was what people saw when they looked at me. I didn't want you to see me like that, a chubby-cheeked nobody. But you just told me to shut up, that you were taking me to the club.

I liked being drunk. I liked being weightless, losing my inhibitions. When I danced, I felt sexy, like I had stepped outside my own body and become someone else. Someone I wanted to be, someone like Trixie. Trixie, who liked to wear little backless tops that showed her sharp shoulder blades, and sometimes grinded against random guys.

When summer started, we went out more often. Mom wasn't around to make comments about how late I slept in, and I didn't care if I was hungover, because I never had school the next day. And it's not like I was going to cheerleading camp, like I had done for the past three summers, even though Mom left the brochure on the counter like it would make me change my mind. The days stretched on, sated with food and wine coolers and bright pink sunsets.

Until the day my aunt Leslie dropped by unannounced when we were lounging on the couch, watching bad reality

TV in our pajamas. Aunt Leslie's jaw practically dropped when she walked in the room and saw the mess. Pizza boxes and fast-food wrappers and two girls in the middle of it.

I froze in panic. I had convinced Mom I didn't need a chaperone, and I knew Aunt Leslie would report back to Mom that I had been wasting my whole summer on a junk-food bender.

But Trixie somehow saved the situation. She got up and said hi to Aunt Leslie and asked her if she wanted to come shopping and out for lunch with us. She was perky and cheerful and so totally not herself. On our way out the door, Aunt Leslie stopped and asked Trixie her name.

"Sarah," she said, without a pause or any hesitation. "Sarah Brown."

I didn't know why she lied. Obviously Mom would find out when Aunt Leslie described her. But then again, maybe not. She wasn't the bleached-blond pixie-cut, lip-ring-wearing friend I first brought home. She had black hair extensions that week and fake eyelashes that made her eyes look enormous. Maybe Mom would think I made a new friend, someone who was a better influence.

So we took Aunt Leslie to a burger place by the pier. Trixie talked the whole time about her big plans to study law at Harvard and her volunteer work with underprivileged kids and her parents, who were abroad building houses. "You should see the pictures they send me of Africa," she said. "It's so serene. I'd like to join them there one day." She told lie after lie without even stopping for a breath. She lied the same way she ate. Fast, without even chewing the pieces before she swallowed. Without letting anything digest.

When Trixie got up to use the bathroom, Aunt Leslie

placed her hand on mine. "Your friend seems very nice, sweetie. But you need to take care of yourself, okay? You can't live on junk food all summer. Promise me you'll have some veggies, okay?"

I nodded, and it was that easy to get her off my back.

Afterward, we waited in the driveway and waved as Aunt Leslie drove away. I glanced over at Trixie and she was wearing this gigantic smile that I had never even seen before, a smile that showed all her teeth. The second Aunt Leslie's car turned the corner and disappeared from view, that smile started to deflate.

"What was that all about?" I said. "Why didn't you just tell the truth?"

She started walking back inside. "Because it was easy. Sometimes it's fun to be someone else."

It was easy, she said.

But it was way too easy for her.

32

TWO HUNDRED AND sixty-three million.

That's how many Sarah Browns exist, according to Google. Too many to ever track down, even if I had a lifetime to do it. I almost don't want to mention it to Jasper because I know he's determined to move on, and also because after he lied about Toby being Trixie's lab partner, I wonder what else he could be hiding from me. And why.

I'm sitting in my car eating lunch alone the next day when the passenger door opens and Beau is standing there, wild-eyed and frantic.

"I did something bad," he says. "Something real bad. I need your help."

I motion for him to get in and a bag of chips falls off my lap onto the floor. It's hot in here, the kind of heat that makes you feel perpetually sticky, and the air gets even thicker once Beau gets in and shuts the door. He smells like alcohol and body odor, and his eyes are bloodshot.

"You need to hide this." He thrusts a bag into my lap. It's a black backpack and for a second, my stomach lurches because it looks exactly like Trixie's backpack, right down to the white trim.

"Where did you get this?" I say. "This isn't yours."

He looks at me like I'm insane, and maybe I am. Then he flips the bag over and I can see that it's not the same, that it has pockets where Trixie's didn't, and my breathing starts to go back to normal.

"I just need you to keep it here." He leans in a bit closer, and the sour smell on his breath makes me want to gag when he whispers against my cheek. "I'm in trouble."

"What kind of trouble?"

"It's not important. I just need your help with this, okay?"

"No, it's not okay." It feels good to put up a fight. "Tell me what's in the bag, or else I'm going to open it for myself anyway."

He looks frantically behind him, in front of him, to the side, to make sure nobody is watching. Then he unzips the bag and pulls a bottle of vodka out. And then a bottle of something amber-colored. Finally, at the bottom, a baggie of weed.

"There, that's it. Just stuff. It's not a murder weapon or anything."

Yes, *it is*, I want to say. *You're killing yourself.*

"What if someone finds it here?" I say instead. "I can't keep this in my car."

"I don't have a car to keep it in." His voice is rough and scratchy, like he's about to cry. "My dad drives me to school. I keep this in my locker and I'm the only one who knows the combination. But Coach Mortimer, he's doing locker searches today. He heard a rumor from some narc that there are guys on the team doing drugs."

I shake my head slowly. *How could you be so stupid? How could you be so careless?* But I guess I already knew that Beau is both of those things.

The worst part is, this isn't the first time he's asked me to store something for him. That was two years ago, when he had a bunch of books he'd taken out from the library that he told me he didn't have time to stick in his own locker, because he was running late for practice. When I took the books from him, I got the feeling he just didn't want anyone else to see that he had them. They were books of poetry by Lord Byron, who we had studied briefly in freshman-year English and whose poems I had glazed over, more preoccupied with cheerleading and my friends than the words of yet another long-dead white guy. But that day, I stood by my locker and read the poems, and with every line, it was like I knew more about Beau.

"Nobody will check here," he says now, and he's already shoving the bottles and the baggie underneath the passenger seat. "You won't get into any trouble. I promise, nobody will ever know."

He looks right at me and it makes my heart hurt. Beau is the only person who can do this, who can make me feel like he sees what other people never will. I don't even have to say yes, because he already knows.

You have a problem, I imagine myself saying. *You need help.*

Anger starts to build up inside me and that's what scares me, how it can come out of nowhere and clot everything else. I want to grab his shoulders and shake him and tell him I'm not always going to be here to cover for him. My body is about to capsize, like a punctured life raft. *I can't be your life raft because I'm sinking too.* But instead, I just nod. Only when he's already gone do I mutter under my breath, "I hate you."

I find Jasper after last period. He's coming out of the computer lab, staring at his phone, and I stand in front of him on purpose, knowing he'll crash into me.

He whips his phone into his coat pocket and curls his lips into a smile that looks more like a grimace. "Fiona. Hi. I've been wanting to talk to you."

For some reason, maybe because he's the only person who wants to talk to me, everything I wasn't planning on telling him all spills out. "I want to talk to you too. Did you ever hear Trixie mention Sarah Brown?"

He shakes his head. "No. Who is she?"

"I don't know. Maybe nobody. Or maybe the person we're looking for."

I tell him the whole story, about how she already had the fake ID when we met. About how she never told me where mine came from, and never asked me to pay for it. Almost like she had been waiting for a Beth Winchester to come along the whole time.

"We should go to the police," I say. "This is proof."

Jasper shakes his head again and hair falls into his eyes. He leaves it there. "This isn't proof of anything. So she had a fake ID. Lots of kids have them. It really doesn't prove anything." He lowers his voice. "I just think this trail you're trying to follow leads nowhere."

"Maybe it does. But let's say she could turn into Sarah Brown. What else would she need to disappear and have nobody find her? A new passport? Credit cards? Maybe that's how it was with Toby Hunter. Maybe he got fake IDs too, and he could have told Trixie where he got his."

Jasper blows out a breath. "Toby Hunter is dead. And you

said it yourself—Trixie didn't ever mention him. So they have nothing to do with each other. All of this is a series of really bizarre coincidences."

"I need to know for sure. We need to find out where she got it," I say. I realize I'm using *we*, not *I*, and that it's because I'm scared to do this myself. Scared of what I might find, or what I won't.

"Well, I can't help you with that. Maybe you haven't noticed, but I'm not exactly the kind of person with any use for a fake ID."

It's not what he says, exactly. It's the way he says it, like he knows he's not cool and he's never going to be cool. I guess I always thought that Jasper was immune to the comments people make about him at school, things like *freak* and *weirdo* and *loser*.

"There's one place we can look," I say. "But I'm kind of freaked out about going there. Maybe we can go together."

Jasper sucks in a breath and bites his bottom lip, making it shiny and red. "Okay," he says, and all I hear in his voice is hesitation. Not that I blame him.

We get in my car and I start driving. The passenger seat is still pushed back from the last time Jasper sat there, so this time his legs fit better. When I pull away from the school and make a sharp right-hand turn, the bottles Beau gave me roll out from under the seat. Jasper stops one with his foot.

"I didn't take you as the type of person who kept an alcohol stash in her car," he says, rolling the sole of his boot over the bottle. "Actually, I never pegged you for a drinker at all. This seems like more of a Trixie thing."

"I'm not," I say quickly, wondering how he could possibly peg me for anything when we've only really known each other for a handful of weeks. "I mean, I've had drinks. I've been drunk. But that's not mine. A friend asked me to keep it there."

"Okay," Jasper says. "I've never liked the idea of alcohol. People drink it for an excuse to let their monsters loose."

I wonder if he's talking about Trixie or me or just people in general, if he has had personal experience with what alcohol can do. He clears his throat and changes the subject. "So where are we going?"

"We're going to the one place she might have left a clue."

Jasper taps his fingers on his leg. "And where's that?"

"Her bedroom."

33

YOU DIDN'T KNOW who I was before you. Maybe because you never bothered to ask. It was like you didn't want that girl to exist anymore.

The Robson Red Flag pep rally was the school's biggest pre-season event. The cheerleaders got dressed up in their game-day outfits and showed off the routine they had been working on for weeks, the tumbling passes they knew would have people on their feet. It was their turn to get the glory. I had already missed a few practices at that point, but I couldn't miss the rally. The girls were counting on me.

"You could come," I told Trixie, but even as I said it, I knew she wouldn't.

"I have a shift at Cabana Del Shit," she said, staring at her face in our locker mirror. "Besides, I'm not into the school-spirit thing. I thought you could come and hang out, and we could do something after. I'll make you one of those chocolate milkshakes you like."

Trixie had been working at Cabana Del Shit all through high school. Which was actually a little hole-in-the-wall restaurant near the beach called Cabana Del Sol. She was a dishwasher, a job that left her hands perpetually dry and cracked. She hated working there but loved complaining about her coworkers: Skylar, the bitchy waitress who had it out for her. Max, the hot but dumb bartender. The pervy line cooks who brought porn magazines into the bathroom.

"Oh." I leaned into the locker beside ours. "That would be great. But I can't miss the rally. Can I just come after?"

"Don't bother." She snapped her gum while she applied eyeliner in quick little strokes. "We don't have to do everything together."

"I'll text you when it's done," I said.

"I have to go. See you later." She scuffed down the hall in her flip-flops without looking back. No signature peace-sign wave, no smile.

The panic was instant. I knew I had screwed up, with Trixie and with everyone else. Getting ready for the rally was something Jenny, Alison, and I had done together since freshman year. We would braid each other's hair and admire how good we looked together, my auburn head next to Jenny's dark-brown one and Alison's blond. We complemented each other, the perfect trio. Things had changed, but Alison had asked me that morning if I was going to be there and I told her I would. I wasn't ready to not be part of that anymore.

I put on my makeup with shaky hands and changed into my uniform in the bathroom. It still fit, even though I hadn't been taking care of myself. I had been eating all of Trixie's favorite foods, the ones Mom never kept in our house. The fact that the uniform still fit made me think I could still fit. I could be a cheerleader and be friends with Trixie. I could have it all. I'd see Trixie later and make it up to her, tell her we could drive anywhere.

But something told me that wasn't true. I had never been good at making decisions. Even the smallest choices, like whether to have garden or Greek salad for lunch, practically paralyzed me. I always knew that whatever I ended up choosing, I would want what I didn't pick.

I wore my uniform out to the parking lot and saw Jenny and Alison jogging on the track, braids bouncing in unison on their shoulders. Jenny leaned in and pulled on the end of Alison's hair, said something that made them both laugh. I wasn't there, and it didn't matter. They were still laughing. Probably at me.

I rubbed the red lipstick off my mouth and darted into my car, still wearing my uniform. I drove away from them, just like I did that day when I met Trixie.

When I showed up at Cabana Del Shit, Trixie looked surprised to see me. She was wearing a stained apron and baseball cap and carrying a giant bin full of dishes back to the kitchen, and her arms were shaking hard, like the bin could fall any minute. She made me a chocolate milkshake, just like she said she would. I sat at the bar, still in uniform.

"I thought you had some big rally," she said.

"I did. But I decided not to go. I don't think I'm a cheer-leader anymore."

She smiled. "You know, I used to wish I had a sister, when I was growing up. This is how I thought it would be."

And just like that, quitting the squad was the best thing I had ever done.

A week later, Alison tried to pull me back. She thought I was sinking and wanted to throw me a life preserver, give me one last chance to get on the boat. She had it all wrong. She didn't understand that I was flying, high as a kite, light as a balloon, and it really pissed me off that she wanted to yank me down.

"Fiona," she called across Mr. More's algebra class at the end of the day, over the sound of thirty students throwing books into their bags and gunning for the door.

"Hey," I said, shoving my backpack over my shoulder.

"Can we talk for a second?" She sat on the edge of my desk, her stupid toned leg in my face. I didn't want to be that close to Alison. It was easier when I was with Trixie and she was my shield, impervious to dents.

"Sure," I said warily.

Alison stared at the ground, and that's when I could tell she was nervous too. Usually, she was great at making eye contact and speaking her mind. That was why parents loved her so much. That was why she was a great student and the newly minted captain of the cheerleading squad. People like Alison had nothing to hide.

"I just wanted to say that we miss having you on the team. It's not the same without you. And I miss hanging out with you. Did I do something to make you stop wanting to be friends?" She curled her fingers up in her lap, waited for me to speak.

I had no idea what to say. I couldn't explain it to her. I couldn't tell her that Jenny had ruined my life, that every time I saw her with Beau I felt like I was being kicked in the gut. Alison would say *Friends always come before boys*, even though she knew I loved Beau first and that Jenny didn't pay me the same courtesy. I'd have to shake her until she realized how easily Jenny let me go, as if I were never even there to begin with.

"It's not you," I said, and I almost laughed because it

sounded like the start of a bad breakup line, just like Brad Colton gave Alison when he dumped her last year. "I made a new friend, that's all. And cheerleading isn't for me anymore."

"Okay," Alison said. "But I'm worried about you. You kind of just shut us out of your life, right after you started hanging out with her."

I couldn't ignore the way she said *her*, like it was a wad of poison she had to spit out. I bristled, like a dog sniffing out an intruder. She didn't know Trixie. How dare she blame her, when everything was Jenny's fault?

"*She's* my best friend," I said, surprised by the anger in my voice. "*She's* always going to be my best friend. You already have one. Now I have one, and it's just the way it should be."

Alison's cheeks reddened and she started picking at the skin around her cuticles. I knew her well enough to know it was a nervous habit, one that her mom admonished. *Put this oil on them*, she would say when I was over at Alison's house, doing homework at the kitchen table. *Don't ruin your fingers.*

"All right," she said, standing up and smoothing out her skirt. "As long as you're happy, I guess I'm happy for you."

I stayed rooted in my chair and watched her leave. A tiny part of me wanted to call after her and tell her to fight harder for me, but that tiny part was extinguished by a bigger part, an inkblot inside me staining everything else, covering the old memories in film.

When I got up to leave, Trixie was outside Mr. More's classroom, scuffing her flip-flops on the ground and smiling. And even though she never mentioned it, and I didn't either, I wondered how much she had heard.

34

JASPER HOLDS OUT his hands. "No. Stop right here. I didn't say I'd do this."

I slam on the brakes. Jasper lurches forward, straining against his seat belt. "You told me you'd help. What better place to look than her room?"

He rubs his hands over his face. "I can't do it. I can't be there. It's way too bizarre. Look, I told you, we should go back to my house. I have that globe that she liked. It might trigger something. A memory, maybe."

"I don't want to look at a globe," I snap. "It's pointless. I need to do this."

He reaches over and grabs my shoulder, breathing heavily. Behind us, a car horn blares, but I don't move. Our noses are an inch apart and then he's kissing me. But not softly, like we did at the beach. Harder, more urgently, the palm of his trembling hand hot against my face, his thumb under my chin. I kiss him back even though it's the worst form of betrayal. Or maybe that's why I do it. Because she left me, she decided I wasn't worth staying for. She sprinkled lies over everything and watched me eat it up and ask for seconds. I'm still asking for more.

My eyes are closed when he pulls away. When I open

them, he's undoing his seat belt. "This is a mess," he says, his voice thick. The next second he's gone, the door slamming behind him. I watch as he gets smaller and smaller in my rearview mirror, his coat flapping behind him.

I take a series of long, shaky breaths. My hands are all over the steering wheel and I probably shouldn't even be driving, but Trixie's house isn't far away now. And as much as I don't want to face Mr. Heller, this is something I have to do.

Turns out, Mr. Heller isn't even home. His station wagon isn't in the driveway, but I ring the doorbell about ten times anyway. I consider just leaving, but then I remember that I have a key. Trixie gave it to me ages ago when she asked me to pick up one of her textbooks that she needed to study for a test. When I went to give the key back, she told me to hang on to it. "In case of an emergency," she had said, and this counts as an emergency.

I open the door slowly. "Hello?" I call, knowing that nobody will answer. I tiptoe inside, glancing around the foyer into the cluttered living room. Trixie once referred to her dad as a hoarder, and the description fits. He collects just about everything there is to collect. Old newspapers with articles about Elvis. Antique teacups. Brass animals. Prints of the walls of the Egyptian pyramids. Shot glasses from countries he has never been to. Mom would have a conniption if she ever saw this mess.

Seeing the mess, for some reason, is the most heartbreaking thing of all. He hasn't moved a single thing, just added to it. There are rolled-up rugs piled in one corner and a bunch of lamps lined against one wall and a coatrack piled high with different hats. And Trixie's not here to roll her eyes and tell him to get rid of it, that it'll bury him if he keeps buying stuff and having no place to put it.

I slink up the stairs, gripping the railing with sweaty hands. Trixie's bedroom door is the first one at the top of the stairs and it's open. I walk in with my heart pounding, half expecting her to jump out from behind her closet door and yell *surprise!* But there are no surprises here. The room is neat and tidy, bereft of anything personal. A desk and a bookshelf and a closet full of clothes hanging neatly on hangers.

I don't know what I'm looking for, exactly. Something, anything. A clue, a sign, a scrap of paper, a compass pointing me in the right direction. I open each drawer and rummage through the notebooks in them, but they're all blank. There's a photo album in the bottom drawer with no pictures in it. I think back to what the police said. *People detach themselves from the past when they decide to end their lives.* But they were all wrong. Maybe Trixie clung to the past, to Toby, like a barnacle. Maybe she wasn't ending her life so much as starting a new one.

Underneath the photo album are our yearbooks. All four years of Robson, not a single signature in any of them. No *Have a great summer* or even a *See you next year.* I flip to the page she shared with Toby Hunter, year after year. I don't know what I'm expecting. A heart around his face, or maybe a love letter scrawled between pictures of the chess club and the tennis team. But there's nothing. The yearbooks don't even look like they have been opened before.

There's another yearbook underneath the rest, and when I pick it up, I see what it says: *Sunnyside Middle School, 2012–2013.* When Trixie was in the seventh grade, before she ever started at Robson.

This yearbook has a cracked spine. This one has been opened and closed, and when I flip it open, I see that the front and back pages are covered in signatures and well-wishes. I keep flipping until I get to Trixie's picture. She has braces and a bad haircut and a fake smile and there's no Toby Hunter beside her, just a dorky kid with bad skin.

I grip the page between my fingers and let out a long breath. This is getting me nowhere. I should have known going back into Trixie's past would be a dead end.

Then I see something on the bottom of the page. A purple arrow pointing to the next page. I turn it over, and there's purple pen surrounding a picture of someone I know. Someone who was still the most beautiful girl in the room, even in eighth grade.

BFFS FOREVER! Love you like a sister! xoxoxoxo
Gabby Reynolds, the girl Toby loved.

35

I LIKED THAT it was only ever you and me. Maybe that was my problem all along with Jenny and Alison. We were one girl too many, unbalanced. I never considered that you were teetering on the edge the entire time, or that you might have your own friendship ghosts.

We were at Cabana Del Shit at the beginning of last summer, on a random Monday after her shift. It was the end of the night, and Trixie got one of the guys in the kitchen to make us a giant batch of nachos full of beef and melted cheese. I knew we'd eat it until we felt sick, but I kept shoveling gooey chips into my mouth and wiping my greasy fingers on flimsy paper napkins.

Trixie was telling me about all the gross things she found while busing tables that day when the little bell at the door rang and Gabby Reynolds walked in, lingering by the hostess stand.

I turned my face away and shrunk back in our booth. I didn't want Gabby to see me pigging out on nachos like some kind of freak. When I tried out for the cheerleading team, Gabby had gone just before me, with a routine that brought the cheer captain to her feet. I expected her to be bitchy and mean, and when I wobbled during my routine, I figured she'd tell me to try out for a sport that requires less coordination.

But she didn't. She smiled at me and it didn't look fake, and when the list was posted and my name was on it, she told me she was happy we were both on the team.

Gabby had this perfect body, curvy in all the right places, and the thickest, glossiest blond hair I had ever seen. I figured somebody that beautiful must have a flaw. Somebody that sweet must have a secret.

But Gabby was also head of the math club, a peer mentor, first chair in band, and volunteered after school with disabled kids. And Toby Hunter loved her. They were the golden couple. King Toby and his leading lady.

The Gabby standing at the hostess stand wasn't perfect. When Toby died, she turned into a shadow of who she used to be. She quit cheerleading. She got pale and bony and her hair started falling out in giant clumps. Jenny said it was because half of her was gone and never coming back, which was such an overly dramatic Jenny thing to say. To Jenny, they were a soap opera instead of real people.

I listened as Skylar approached the hostess stand, her shoes clacking on the ground. "Can I help you?"

A fly buzzed around my face. I swatted it away.

"I'm just picking up takeout," Gabby said. "I forget my order number. It was a cheeseburger and fries."

For some reason, Gabby doing something as simple as ordering a cheeseburger and fries made me want to burst into tears. I wondered if that was the hardest part for her, just doing normal things. The old Gabby would have been here with her friends. This Gabby was bringing food home, probably to an empty house. I pictured her eating it in tiny bites, trying to stomach it.

Finally, I realized Trixie hadn't said a word since Gabby came through the door. She had stopped eating and was staring at her with this look I had never seen her wear before. It wasn't pity and it wasn't curiosity and it wasn't sadness either.

It was pure and undiluted contempt. Her eyes narrowed into little slits and dents appeared in her forehead and she was biting her lip so hard that it was turning white around her teeth.

"Are you okay?" I asked. I figured her mind must be somewhere else, that that look was reserved for something besides Gabby Reynolds.

"Yeah," she said, snapping back to reality. "Life's just fucking peachy."

Trixie stared at Gabby until she paid for her food and left, scurrying for the exit in worn-out ballet flats, Styrofoam container in hand. She saw us sitting there and gave a little wave, which I weakly returned.

"I need more sour cream," Trixie said abruptly, getting up and darting back to the kitchen. I looked down at our plate. There was plenty of sour cream left.

When she came back to the table, her eyes were bloodshot. She said it was because she smoked a joint with one of the kitchen guys behind the restaurant. Except she didn't smell like pot and I was pretty sure she had been crying. I didn't call her out on it because I had no idea what had just happened, why she had turned from regular Trixie into somebody I didn't know.

Maybe it wasn't impossible to hate Gabby Reynolds after all.

36

JASPER IS WAITING for me at my locker—*our* locker—when I get to school the next day. "Sorry I got a bit wound up yesterday," he says, pushing his hair behind his ears. "I just—I mean, I never even went over to her house when she was alive. With her. It seemed too strange to go there without her. Does that make sense?"

I nod. It does make sense. I try to picture it the other way around, me going to snoop around Beau's bedroom without him, and that doesn't feel right either.

"It's fine," I say, opening my locker. *Eight. Thirty-one. Seventeen.* The same reminder, multiple times a day, that she's out there somewhere. Maybe with him.

"Did you find anything?" His voice is tentative, like he's afraid to ask. Or maybe afraid of what I'll say.

"Not really. I mean, maybe something. Did you know Trixie used to be friends with Gabby Reynolds?"

Jasper shakes his head. "No. She never mentioned it. I can't think of anything they'd have in common."

"Maybe they didn't have something in common. Maybe it was someone."

* * *

Gabby hangs out in the smoke pit at lunch. She fits in there, dark rings around her eyes and yellowing fingertips. My heart pounds as I walk down the stairs and take a seat on the bench beside her.

"Hey," I say. "Mind if I borrow a cigarette?"

She laughs. It's not the normal laugh I'm used to hearing from Gabby, the girly giggle that echoed through the gym. This one is brittle, like straw cracking.

"I believe the correct term is to bum a cigarette." She hands me one with a wink. "It's not like you're going to give it back."

I put the cigarette in my mouth and cup my hands while Gabby lights the end. I try not to sputter on it, the way I did when I first smoked a cigarette with Trixie.

"How are you?" My mouth floods with smoke and my tongue feels thick and fuzzy, like it's too big for my mouth.

"Fine," she says, nodding. "How are you holding up? I'm sorry, you know. That she's gone. I obviously know how it feels."

She stares at the ground, her eyes glassy. I realize I'm a terrible person for never saying anything to Gabby after Toby died. No *I'm sorry* or *I'm here for you* or *I'm thinking of you*. I guess I never thought I was close enough with her to make a statement like that, and I didn't know how to say the words or even what words to say. Everything in my head sounded cheesy and cliché, but maybe it was what she needed to hear.

"I'm okay, I guess," I say.

"I'd tell you it gets better"—Gabby taps the end of her cigarette—"but I don't want to lie to you." Her mouth forms a little O and she drags one of her fingers along her forehead, smoothing a line that appears there.

"I was going through her stuff," I say. "I found an old year-book, from Sunnyside. I didn't know you guys used to be friends."

Gabby takes her hair in her free hand, smoothing it over her shoulder. "Yeah, once upon a time. A million years ago. I had forgotten all about that."

I take a quick drag of my cigarette. "Why did you stop?" I ask, pausing when I realize I don't know how to finish the sentence. "Being friends. Why did you stop being friends with her?"

"I didn't. She stopped being friends with me." Gabby leans in closer. "We were just kids. She had a thing for this guy we went to school with, and he ended up trying to kiss me at this dumb school dance. I didn't let him, of course. She was my best friend. But she never forgave me for the fact that he liked me better than her. She cut me off, just like that. And in high school, we just never talked again." She shrugs. "Girls do stupid things when boys get in the way."

The bell rings and I drop my cigarette on the ground, accidentally on purpose. I watch it glow before grinding it into the pavement.

"As someone who used to be her friend, do you know why she would have done it?" I hate how idiotic I sound. "Do you have any idea why?"

Gabby purses her lips. "I'm coming to learn that there doesn't have to be a *why* involved. It's selfish, is what it is. They leave these people behind and don't realize how bad it hurts, not having them here. I know I'm not supposed to say that because they were obviously messed up, but that's how I see it. It's an easy out, getting swallowed up by the ocean." She tugs on her hair. "I'm sorry. I didn't mean it like that."

"I'm sorry too," I say, even though it's more than a year too late. "For Toby."

She stretches out her arms and sucks in a breath, and I can tell she's somewhere else, a million miles from here. "Me too."

When I'm sitting in geography, I open my textbook to a map of the world. Earth is made up of 71 percent water. I guess if you were planning to get swallowed up by anything, that's what it would be. There are no footprints left behind, no tracks, no clues. That's when I realize how long she might have been planning this whole thing. It could have been arranged with Toby the whole time, him going first and her going after. Maybe she knew that she wouldn't be around longer than August thirteenth.

Or else Toby Hunter came back from the dead.

37

YOU TOLD ME *girls like Jenny were fake, as if the world was divided into two types of girls: real ones, made out of flesh and bones, and plastic ones packaged up like dolls. But you were wrong. Sometimes, Jenny got insecure. Those were the times I loved her the most, because when she got insecure, she got real.*

"I feel like I'll never fall in love," she told me. It was just the two of us, on Alison's deck. Alison had gone inside to get marshmallows so we could roast them over the fire pit. Jenny had a tendency to make big dramatic statements like that, to leave them hanging in the air, open for interpretation. I was supposed to say something like *Sure you will.* But that night, I said something else.

"I think I'm already in love. With Beau."

Jenny grinned and threw her arms around my neck. "I knew it! You guys would be so cute together. Seriously, ask him out. He's so shy, you'll need to do it. Ali and I have been wondering when you two would finally hook up."

I smiled too, but I wanted to know when she and Alison had been talking about me behind my back. And when Alison started liking the nickname "Ali" after previously telling us how much she despised it. I shook off the feeling that it was always the two of them in step, with me lagging just a little bit behind. It was me and Jenny now, no Alison.

"What does it feel like? Being in love?" she asked. "Tell me all about it."

"Different, I guess. But I just know. It's hard to explain."

It really was hard to explain. I couldn't exactly tell someone that it felt like I had swallowed the stars, that I was filled with the sky.

"I just hope it happens soon for me," she said. "I'm sick of waiting around for it. Maybe there's something wrong with me."

"There's not. You'll find someone. And when you do, it'll be great."

"And we can one day tell these stories at each other's weddings."

That made me laugh. It was just like Jenny to think ahead to marriage when the rest of us just wanted to get through prom.

When Alison came back with a bag of marshmallows, Jenny didn't tell her about Beau. Alison already knew I liked him, but not that I had used the word *love*. It was a good feeling, that I could trust Jenny with something huge like that. When I looked at her face across the fire and passed her my burnt marshmallow because I knew she liked them that way, I had this surge of loyalty toward her, like I'd be her friend forever.

But our forever had an expiration date.

38

DURING THE MORNING announcements, there's a special broadcast about the big football game after school today against the Tasker Titans. Part of me wants to go, but I know it will hurt too much. It will be a reminder of everything I used to have. Everything I decided was worth nothing when Trixie came into my life.

I find a note in my locker at lunch. *Meet me at the parking lot after school. I'll take you somewhere. J.*

I used to see the notes Jasper left Trixie, sticking out the door of our shared locker like white flags. She tore one up like confetti in front of me once and tossed it in the garbage can. When I asked her what it said, she just laughed. "He's too in love with me. I need to make him hate me more. That's the only way you can be with a guy."

"Weren't you just with him last night?" I had asked. "Don't you want him to be thinking about you?" She shook her head and smiled knowingly, that Fiona-you-have-so-much-to-learn smile that drove me insane.

"I fucked him last night. But that's all he is to me, and all he'll ever be."

I felt sad for him, because I could tell she meant it. Once, I opened one of the notes and shoved it in my pocket before she could see it and destroy it, because it didn't deserve to rot in the garbage with banana peels and wads of gum.

It said: *You're the moon because you only come out at night and aren't there in the morning. Maybe one day I'll wake up and you'll be the sun too.*

When I open my car door to wait for Jasper after school, I'm hit with a dizzying wave of hot air. I barely have a chance to sit down before someone grips my shoulders.

"Jasper?"

Beau swims in front of my vision. "Hey," he says, prodding me gently, and there's concern in his eyes that makes me hold my breath because he's here, whole, not the broken version he shattered into. "Earth to Fiona. You okay?"

His voice is rough, coarse. And *You okay* isn't the nicest thing anyone could say. But somehow it sounds like the sweetest thing anyone has ever said to me. Because it's coming from Beau and everything coming from Beau is amplified a thousand times.

"I'm fine. Just hot."

"I can get you some water," he says, but it's more like a question. Even though my mouth is parched, I shake my head because if he goes somewhere to get water, he might not come back and it will be like this never happened.

"Look, I need something," he says, and suddenly I feel like an idiot, because I know exactly why he's here. Because of the bottles under my passenger seat. The ones I should have gotten rid of but didn't because secretly I hoped a variation of this exact moment would happen. That I would have something he wants.

"No," I say, even though it would be easier to just say yes.

"I need it. I'm having a terrible goddamned day. Look at

my hands." He places his hands, palms down, in front of my face. And sure enough, they're shaking violently. Maybe he's doing that on purpose, faking it so I'll cave.

"You need help," I say. "It's obvious, what you're doing. You have a problem. And people let you get away with it because Toby . . . But you can't keep doing this."

Beau claps his hands together so loudly that I jump. "I do whatever I need to do to keep breathing. Nobody knows what actually happened that night. Especially not you, because you weren't there."

My heart falls into my stomach. *You weren't there.* It's an accusation, a dagger, something that punctures my skin and settles underneath. I wasn't there. I stayed home the night Toby disappeared. If I would have gone to that party, would everything be different?

"He's not coming back," I say gently, even though I'm not sure exactly what I believe anymore. "You know that."

"Says who?" Beau says, his voice rising in a crescendo. His hands ball into fists and I wonder if he's going to smash the hood of my car.

"Says you," I shout back, my voice louder and angrier than I thought was possible.

Maybe he doesn't remember saying it. There's probably a lot Beau doesn't remember saying.

"And you should talk," he spits out. "What a coincidence that she disappears too."

Beau abruptly stops talking and sets his lips in a thin line. He bows his head and scratches his hair with his hands, runs his fingers through the roots like he wants to yank it out.

"What do you mean, what a coincidence?" I say, my voice shrill. "What do you mean by *too*?"

"Nothing," he says, rubbing his hands over his face, the word coming out in a muffled thud. "Nothing. Fucking nothing."

My heart beats so hard I can feel it everywhere inside me. I'm a ticking time bomb and I'll explode any second. I know he's lying, that he didn't mean *fucking nothing*. I know that Beau swears when he lies, probably to cover everything up in something slick, making it easier to swallow. He never even used to swear. He had the perfect word for every situation, words that bloomed on his tongue. Now it's like he can't be bothered to find them anymore, so he layers them in ugliness on purpose.

"I'll give you those bottles," I say, even though I'm just hurting him, wrenching the sword in deeper. "I'll give you what you want if you tell me what you meant."

When Beau takes his hands away from his face, his features are twisted in pain. A whole new layer of guilt wraps itself around me like a too-tight hug. I'm using him to find out something I can't figure out myself. It's not fair. But maybe now we're even.

"Forget it." He shakes his head. "Just forget about it. I thought I could trust you." His eyes go wild. "You said I could trust you."

"You can trust me."

A car door slams behind us and both of our heads whip around. But it's just Mrs. Carson, the white-haired music teacher, who smiles at us. Mrs. Carson, who wears giant bottle-cap glasses, probably can't even make out who we are. Even so, Beau darts around the passenger side of my car and pulls the door open, and before I can stop him, he gets in and grabs one bottle from under the seat. His fingers fumble with the cap. His eyes are greedy and his face is sweating and it's lust I see all over him.

Beau is fully, impossibly shattered, just like that bottle he smashed in Alison's kitchen the night Trixie disappeared. He looks at the bottle like he has never looked at a girl before. Not Jenny. Definitely not me. Not back when we looked up at stars together, or when we almost kissed on Alison's deck, light-years ago. Everything between us up until now has been the biggest lie of all because Beau will never want anything more than he wants what's in that bottle.

Maybe they shouldn't call it heartbreak, because everything else feels broken too.

Beau swears under his breath. "Fuck," he says, crouching down and stuffing the bottle back under my seat. But the cap isn't on properly and liquid seeps out, soaking into the rubber mat and the dingy carpeting underneath. The smell sets my throat on fire and brings back everything about the night Trixie disappeared.

But it's too late to care, because Principal Shepherd emerges from behind a blue van two spots down. His smile turns into a frown as he starts walking toward my car.

"Fuck fuck fuck," Beau chants, and I know he's looking for a place to run, but there's no way out of this. This is the moment he gets caught. Unless I save him.

I rev the engine and drive away.

39

YOU MIGHT HAVE known, the night you went away, that you were leaving. But both times my world was upended after Alison's parties, I was caught off guard. Jenny, Alison, and I went shopping the day of Alison's first party. We had no idea that less than twelve hours later, Toby Hunter would be underwater.

We were at the mall trying on clothes. Alison was excited because she'd heard some seniors would be at the party, and she wanted to look cool. "I've been working out hard all summer. I think I should get something sexy to show off."

"You totally should," Jenny said. "We all should."

So we did. It was the perfect day, going in and out of mall changing rooms, asking each other what looked good and knowing pretty much everything did. After we each picked a new outfit, we went to the food court for ice cream.

"It's my cheat day," Alison said. "I'm getting two scoops of Rocky Road. With extra chocolate sauce."

My stomach started to hurt while we were waiting in line, but I chalked it up to period cramps. I'd take a Midol when I got home and everything would be fine.

"Look who it is," Jenny said, nudging her hip into mine. "Lover boy, across the food court."

I spun around so fast I practically gave myself whiplash. Beau was sitting at a table with a couple guys from the team, eating what looked like Chinese food. I had this vertigo sensation like I might fall over, and my heart pounded like it used to on Christmas morning when I was a kid. I wanted to run to him but also to stay rooted where I was, like some kind of tree, where it was safe.

"You should go over there," Jenny said. "Show him your outfit for the party. He'll be taking it off later."

She was kidding, but I still felt my face go as red as the dress in my bag. Jenny giggled.

"If you have sex in my house, just don't do it in my parents' room," Alison said. "I have to clean up this party before they get home and pretend like it never happened. Remember? You guys said you'd help me. That was the whole point of telling your parents you're sleeping over."

"I won't be having sex anywhere," I said. "But maybe we'll kiss. If he's even coming."

"It's about time," Jenny said, slinging her arm around my shoulders. "Maybe I'll meet my soulmate too. I just have a feeling this is going to be the best night ever."

I looked across the food court at Beau. It was like he knew I was staring at him, because he raised his eyes and smiled directly at me.

"You should go say hi," Jenny said. "Seriously. Look how much he's smiling. You can see his adorable little dimples from here. He wants you."

"I'll see him later," I said. I would have gone over if it weren't for the other guys. It seemed like Beau and I had so few moments alone together. He was always flanked by his football friends and I was always with Jenny and Alison, the tight knot of our little trio. Sometimes I wished everyone else would just disappear so we could say everything we wanted to say to each other.

"You'll see him now, because he's coming over here," Alison said. It was her turn to order, so she grabbed Jenny and turned away from me.

I smoothed my hair down and looked at the ground, because it was easier than watching him walk over. I imagined what would happen if I ran toward him and threw myself into his arms, like girls did in the romantic comedies Alison liked. I didn't have the courage to find out.

"Hey," he said when he was standing in front of me. Now I glanced up and met his eyes, matched his smile, and suddenly it was just the two of us, not Jenny and Alison and the football team and the rest of the food court.

"Hey. Hi. What're you up to?"

"Matt needed a birthday gift for his mom, and I guess he thought I'd be good at that kind of thing, so he invited me to come along."

I smiled. Beau would be good at that kind of thing because he was thoughtful, because he remembered things about people. He took the time to listen, not just nod and pretend.

"Cool. How's your summer been going?"

He bobbed his head. "Okay, I guess. I'm kind of glad it's almost over."

I hadn't seen Beau in a while. The same parties were happening just like every summer, but he wasn't at most of them. We texted back and forth, but I got the feeling he was distracted, and I convinced myself he probably had a girlfriend, that I had lost my chance. I wondered again if I would see him at Alison's.

"You'll be there tonight, right?" He said it, not me. I was so surprised that I almost forgot to answer.

"Yeah, I'll be there. We just went shopping for new outfits, actually." I held up my shopping bag as proof. I hoped he would like the red dress inside.

"Sweet," Beau said, nodding. "So you're going to be there."

"I'm going to be there."

"I guess I'll see you there."

"I guess you will." I had turned into an echo, but he was smiling, so it didn't matter.

But later, the stomachache that started in the food court turned out not to be period cramps but food poisoning, which Mom had too. It must have been the takeout we ordered the night before, because we both spent a good portion of the evening hunched over the toilet. Good thing our house had two bathrooms.

I texted Jenny and Alison, telling them I couldn't make it. I texted Beau too. He never messaged back. And the next time I saw him, he was somebody I didn't even recognize.

40

I DON'T EVEN know where we're going, sort of like I didn't the day Trixie first got into my car. Beau doesn't tell me either, so I end up driving past my house. When I see Mom's car in the driveway—she must be home between meetings—I keep driving.

"Turn right here," Beau says. "Then your first left, and right on Whisperwood. The big yellow house. Nobody's home. Nobody's ever home anymore."

We're going to Beau's house, something I always imagined, but never like this. Everything I imagined with Beau now falls into the but-never-like-this category in real life. In my head, he brought me over for dinner. He would say "This is my girlfriend, Fiona," and I would be wearing a dress I had made, and Mrs. Hunter would comment on how nice it was, and we'd eat comfort food like shepherd's pie.

In reality, he gets out and slams his door and I do the same, then I follow him as he fumbles to get the front door open. It's weird when we're standing in Beau's foyer. His house isn't much bigger than mine and it's messy, with shoes piled on a dirty mat near the front door. The big white sneakers Beau wears to school, plus a bunch of pumps like Mom wears to work. The hallway is lined with photos, formal family photos.

It looks like the same picture, year after year. Mrs. Hunter sitting, Mr. Hunter standing behind her, Beau and Toby on either side. Matching white smiles and dimples.

"I always wondered how you'd look in my house," he murmurs, leading me into the kitchen, and just like that, he's the old Beau again, not the raging one from the parking lot. "I guess I just thought it would be under different circumstances. Like, a regular dinner. My mom makes good lasagna. I mean, she did. She doesn't do much of anything but hide at the office now."

It makes me want to smile and cry. Beau thought about how I'd fit here. He imagined me at that kitchen table, eating his mom's food.

"I like lasagna," I say, and my heart breaks a little more that our entire lack of a relationship has been one giant missed connection.

Beau straddles a barstool at the counter and smiles. "Maybe she'll make it again sometime," he says. I want to throw my arms around his neck and tell him there is still hope, that we can be what we were always supposed to be, but a second later his face falls. "But I doubt it. This family is just one big fuckup after another."

"Everyone makes mistakes," I say. "They're inevitable."

"Not as big as mine." He leans forward and buries his face in his hands. Then he gets up and pulls a water bottle out of the fridge. A big plastic one, like the ones the football players keep on the sidelines during games. He takes a long swig and his face relaxes, and I realize that it's not water in there. I think about what I read on the internet about alcoholics, back when I was trying to figure out what made him change. *Addictive personalities. Sensitive to emotional stress, with difficulty trusting people and managing feelings. Insecure. Lonely.*

"I can help you," I say. "We can help each other. We can figure out what happened. I know Trixie isn't dead, and I want to find her." *Find them*, I add in my head.

Beau squeezes the bottle until his knuckles turn white. "You never will. Just forget her."

"Like you're doing such a good job of forgetting him?" I say, my voice turning into a shrill crescendo. "Like it's something you can just push out of your brain?"

Beau stares at the water bottle, then pitches it across the room. I duck instinctively, even though he tossed it in the other direction. It hits a clock hanging against the floral wallpaper. The clock comes crashing down and hits the floor.

I grab my purse from the kitchen chair and turn around to leave, tears blurring my vision. It's the second time Beau has made a scene in a kitchen, the second time he has thrown and broken something. Except he's the one who's really broken. Maybe that's how he covers it up, by breaking other things. Bottles. Clocks. Hearts.

"Don't go," he pleads, his voice soft again. I stop but don't turn around. I should keep walking, because there's nothing for me in this kitchen. Nothing but being stuck in the past. And I'm not sad as much as I'm angry, pissed off, my skin too tight for my body. The anger rolls off me in waves, and I know he feels it and I hope he chokes on it, the same way I do.

"I'll tell you," he says. When I turn around, I see that he's in a heap on the floor, crunched against the counter, his face streaked with tears, and the anger drains out of me like it was never there at all. He's holding on to a blue baseball cap, and I'm sure it's the same cap Trixie put on the day we met.

"Where'd you get that hat?" I ask.

"It was his," he says, squeezing his fingers around it defensively.

I sit down on the floor across from Beau, wrapping my arms around my knees. "But I know that hat. Trixie had it. Why did she have it?"

"I owe it to him not to tell," he says. "He would kill me for this."

"But if it can help us find him, you have to tell me," I say. "He'd want that. He would understand."

"He wouldn't understand," Beau says, a vein emerging in his forehead. "He jumped off that pier, hating me more than anything. And it was my fault that it happened."

I hold out my hands. I don't expect him to take them but he does, dropping the baseball cap and clutching my fingers so tightly that it hurts. "He didn't hate you. You're his brother."

"Not that night," he says, squeezing my hands tighter, almost like he's sending a message in Morse code. "That night, he said we weren't brothers anymore. Because I kissed his girl."

"You kissed Gabby?"

He doesn't answer, and suddenly it makes sense. *I kissed his girl.*

"Trixie was his girl," I say, and even though on some level I already knew, it's so much worse now, radiating off Beau like a fever. *Eight. Thirty-one. Seventeen. I had this thing with my lab partner.*

Beau kind of nods, his chin trembling.

"She was his girl," I say again, letting go of his hands, the sweat on my back turning clammy. "And you kissed her."

41

YOU IGNORED BEAU at the party the night you disappeared. Even when it became painfully hard to ignore him, after he got so drunk that I thought Alison would have to kick him out. When he started calling everyone an asshole and an idiot and saying he hated everything.

I was standing in the kitchen when he came in from Alison's deck. He was barefoot and his baseball cap was gone, so his hair was standing straight up. His face was flushed red, the same way mine had looked when I caught him and Jenny in the bathroom an hour ago.

An hour, or maybe it was two, or three. It was all spinning. The ugly wallpaper in Alison's kitchen. The stainless steel of the fridge, adorned with a thousand sets of sweaty fingerprints.

But something had happened in that hour or two or three. Jenny had come in thirty seconds before Beau, her face down. I could tell she was crying. A thought had flashed through my mind. If this was a year ago and I had seen Jenny crying, I would have dropped everything to make her feel better. I would have sat with her and passed her tissues while she complained about some guy, and I would have said all the right things. *You're so much better than him. He's an asshole. You're better off without him.*

Not that night.

That night, when I saw her make a beeline through the kitchen, down the hall, and out the front door, I felt this little tingle of excitement. Maybe that makes me a terrible person, but part of me wanted to jump in front of her and say, *Serves you right*.

I had looked around to see if Trixie was there to witness this, but she wasn't anywhere.

When Beau came lumbering in, I barely recognized him. Of course I knew about Beau's drinking. I had seen enough of him at school to know the rumors were true. But he had never been like that before, completely unhinged, like a wild animal. He had a bottle of something in his hand and was calling after Jenny, waving it around.

The whole party stopped. Everyone went silent. The thumping bass was in tune with my own heart. Boom-*boom*, boom-*boom*.

"What's everyone staring at?" Beau yelled, and nobody said anything. He waved the bottle over his head and looked around the room, like he was trying to find something specific in every face.

Something, or someone.

When he got to me, he paused. I noticed how bloodshot his eyes were and I wondered if he had been crying. The thought was painful, like a dagger twisting in my gut. In that moment I didn't understand why I loved Beau, and I wished I didn't. It felt like a curse, something weighing me down, like chains attached to my ankles.

Then Alison made the mistake of reaching out and placing a hand on his arm.

He flipped out. Smashed the bottle on the ground, where

it crashed into a bunch of pieces. Some big ones, a bunch of smaller ones, which he crunched over with his feet, apparently oblivious to the pain. One shard had fallen beside me and I leaned down to pick it up. When I stood back up, Beau was gone, leaving a trail of bloody smears on the tile floor.

Then Alison started to cry. She had been too distracted by a flip cup game to notice Jenny barge in before. If she had noticed, she would have done what the old me would have done and consoled her. If she had noticed, she probably wouldn't have been around to try to calm Beau down, and he might not have thrown the bottle and cut his foot open.

And I might not have this scar on my back.

I was just drunk enough to think it was a good idea to go after Beau. But then Trixie showed up and slung her arm around my shoulder and held out another plastic cup.

"Did you see that?" I said, and my tongue felt thick in my mouth. I could tell I was getting drunk, reaching the point where I should probably stop.

"See what?" She clinked her cup against mine. "Drink up."

I drank, because she was. I didn't follow Beau.

"Where did you go?" I asked, and I could tell I was slurring my words, that the letters were strung together crookedly like little Christmas lights.

"Bathroom," she said quickly, wiping her hand on her jean shorts. She did it fast, but I still noticed that her hands were shaking.

Something made Beau angry that night.

Something made Jenny cry.

Something made Trixie disappear.

What if it was all the same thing?

42

"IT WAS AN accident," Beau says, yanking on his hair. "I never planned to kiss her. It meant nothing. But it meant everything to him. I was pissed because he was keeping this epic secret from me. So I found the only way I knew how to call him out on it."

"Tell me. I need to know everything." I'm talking, but I'm numb.

Beau bangs the back of his head against the counter behind him. It makes a dull thumping sound. "He was with Gabby. They were, well, you know. Good. He even had a ring." He stares at the floor. "Then all of a sudden, he started acting shady. All summer, he said messed-up stuff, like he was going to quit the football team, even though he already had scouts from Princeton offering him the world on a platter. He got in a couple huge fights with my dad. And a few nights, he didn't come home at all."

He looks up at me and his face is pale and worn, with bluish half-moons under his eyes.

"I flat-out asked the guy if he was seeing another chick. He looked me in the face and said no. And I believed him. So I dropped it. But he kept acting strange. My dad was pissed. And Gabby was on my back, asking me why Toby was different now, why he didn't pick up his phone and why she hadn't seen him in weeks. I didn't have the balls to tell her that he told us he was out with her. By then I knew he was seeing someone else. I just didn't know who."

"Trixie," I say weakly. I stare at the kitchen floor. It's not tiled like Alison's, but linoleum like the one at my house. Beau is playing with a piece against the counter that has curling edges. I wonder what would happen if we dug our fingernails in and ripped the whole thing up, what secrets would be buried underneath.

"I still didn't know that. I didn't even know who Trixie was until the night of the party. I wasn't even planning on going to that party. I only went because you said you were going to be there and I had this thing I wanted to give you."

You'll be there tonight, right? Except, I wasn't there, the night the world spun while I threw up.

"Anyway, by the time I got there, Toby was wasted. Slurring his words. At first he was happy to see me. He was, like, on top of the world, high as a fucking kite, jumping from one place to the next. I couldn't keep tabs on the guy, even though I should have. Then I had to take a leak and there were a bunch of people lined up to use the bathroom, so I went out behind the back shed. And I saw Toby back there, with her. He didn't see me. His back was turned to me. They were . . ."

"Kissing?" I say.

"Fucking. Right in the backyard, where anyone could have seen them. But anyone was me."

I rub my eyes so I don't have to look at him. It's like he's talking about a totally different girl than the one I knew.

"I wasn't pissed that he was cheating on Gabby. Really, that wasn't my business. What I couldn't shake was that he lied to me. Looked me in the eyes and lied, like it was the easiest thing in the world. It was like our whole fucking relationship was a joke. Like being brothers meant nothing to him. I realized I didn't know the guy at all." He presses his palms flat on the floor and stares at his fingers. "I was going to walk right into the house and tell Gabby exactly what I'd seen. But when it came down to it, I didn't have the balls for that either. I couldn't do that to Toby. But then I did something worse."

"Toby kept drinking and drinking. I let him. He liked to party, and I let him self-destruct. And the second I saw Trixie walk away alone, I followed her. I asked her who she was here with, then I kissed her before she could answer. She must've been in shock or something, because she didn't stop me. Not for a few seconds. And when she did, she was looking past me. Toby was standing there on the deck. I'd seen my brother mad before, but I'll never fucking forget how he looked that night. No matter how hard I try to get it out of my head."

I stare at the broken clock, at the crooked clock hands and the water bottle on its side on the floor. I beg the clock to turn back time, plead with the water bottle to be just a water bottle and not a disease. I bargain with nobody and wish so badly I could erase Beau kissing Trixie, and Trixie covering it up by telling me how much she hated him.

"So what?" I ask. "You fought with him?" I already know this from what Jenny told me about the party, from the rumors that had ripped through the school. The fight between the Hunter brothers. Everyone had a different reason for what it was about. Most people thought it was about Gabby. Only Beau, Trixie, and Toby know the truth.

"That came later." Beau rubs his eyes with the heels of his hands. "First, he just looked like I'd broken his goddamn heart. And Trixie, she tried to calm him down, but he went off like a fucking loose cannon. Started smashing bottles against the back of the house. Grabbed my neck like he wanted to strangle me. Told me whoever I was, I wasn't his brother anymore. And that was the last thing he ever said to me."

I press my hand against the floor and inch it forward to where Beau's right hand is planted. I push my fingers into the open spaces between his. He doesn't stop me.

"Did you have any idea what he was going to do?"

Beau stares at the ceiling and blinks. "I didn't even see him leave. I ended up getting loaded for the first time ever that night. And then it was every night after that. Want to know the reason why? Because Toby was the one who always told me I should take up drinking. He meant it as a joke, but I remember him saying it was a great way to clear your head. I guess I just decided to take his advice."

"But you don't think he's dead."

Beau clenches my hand so hard it hurts. "He's not dead. He's out there somewhere. Toby used to swim in the ocean for fun. He didn't go out there to die." He sucks in a breath and holds it, almost like he's underwater. "I think he planned it. He wanted out. Princeton, Gabby, the ring, the whole deal. And that was the only way."

I focus on a muddy footprint near the door, feeling sick to my stomach. I think about all the headlines about Toby, about how rough the water was that night. About the person who almost drowned trying to save him. How the police said there was no way he could have made it back to shore. How the chances of finding a body were almost none because of the undertow. I thought about it last year, about what happened to what was left of Toby. If he sank in the middle of the ocean or was ripped apart by sharks.

But what if Beau is right? What if Toby planned the whole thing?

"So if he's alive," I say slowly, "why haven't you tried to find him?"

Beau's eyes are unfocused. He's looking past me, to the water bottle on its side. "You don't think I have? But it's pointless. One thing people never knew about Toby was how good he was at disappearing. When we were kids, we used to play hide-and-seek. But Toby took it to another level. Nobody ever knew his hiding spots. He'd come strolling back hours after everyone else gave up, with this big goofy smile. My mom even called the police to report a missing person once. She was hysterical."

"This is different," I snap. "This isn't some game of hide-and-seek."

Beau laughs, a sharp, miserable sound. "Isn't it?"

For a long time, I don't say anything. I listen to his long, rattling breaths and think about how completely bizarre and messed-up this is. That it took two people to disappear—the two people who meant the most to both of us—to even get us in the same room after last year. To give us back the common ground we lost.

"But you think she's with him," I say, a sliver of relief opening in my chest that he could believe it too. "You think somewhere, they're together."

Beau pulls his hand away, leans his elbows on his knees. "I don't know if they're together. But I think she wants to be."

I remember the time I came up behind Trixie when she was at her computer. She didn't seem as mad as she did something else. Scared. Freaked out. All the time she spent on her phone, when she told me she was talking to Jasper.

It was Toby the whole time. Convincing her to disappear.

Beau starts to laugh again, and it sends shivers up my spine. "You know something else really messed up? She warned me not to go near you. The night she left. I told her to leave me alone."

Fragments of the party come back, each one sharper than the next. Beau smashing the bottle. Jenny crying. Trixie walking in after them like nothing had happened.

"Is that why you and Jenny fought that night?" I ask quietly.

"Probably. Maybe. I don't know."

The sound of a car door slamming makes Beau jump up fast enough to smack his head on the underside of the counter. He runs to the front door and peeks out the curtain, then comes back rubbing his forehead. I grab my purse and prepare to leave.

"Don't go," he says. "Please. Just stay. Don't leave me."

But I can't stay. Because there are questions I need to ask that I can't possibly say out loud. There's poison creeping over every memory of her, charring the edges, blocking out the light like a dirty finger over a camera lens. Everything is becoming thick and tarry, and I'm sinking in the muck.

Did Trixie only become my friend to get back at you?

Has my life for the last year been a lie?

Maybe Beau knows the answers, or maybe he doesn't. Either way, I can't stomach the truth. So I ask something even more sickening.

"The baseball cap," I say. "She had it, and now you do. Were you with her? Did you ever sleep with her, after?"

He hangs his head. "Don't ask a question you don't want the answer for."

It's a thousand times worse than being betrayed by Jenny. It's the worst pain I have ever felt, so intense I'm almost on fire. I pinch my skin, hoping it hurts badly enough to make everything else go away. I'm suddenly glad Trixie's gone, because I honestly never want to see her again.

"Look, I was really messed up," he says. "There was only one person who knew how messed up. I was only supposed to go over to get Toby's cap. It meant nothing."

"Who started it?" I blurt out, unable to stop myself from asking. "How many times did it happen?"

Beau shakes his head. For the first time, he actually looks scared of me, and for the first time, I'm glad to see him like this. Speechless. Ruined. Lost.

"When? When did it happen? I need to know when." I need for it to have happened before I told her how I felt. *I need I need I need.*

"I don't know. Like, October. I didn't keep track of the dates."

October. After she had listened to me that day in my car, after she told me he was a loser. A sob rises in my throat, and it's like I'm naked and exposed except worse, like my skin has been stripped off and my insides are showing. When I speak again, my voice shakes and there's a ringing in my ears.

"Did you know she was going to disappear? Did you have something to do with it?"

He blinks repeatedly. "I don't know. But trust me, there

are some things about me you don't want to know. I'm not the same as I was. I won't be."

He's not going to tell me anything else, so I force myself to stomp down the hallway, out the front door, to my car. It feels like I have weights strapped to my ankles, tethering me to the driveway. When I open my car door, hot air puffs out, just like it did the day I met Trixie. But this time, I beat the steering wheel so hard with my fists that my hands turn red. I guess I always thought it was an accident that she was beside my car that day, that I was just in the right place at the right time to be her getaway.

But she was waiting for me. She already knew who I was. Maybe she had been waiting for days, weeks, for me to be alone out there. I'm coming to believe that there are no accidents at all.

43

I HEARD YOU in your bedroom with him once. I came over with two pints of Cherry Garcia because that was your favorite ice cream, and now I couldn't get enough of it either.

I knocked on the front door and when nobody answered, I let myself in. The ice cream pints were starting to sweat in my hands and besides, Trixie let herself in to my house all the time, barged in like she lived there too. I figured she was doing homework in her room with the music cranked. Her blue baseball cap was hanging on the newel post, but I didn't think about what that meant.

I heard the music when I started walking up the stairs, something loud and gritty. I hovered outside her door and almost put my hand on the doorknob when I heard something else coming from inside. A banging sound, something hitting the wall. Then I heard her, moaning. And grunts that were distinctly male.

I almost dropped the ice cream as I retreated back down the stairs. I couldn't get out of there fast enough. I was embarrassed, even though I hadn't done anything wrong. As I got back in my car and drove away, the Cherry Garcia on the floor in front of the passenger seat—Trixie's seat—I felt irrationally sad, like there was this huge part of her I would never know. In that moment, she seemed years older than me, years wiser, years more experienced, and I wondered if I'd ever catch up.

The ice cream was going to melt, so I pulled over on the next street and ate both pints with a crappy plastic spoon. I ate until my brain was frozen and my stomach was about to explode, until it stopped tasting good and started making me feel sick. I ate until I couldn't hear Trixie and Jasper in her bedroom anymore.

But I never saw who was in there with her, and Jasper told me he had never been to Trixie's house. What I never considered is that somebody else had.

44

I HAVE TO train my brain to not think of Trixie, but I had a life before her and I'm having one now, after her. I don't even care where she is, if she really is caught in the tide somewhere, her hair slimy with seaweed, or if she and Toby Hunter are shacked up in a cheap motel, making fun of all the suckers back home whose lives they tramped over.

Jasper was right when he kept saying that we need to move on with our lives. But now it's not enough to just move on. I don't want to do anything on Trixie's terms. Wherever she is, I want to hurt her. If she ever comes back, I want her to stare at me like she has no idea who I am anymore. And she won't. I'm not her sister, and I never was.

I don't want to see Beau either. He sends me a two-word text: *I'm sorry.* But he has said those same words so many times that they have completely lost their meaning. I want to hurt him too, every single time I think about when he walked past me last year and didn't see me at all. I was nobody to him and now I'll make him nobody to me.

Moving on is different from getting even, and I don't think there is a way to get even, to hurt them both like they hurt me. But there's one way I can try.

I leave a note in Jasper's locker.

Meet me at my car after school. I promise, no more searching.

I know there's a chance he won't show, because he left pretty much the same note for me yesterday and I wasn't there. He doesn't owe me anything. He could walk away from me just as easily as Trixie did. There's nothing binding us together except the fact that the same girl pretended to care about both of us.

But he does show up, holding the note between his fingers with a little half smile. I'm standing behind my car because I can't handle having another person hop into it with me.

"What's going on?" he says. "You figured out where she is?"

I shake my head. "You were right. We need to live our own lives. So I figured today is a good time to start."

He slips my note into his pocket. I wonder what he'll do with it, if he is the kind of person who saves anything remotely sentimental. I think about the note I found that he wrote for Trixie and wonder if it's still in my bedroom, buried in a desk drawer.

"What do you have in mind?" he asks.

"I don't know; what do people do around here when they're not searching for missing girls? We could go get some food. Or see a movie." For some reason, I can't picture Jasper doing either of those things, and I immediately feel bad for thinking it, because he's used to people seeing him as some kind of freak.

He doesn't say anything at first and I think I have horribly misread the situation, and he only kissed me because we were both missing the same person and wanted to somehow feel closer to her by getting closer to each other. Then he

155

takes a deep breath, like he's relieved, and I let myself consider that he might actually like me, and that I might actually like him back. "That sounds really good. Maybe we can skip the movie, though. I think we've both had enough drama lately."

It's his attempt at a joke, at least I think it is. I guess Jasper might have a sense of humor. Everything I know about him is tied to Trixie, and I want to break him out from under her spell.

"I'll pick you up at seven," I say, my mouth so parched that my words almost get stuck there.

Later, when I'm alone in my room, I pretend it's a real date, that he asked me. I put on makeup and style my hair and pick one of my favorite outfits from last year, a shirt I added ruffles to and a corduroy skirt. I don't even give myself time to worry about whether they'll fit, and to my surprise they do, even if the skirt cuts into my stomach more than it used to. Maybe it really was all in my head, my weight gain, and the girl—the girl who snatched me out of my old life so she could prop me up on her shelf with the rest of her unsuspecting victims. I stare at the spot where my sewing machine used to be and remember the day I got rid of it. *It's just a hunk of metal taking up space,* I told Trixie when she noticed it was gone. But it was more than that.

Mom knocks gently on my door before letting herself in. "You look nice," she says, sitting on the edge of my bed. "Are you going somewhere?"

"I'm having dinner with a friend," I tell her. "Her name's Sarah."

She looks so excited that I feel bad that Sarah doesn't exist. I should have known she would glom on to the mental picture of me and a new and improved best friend. I wait for some underhanded speech about how I should *think for myself* and *not be so impressionable,* but it never comes.

"I'm glad you're going out," she says. "You know I was worried about you starting senior year without a close friend. Sarah sounds really nice."

I haven't told Mom anything about Sarah, who is obviously fictitious, besides her name. That's how desperate she is for me to be normal, how badly she needs to not imagine me eating lunch alone in my car.

I text Jasper when I get to his house, and when he doesn't answer right away, I wonder if I should go ring the doorbell. My heart starts to hammer erratically. *I should have worn something nicer. Maybe I'm supposed to meet his parents.* But then I see him bounding down the driveway in his typical all-black uniform, hands in his pockets.

"What kind of food do you like?" I say after he gets in the car. "There's a vegan place that just opened up on Ramsay. Green Machine. We could try that."

I don't actually want to eat vegan food, especially since Mom seems determined for us to eat it at home. But almost every other restaurant has some association with Trixie, and I don't want her there, the invisible third person on this date.

"Sure," Jasper says. We spend most of the ride in silence, which I punctuate by changing the radio from station to station, trying to find a song but only getting news. Jasper surprises me by turning it off.

"Ever notice the news is only ever bad?" he says, and then his hand is on my leg, just resting there on the bare skin below my skirt.

"I guess," I say, pulling into the Green Machine parking

lot, which is small and dark and empty besides my car and a white minivan. I don't want to think about bad news or bad friends or bad decisions. Before I can say anything else, Jasper undoes his seat belt and leans over, his lips grazing mine. He cups his hands around my cheeks and I make the mistake of keeping my eyes open when he kisses me, softly at first, then urgently, like there's something inside me he's desperately trying to suck out. I fixate on the skin between his eyebrows, how it's pinched together, a world of tension. I kiss him back and wrap my hands around his neck and finally shut my eyes, and then I feel his body on top of mine. One of his hands slides from my face and into the neckline of my shirt, and I should stop him but I don't because it feels good and he's touching me like he wants to touch me, not like he only wants to touch me because he won't remember it in the morning.

I only pull away when he takes his other hand from the side of my face and slips it up the front of my skirt.

"What's wrong?" he says, a line appearing between his eyes. I push my hair off my face and pull away from him, and Jasper settles back into his seat and stares straight ahead. "I'm sorry. I didn't mean to take things that fast. You're a virgin, aren't you?"

Little pieces puncture me, shards of broken glass that used to be something whole. I don't know if I'm happy or mad that Jasper kissed me, that he wants to do more than kiss me. I don't know why I pushed him off me, if it's because I still feel loyalty to the one person who did the worst thing a friend could do, or because I still love somebody who will never love me back. I don't owe them anything. I want them to see this, to feel everything I felt because of them.

"There's something you should know," he says, and this

time I lean over and kiss him. I don't want to talk anymore. I press my lips against his and open my mouth slightly at first, then more, until I hear him moan into me and pull on the back of my hair gently.

We never go into the vegan restaurant. We don't say another word for the rest of the night, and I don't open my eyes again. I run my fingers over his jawline, memorizing its sharp edges. I press my palm against his chest and am shocked at how light and fast his heart beats. I take his bottom lip between my teeth and bite gently and he reacts by grabbing my face and covering my cheeks with his hands again, which are still cold. I don't let him take my shirt off, but I let him bury his face between my breasts and plant tiny kisses there.

By the time I get home, my lips chapped and swollen and my head spinning, I understand more than ever that you don't have to say anything at all to tell a lie. Lies come in many forms. A nod. A kiss. A caress.

I don't know how many lies I told Jasper tonight, or how many he told me. Maybe one side of the scale is tipped and one of us is about to fall off with no safety net.

Or maybe we're even.

45

"THERE HE IS," you said, ducking down in the front seat.
"No, don't look. I don't want him to know we're looking."

I bent my head down obediently but I peeked anyway. He wore all black, helplessly out of place in a pastel school like Robson. He took giant strides when he walked and his head bobbed constantly, like there was music playing in it.

"Tell me again why we're spying on your not-boyfriend?" I asked.

Trixie hunched over her knees and smiled. "Pure curiosity. I just wonder who he is when he's not with me. If there's any hope for him to be normal."

I felt sorry for Jasper in that moment. He was an experiment to her, a sideshow freak who she wanted to see perform on command, a specimen she wanted to study under a microscope. I wondered how she kept up the charade, how she acted when she was in bed with him. I wondered if he had any idea he was being used.

But I guess now I could ask myself the same thing.

46

DR. ROSENTHAL ISN'T all that bad, for a middle-aged man I have been forced to talk to about my life. He mostly lets me talk and doesn't seem to care when I stumble over the answers to the questions he does ask. He's nice, kind of fatherly, which is weird for me to think, because I've never had a father in my life and don't know what one would actually be like. The only real example I have to go by is Mr. Heller, and I don't want to think about him.

We don't spend that much time talking about Trixie. Maybe Dr. Rosenthal thinks it's because I blame myself, that I was her best friend and should have known she was hurting. What I almost want to tell him is that I'm the hurt one. I'm the girl with the knife sticking out of her back. He doesn't make many notes but when he does, I imagine he's writing something like *Seems disaffected by tragedy*. He probably thinks I'm blocking it out for self-preservation. Or that I'm a psychopath.

Mostly, we talk about me. About what I think of myself. About my fear of getting on the scale and my avoidance of the clothes I wore last year. He reads a lot into the fact that I dumped my sewing machine at Goodwill, even though I tell him it's no big deal, that I was just getting rid of things I didn't use anymore.

"It seems like fashion has been a big part of your life," he says, and it's embarrassing hearing it out loud, like he's talking about someone else.

"It was just a phase," I tell him.

"But now you're avoiding your closet, and by association, the person you were before Trixie came into your life. Fiona, it seems to me like you're struggling with poor body image and your self-confidence has taken a nosedive with everything else you've been through."

I put my hands in my lap and hunch my shoulders in, like that'll make my body smaller and easier to hide. *No shit. It's all her fault.* I want to be alone with my thoughts but there he is, wanting a response, maybe expecting me to thank him for figuring me out.

He keeps talking. "Negative body image affects a lot of teenage girls. It's easy to feel the need to compare your body to those of your peers, or seek reassurances from them."

How the hell would you know? I want to say, but then he might think I have anger-management issues on top of everything else. But he doesn't know what it's like to be a girl. Life is one big comparison, no matter who you're friends with or not friends with. When it was me and Jenny and Alison, I wanted Jenny's skinny legs and tiny waist, along with Alison's perfectly toned arms and her collarbone that protruded just the right amount. When it was me and Trixie, I wanted her confidence, her ability to wear whatever she wanted, to not have to dress up for life. I wanted her complexion, which never seemed to break out like mine. I wanted to live in her skin, cover myself with it like a blanket.

"I'm going to give you some homework, Fiona. I want you to do some research on negative body image and write down some things you *like* about yourself, both physical and otherwise. Be honest about it. We don't have to talk more about this if you don't want to, but I think it would be a good idea."

I leave his office without a prescription, no miracle cure for everything that's wrong with me. I'm not sure what I was expecting. Now I'm supposed to go home and ask Google why I hate how I look, and that wasn't part of the plan.

But Dr. Rosenthal doesn't seem to think I'm fat at all. Not that he'd tell me if he did. Maybe it's all in my head, and it's not that I'm trapped in the wrong body but that my body is trapped by the wrong brain.

I'm walking toward the elevator when the door from the stairs opens and Alison bursts through, her gym bag that she brings to cheerleading thrown over her shoulder. She must have come directly from practice, which also explains why she's in leggings and her hair is in a wet bun on top of her head.

"Fiona," she says. "Hey. How are you?"

I mean to say "I'm good," because that's what people always say, but instead I say, "I'm here." That makes her laugh.

"Yeah. I know what you mean."

There's an awkward silence and I realize for the first time that she's here too, that she must be here to talk to somebody, same as I am. Besides Dr. Rosenthal, there are three other doctors whose names are on the waiting room door.

"Look," she says. "I know a lot is different from how it used to be, and we haven't hung out in ages, but I meant what I said at school. I'm still here if you need someone to talk to. You know, someone you don't pay to see."

I stare down at my ballet flats. "Thanks. Same." I wonder why someone as perfect as Alison has to be here at all.

"My mom's making me see someone," she says. "She's convinced I'm, like, damaged somehow, because of what happened at my parties. Maybe I am damaged. I heard a girl at school call me Sister Suicide. Like it was my fault."

"It's not your fault," I say, with a bit too much venom. "People are going to do what they're going to do. You couldn't have changed anything."

"Thanks," she says. There's a pause, and maybe she's waiting for me to tell her why I'm here, because she told me, but I can't bring up the words *negative body image* in front of her perfect body, the thigh gap in her leggings that I'll never have and the fact that when she takes her hair out of that bun, it'll magically form perfect beachy waves.

"I should go," she says. "I'm pretty sure they charge by the minute, not the hour."

"I should go too. See you around." When I'm standing in front of the elevator, I get a burst of courage and whip around. "You're right. We should hang out sometime. If you want."

She turns back and smiles. "Yeah. I think I would."

47

YOU AND I had our rituals—our fake IDs, our random drives, our lazy sprawl across your bedroom carpet with convenience-store junk food cellophane-shiny between us. But before you, I had traditions too. I was a creature of other people's habits.

Jenny, Alison, and I did the same thing after each football game. We'd head to Alison's house and take off our makeup, our Robson red lipstick, and we'd put on face masks and make nachos. My half was only ever cheese, because I didn't like the other stuff Jenny and Alison added. Onions and black olives and peppers and—gross—artichokes for Jenny. When the nachos were done, we'd eat them standing over Alison's kitchen counter.

"I wish cheese had no calories," Alison always said. "I'd live off it if it didn't all pile up right here." She put her hands on her hips, trying to force them inward.

"I'd live off chocolate pudding," Jenny said one week, then changed her mind to cheesecake the next. "I just wish my ass wasn't so lumpy. And I swear, my arms are getting fat."

"You're both perfect how you are," I would say every time, because that was my role. I was the physical support during games and practice and the emotional support the rest of the time.

One night, Jenny hugged me after I said it. "You're the perfect one. Do you even know how awesome you are?"

It was over-the-top, but that was Jenny. She gave out hugs and compliments like they were nothing. Sure, they cost nothing, but they were also the hardest things to give, because they meant letting your guard down, exposing your insides.

"I love you guys," Alison said, wiping crumbs off her lips. "I literally have no idea what I'd do without you."

I felt the same way, although I never said it back. I never thought I'd have to find out what I'd do without them. But when Trixie came along, there wasn't room for everyone. There were only so many dolls that could fit on her shelf.

48

THE PARKING LOT behind the Green Machine becomes my and Jasper's spot. He says his parents are always home at night, and I don't want to risk Mom finding him at my house, so I pick him up and we drive there on nights that I know Mom won't question where I'm going or who I'm with. It's easy to lie to her, as long as I text her and let her know where I am. *I'm at the movies with Sarah. Sarah and I decided to go shopping after school.*

"Sarah really sounds great," she says absentmindedly while she's stirring a pot of whole-wheat spaghetti one night. "You should bring her around sometime so I can meet her."

"Sure," I say weakly. But I know what she really means. She doesn't want a repeat of the arguments we had about Trixie. She wants to know my friends, know the influence they have on me.

I try to lose myself in Jasper, in the darkened car. I let his hand creep up the back of my shirt. I get used to the way his hair feels between my fingers, the way his neck smells when I press my face against it.

I don't know why we always come here, why everything is such a secret. I sometimes fantasize about Trixie walking up to the foggy car window, tapping on the glass and shaking her head. I'd pull away from Jasper long enough to smile and wave, or maybe just give her the middle finger she deserves.

I'm the one who suggests going out in public together, because being together in secret stops being enough. I want the world to know that I don't give a shit what happened to Trixie Heller anymore. I want everyone to know that I'm over it, over her.

"I'm hungry," I tell Jasper, sliding off his lap.

"Yeah," he whispers in my ear. "I can tell."

"No, I mean for actual food. Let's go have some."

"Here?"

"No. I have a better idea. Do you like surprises?"

"Not really. I'm not so good at dealing with the unknown."

It's such a Jasper thing to say. Sometimes it sounds like he swallowed tarot cards or a crystal ball and he's fated to spew out their lines at random times. I'm not sure what he's going to think about where I'm taking him, but it feels right somehow, my idea of flipping off the universe and Trixie, lost somewhere in it.

When we get to Cabana Del Shit and park, Jasper sighs. "Of all the places, you want to eat here?"

"They have the best quesadillas." Not that I'm going to eat a quesadilla in front of Jasper. I'm sure he wishes I was in better shape, that when his hands are on my skin he wants there to be less of it. The last girl he was with was Trixie, and we're still competing, even though she's not here for me to compare myself to. Those were Dr. Rosenthal's words.

"Okay," he says. "If you want."

Honestly, I don't really want. I lean over and kiss him again, and I almost want to frame his face, his lips and flushed cheeks and messy hair, and keep it that way forever, just to remember that somebody felt lust for me.

Cabana Del Shit is empty, and there are black paper lanterns fluttering in the wind that look almost like shadows. Skylar is behind the bar, wiping the surface with a rag, and she looks up and arches an eyebrow when she sees us come in.

"We're closing soon," she says. "But sit anywhere."

Trixie always complained about what a bitch Skylar was. I wish Skylar wasn't a bitch so I don't have to agree with her, but when she practically throws menus down in front of us and rattles off the specials, I have to admit that Trixie was right.

"I'll just have a Diet Coke and a salad with dressing on the side," I say, taking smug satisfaction that I made her waste her breath telling us the specials when I knew I wasn't going to order anything besides salad.

"Same here," Jasper says.

When Skylar is gone, I raise an eyebrow at him. "Are you on a diet?"

He nudges my knee under the table. "Are you?"

"I'm a girl. I'm always supposed to be on a diet." I roll my eyes like it's a joke, like I'm okay with it, but I'm not. I wish he would tell me I'm beautiful, but I know he won't.

He drums his fingers on the table. My hands are in front of me, clasped together like a fleshy seashell. If this is a date, shouldn't our hands be entwined across the table, or at least touching? But he doesn't make a move to touch me so I don't either, and maybe he's embarrassed to be seen with a girl like me in public, even though this barely counts as public because we're the only two people here.

We have nothing to talk about. In my car, in the dark, we

don't have to talk at all. We let our bodies do the talking, our lips and hands and skin. But here, under the harsh Cabana Del Shit lighting, there's absolutely nothing to say. We share one thing in common and it's not even a thing but a person, and she's this giant elephant in the room that I don't want to give the chance to step all over me again.

"I'll be right back," I say, because I need to be alone to think of things I can talk to Jasper about. Things that are safe.

I duck into the bathroom and stare at myself in the mirror, fixating on how greasy my face looks. I use a brown paper towel to blot my forehead. I wish I had makeup with me, powder and concealer to even everything out. Jenny never went anywhere without a makeup bag, which used to clank around in her purse, and Alison and I would tease her for it. Now I get it. She didn't want to get caught anywhere looking less than perfect.

The door to the bathroom swings open, almost smacking me in the face. It's Skylar, who makes a beeline to the sink beside mine, where she starts scrubbing her hands with soap.

"Be careful," she says when I stick my hands under the dryer on the wall.

"I think I know how to use a hand dryer," I snap.

She rolls her eyes. "No, not that. The guy you're with. Be careful. I'm surprised you're even here with him. Don't you know who he is?"

"What do you mean?" I say, my chest tightening. I rub my arms, where goose bumps have started to rise, despite the heat of the hand dryer. *Of course I know who he is. That's his smell all over my skin. His hair is messy because my hands were just in it.*

"Shit. You don't know," Skylar says, and I can tell by the

way something softens in her eyes that she's preparing to take me into her confidence. "I guess it's a good thing I'm here to tell you. He used to hang around here, like, all the time."

I continue to stare at her blankly.

"He's the guy who was obsessed with your best friend."

49

"OBSESSION," YOU SAID, *standing in front of the vanity in your bedroom with purple lipstick in your hand.* "A three-syllable euphemism for its ugly older sister, stalker."

I was on her bed, flipping through a magazine. "What are you talking about?" I said. "Who's obsessed with you?"

She applied the lipstick expertly, with her eyes closed. She didn't even need to use the mirror.

"Nobody. That's just the name of the lipstick."

I didn't quite believe her.

50

I TRY TO forget about what Skylar said, but her words are on repeat in my brain, like an annoying chorus from an over-played song on the radio. *He's the guy who was obsessed with your best friend.* Jasper and I ate salad and drank Diet Coke together, and I dropped him off at home and didn't say a word about what Skylar told me, but now what she told me is all I can think about. Jasper said he and Trixie were just friends, that he didn't care about having an actual relationship any more than she did.

But maybe he lied. I read the note he left in our locker. I already know Jasper cared more about Trixie than he admit-ted to me, but it feels different now, because somebody else knew too. Maybe he's the kind of guy who needs to be obsessed with someone.

As much as I don't want to care, I need to know the truth. Except, I have no idea how to bring it up. It's not like I'm going to approach him and say, "The waitress from last night told me you used to be obsessed with Trixie. Can you elaborate?"

I don't owe it to Trixie to investigate what Skylar said. I don't owe her anything. She slept with the one person she knew meant everything to me. But maybe whatever I'm doing with Jasper isn't revenge at all. He didn't mean anything to her, and she'll never know what we're doing anyway. I guess I need to figure out if Jasper means anything to me.

A week after the Cabana Del Shit date, or whatever it was, Jasper asks me if I want to come over after school. I'm terrified that it's because he wants to have sex with me, and more than that, I realize I'm scared to be alone with him—actually alone. There's a comfort in being in my car in a parking lot, because I could open the door and let myself out at any time, and people are close by without being too close. But being alone in his bedroom is a whole other beast. I've been using him to move on, to do what I think I should be doing, but we're still tied up in the same person, the uninvited third party in the passenger seat with her arm hanging out the window, smoking a cigarette, asking why we're taking so long.

I end up saying it on the drive to his house. "How did you really feel about Trixie? I need to know."

"I've already told you. We were friends who hooked up. That's all."

I flush, embarrassed. That's exactly what we are, except minus the friends part. I don't even have what Trixie had with Jasper. I'm sloppy seconds, a hasty replacement.

"Did you hang around Cabana Del Shit after you stopped seeing Trixie?"

I can tell by the way his eyes widen that he wasn't expecting that, and part of me expects him to get mad and tell me off. But he doesn't get mad. He starts to talk.

"No. I mean, sort of. I went there a few times, just to make sure she was okay. She wasn't returning my calls or texts. I figured something might be wrong. It wasn't like her to just blow me off."

"But you were only hooking up. That's what you said."

"Yeah, but she still owed me an explanation."

I want to tell him she didn't owe him anything. I try to remember the conversation we had on the way to the beach that day, which feels like forever ago. He said Trixie wouldn't give him a ticket to her graduation. Why would he even want one, if they were just friends with benefits?

"I just need to know the truth." My voice is small, but my desperation feels huge, big enough to swallow me up. "Were you in love with her?"

"The truth is," he says, leaning against the window. "The truth is, I don't know. I think I felt more for her than she felt for me. It was unbalanced."

I know the feeling, I want to say, but I don't.

"But if you loved her, and you think she's still out there, how can you just move on? Don't you need to know what happened?" That's what I actually say. I try to imagine it the other way around, if Beau went missing. Even though I'm pissed off at him—it feels like he cheated on me with Trixie, even though it was actually Jenny he cheated on—I wouldn't stop looking until I found him.

"I don't know," he says. "I haven't moved on. It's complicated. I mean, I don't *think* I loved her. I've never been in love. I just don't see the point in following all these dead ends that lead nowhere and leave us more frustrated than when we started."

"You were obsessed with her. You were, weren't you?"

"Who told you that? It's not true. I just thought she was

cool. We had fun together." He rubs a hand over his face, pulling his eyes and nose down, making himself look grotesque. "Look, I have an idea. That's why I wanted you to come over today. I have a theory about where she could be, but I didn't want to get your hopes up. I was looking at that globe in my room and remembered a place she mentioned she wanted to go. Tijuana."

I narrow my eyes. "She never mentioned Tijuana to me."

"Well, I'm sure she didn't tell me everything you guys talked about either. She used to say to me, *How nice would it be for us to get away and spend a weekend in Tijuana?*"

That doesn't sound like something Trixie would say, I want to scream. Especially since she spent all her weekends with me. But maybe he's right. We knew two different girls who somehow make up the same person and that's why we need to work together, to build the actual girl.

"Okay," I say, and somehow we're back here, back to wanting to find her, even though I'm still so mad. Maybe that's why I want to find her, because I'm full of all this hate, and I need to spew it somewhere. I picture us finding her in Tijuana, maybe with Toby Hunter, walking on the beach, skinny and tanned. I'd act shocked to see Toby, of course, because I'm not sharing with Jasper what Beau told me. I imagine my hands making contact with Trixie's back, pushing her down, watching her crumple in the sand. I hear myself telling Toby what she did with his brother and watching him abandon her too.

"She told me about New York too, you know," he says, his fingers brushing over mine. "She told me you were going there together."

A flicker of hope opens up somewhere inside me, and I

wish I could fill it with cold, hard hatred, pour it into the void like cement. She slept with Beau and didn't tell me, and might have only become my friend as some sick little vendetta to get back at him. I may have been the biggest pawn in a game I didn't know I was playing. But little things like this, her telling Jasper about me, somehow mean something.

"So, Tijuana," I say, changing the subject back. "When are we going?"

51

MAYBE YOU WERE *the one with negative body image, because you were obsessed with the size of everything. Your ears were too small. Your nose was too big. Your toes were too skinny and your kneecaps out of proportion to your body.*

Morrison Beach didn't fit.

"I'm done here," Trixie said one day when we were walking from my car to the school. "Don't you think we need something bigger?"

I thought everything was big enough already. If anything, I wanted to shrink. Shrink myself and shrink the world down to just the two of us, where nobody expected anything of me and I expected nothing back from them. I wanted our world to become a bubble we could draw curtains around, a snow globe immune to the outside.

"What do you mean?" I said.

"I mean," she said, slinging her arm around my shoulder like she did when she got especially amped up, "New York City big. What do you think?"

I stopped, and she kept walking. "Are you asking me to move to New York with you?"

"Of course I am. I'm not going by myself, silly."

The idea kind of scared me. I always figured I'd end up at

UCLA, like I talked about with my old friends. I had even gone to visit the campus last summer with Jenny and Alison, and we stayed in a dorm room, picturing how awesome life after high school would be.

"Okay," I said, because maybe New York would be the scene of my awesome life after high school. What was anchoring me in California anyway? Or who?

"They have the best cheesecake," she said. "And bagels. And snow, Fiona. Plus, you love fashion. I picked up some brochures about NYU. It's the perfect place for us."

I nodded along with everything. I had gotten rid of my sewing machine and didn't talk about clothes anymore, so I was surprised she even remembered. She was so excited about the possibility of New York that I got excited too, started to feel like maybe I really would have an awesome life after high school, that I could become myself again. Maybe getting away from everyone would be the best way to get back to that girl.

I never considered that if I had an anchor in California, in the form of a boy I wished I didn't love, Trixie might have had a magnet, pulling her farther and farther away. Toby.

How far did she go for him?

52

"WE SHOULD JUST go," Jasper says one day at lunch, plucking blades of grass from the ground and splitting them in half. "If we're going to do it."

Tijuana is an hour's drive from Morrison Beach, but we can't just go there after school and hope nobody notices. It has to be the right time. And thanks to Mom, the right time ends up being the first week in November.

"I'll be back Monday at the latest," Mom says, throwing clothes in her suitcase. Her forehead creases. "I think it would be best if Aunt Leslie comes and stays with you."

My stomach forms a knot. Aunt Leslie would ruin everything.

"No," I say. "I'm fine on my own." *Please*, I beg silently. *Please, believe me.*

Mom purses her lips. "I expect you to call every day. Twice a day. And if you don't call, I'm sending Leslie to the house."

I nod emphatically. She didn't say anything like that during the summer. She has been different since Trixie left, more worried Mom and less cool Mom. Trixie changed more people than she'll ever know.

I wave as Mom's car pulls out of the driveway. She waves back and for a second I feel like running after her, like asking her to stay and make me feel like a little kid, loved and protected and safe. But I can't think about that now. Not when I have a mission.

I pick Jasper up after school. He has a duffel bag with him, which he shoves into the back seat of my car. I raise my eyebrows. "Are you planning on sleeping over?"

He laughs. His incisors are pointy, almost vampire-like. I remember how they felt tugging on my lip. Then I remember what Skylar said, and I shake the thought out of my head.

"I just figured it was best to be prepared."

"Where did you tell your parents you're going? Did you think of a good excuse?"

He stretches out his legs. "Astronomy project. Something about the lunar phases of the moon. I'm a good liar when I need to be."

Jasper's fingertips are perched on the console while I drive. His hand creeps closer and closer to my thigh, where it comes to rest. When I jerk away, he stretches out his palm, which is hot against my jeans.

"Relax," he says. "I just wanted to touch you."

"Why? Why me?"

It's a valid question, but he could ask me the same thing. Neither of us wants to answer it. But Jasper's mouth is edging closer to the side of my face, his breath tickling my earlobe. "Let me tell you a secret," he whispers, and I instinctively clench up, because I don't have room to store more secrets. "You're the most beautiful girl I've ever seen."

My lips twitch into a smile and I let him keep his hand there, resting on my thigh. I push out the fear, the nagging worry that he needs a girl to fixate on and now that's me, because I'm here and she's not.

We park at the sprawling Plaza Río shopping center, because it seems like a good place to start. But as soon as we get out of the vehicle and walk into the open-air mall, I start to think this might have been a really dumb idea. There are about a million people wandering everywhere. Actually, nearly one million, seven hundred thousand—that's what I read online. That's how many people live in this city. And we thought we could drive here and just pluck her out of the crowd. I'm dizzy from the heat, from my own stupidity, from the smells, from so many bodies crowded into a small space.

"She had brown hair," I say, trying to remember exactly how she looked the night she disappeared. "Light brown, I think. Or maybe it was dark."

"But she could have changed that," Jasper says, brushing his fingers through his own hair. "She could have changed everything."

My jaw trembles and I fight back tears. Usually I feel too big to fit in, but here I'm too small, just a speck among throngs of people. Which, ironically, is what I've always wanted. I guess when people say be careful what you wish for, they mean it.

"She mentioned this place for a reason." He grabs my hand. "So let's walk around and see what we find."

We walk through the mall and Jasper doesn't let go of my hand, even when ours both become hot and sweaty. We go into every store and then to the bustling food court. We pass each kiosk, checking to see who is working behind the counter. They're mostly kids our age, pimply-faced and gangly, wearing ugly hats.

Every time I see a skinny girl with shoulder-length brown hair, I hold my breath. Which is every two seconds, because that's how common skinny white girls with shoulder-length brown hair are. About as common as the name Sarah Brown. A dime a dozen. And I know she must have done that on purpose.

We walk laps around the mall until my feet hurt and I'm exhausted. Then we walk all the way down Avenida Revolución, where there are even more people. I try to stare at each face, but there are too many and they're going by so fast, too fast. Within the first five minutes, we could have passed a hundred Trixies without even knowing it. There are lots of little restaurants along here, places exactly like Cabana Del Shit. Maybe we should have made up posters with her face on them. HAVE YOU SEEN THIS GIRL? Maybe I would have, if I had any photos of her left.

I start to laugh. Not because it's funny, but because it's pathetic. The air is getting cold and I wrap my cardigan around my stomach.

"What?" Jasper says.

"We should just go home," I say, shaking my head. "We're not going to find her here. Not tonight. Maybe not ever. It would take weeks, months, even years, and we still might never find her." She probably mentioned Tijuana to Jasper to throw him off. Just like she told me she was going to community college and was still seeing Jasper all summer. Just like she told me she thought Beau was a loser. She doesn't deserve to have people looking for her.

But Jasper stops moving and stares ahead. I swear, my heart comes to a complete stop and the color drains out of my face and the blood rushes down to my feet, even though I have no idea what he's looking at, or who.

"Jasper," I say, my voice shaking. "Jasper, what's going on?"

He holds out his hand slowly, like moving will scare away

whatever he's looking at. There's a cluster of girls and my eyes dart from face to face to the backs of heads. Blondes and brunettes and one redhead, and they're all squealing and hovering over something. One of those monkeys on a leash jumps on one girl's skinny tanned shoulder. I can't see her face. My breath hitches in my throat as I let myself think this could be Trixie.

Then the girl turns around, almost like she knows someone is watching her. She looks straight at me and I deflate. She's not Trixie. The face is all wrong, wide cheeks and thick eyebrows and a dimpled chin.

I grab Jasper's wrist. "Not her," I say, except he's still staring, not saying a word.

Finally, I see that he wasn't looking at the girl at all. He was looking at the guy with the monkey. A shock of blond hair and a lime-green vest, the kind dirt rubs off.

Byron St. James. The man who saw Trixie die.

53

YOU MIGHT ALREADY know this, but Beau was right. Toby did like to hide.

There was a big football after-party once, when we won against the Hutchings Hailstorms. We didn't beat them so much as annihilate them, and it was all because of Toby. King Toby, who scored three touchdowns. One of the guys on the football team invited everyone back to his parents' mansion after. The house looked like a layer cake, people on every tier. People drinking, dancing, swimming in the backyard pool, making out in the hot tub. Everyone was there except the king himself. Jenny, Alison, and I were huddled on a wooden swing, legs sticking together with sweat. As everyone else buzzed about where Toby was, I looked for a different blond head. Beau's. But he wasn't there, and unlike his brother, his absence went unnoticed by everyone but me.

"He said he'd be here," Gabby whined from her perch on a lounger in front of us. I could tell she was annoyed, and maybe embarrassed, because he wasn't where he said he would be. She kept pulling out her phone and shoving it back in her purse.

"What could have happened to him?" Jenny said in a hushed whisper. She wanted a story to tell the next day.

"What if he got in a car accident or something? Or had a brain aneurysm? Those can happen to anyone."

Alison crossed her arms. "I'm sure he's fine. Maybe he decided to stay home and sleep. Who knows?"

An hour or so later, a familiar song started playing on the loudspeakers. "Sweet Child O' Mine," which for some reason, Toby considered his own personal anthem. I figured somebody must need a pretty big ego to have their own personal anthem.

"Toby's missing his song," Braden Baker yelled. "Where the hell is that dude?"

Then the doors to the pool shed burst open and out came Toby, shirtless, with his football number painted in gold on his chest. With his arms up, he proceeded to run the length of the diving board and execute a pretty impressive flip before submerging himself underwater for an extremely long time. We all gathered around the pool, waiting for him to come up. When he did, it was with both fists in the air, like Superman.

"You should have seen your faces," he said later, when he was surrounded by people, a towel over his shoulders. "I was here the whole fucking time."

Nobody knew why he thought it would be funny to pull that kind of prank. But maybe he didn't think it was funny at all.

54

WE WAIT UNTIL the girls clear away. There's noise everywhere, but everything has faded, except the sound of my own
heartbeat in my ears and Jasper's breathing, heavy and measured, beside me.

"I actually don't believe this," he mutters, and he sounds
scared. Scared of what we're going to find out. Or what we
won't.

After the last girl fishes a crumpled bill out of the pocket
of her jean shorts and passes it to the guy with the monkey, I
step forward. I pull on Jasper's hand but he doesn't budge.

"I don't think we should talk to him," he says. "He could
be dangerous."

"Jasper, he has a monkey on his shoulder. Do you honestly
think he's going to do something to us?"

"I don't know. I just have a bad feeling."

"I'm not going home without talking to him. Do you
have any money? Mom gave me a hundred before she left
this weekend, but we might need more. I feel like he's not
going to talk to me unless there's something in it for him."

Jasper is silent, and for a minute I think he's going to turn
around and leave me here. Then he reaches in his coat

pocket and retrieves his wallet. "I have a hundred bucks. You can take it. But I think I'll hang back. I mean, look at me. I'm not exactly approachable. You look a lot nicer."

He has a point. And as terrifying as it is to confront this guy by myself, I need to find out everything I can, even though I have a feeling it will make me hate Trixie more than I already do, that it'll chip away at any of the good memories I still have left of her.

Jasper pulls his hood over his head. "I'll be right here. I won't let you out of my sight."

I take a shaky breath and start following Byron St. James down the sidewalk. He's facing away from me, walking the other way. I notice he has a swagger, like he's the most popular guy at school, like he's strutting down the hallway after football practice, not walking down the street with crumpled bills in his pocket and a sad-looking monkey perched on his shoulder.

"Excuse me," I say, but he doesn't turn around, so I pick up the pace until I'm close enough to realize how badly he smells. Like cigarettes and body odor. Like he hasn't showered in weeks.

He spins around, a lopsided smile crossing his face. His teeth are straight but yellowing and I see, up close, that he's not that much older than me, maybe only a few years. His hair is blond but looks dirty and greasy.

"You want your picture with the monkey, kid?" he says, and he has a dimple, just like Toby Hunter did. Does.

"S-sure," I stammer, and it's already climbing onto my shoulder, the pads of its feet cool on my skin. I paste on a smile as the guy raises a Polaroid camera and snaps a picture.

"Good one," he says. "That'll be ten bucks."

"I recognize you," I say slowly, handing him a ten-dollar bill. "You're from Morrison Beach."

The smile disappears from his face and his eyes dart around. The monkey jumps back onto his shoulder.

"Nah. I've been here forever. Just ask this little guy."

I glance at the monkey, who stares at me with black eyes shiny like marbles.

"Nice meeting you," he says, turning to walk the other way, flipping me a casual wave. "Have a nice life, kid."

Have a nice life. I wonder if that's what he said to Trixie, or if she said it to him.

"How much did she pay you?" I say, following him down the sidewalk. "How much did she pay you to tell people she drowned herself?"

He stops so fast that the monkey nearly topples off his shoulder. "I don't know what you're talking about."

"You were all over the news. Telling everyone what happened. But something just didn't add up."

"Look, kid, you have me mixed up with someone else." He turns away, pulling his vest closer to his body.

"A hundred dollars says I don't," I yell after him. "Your name is Byron St. James. Just tell me what you know. All I want to do is find her."

He hesitates but keeps walking, and I trail him, hoping Jasper is right behind me like he promised he would be.

"I won't tell anyone," I shout. "Whatever you say stays between you and me."

"Two hundred," he says, stopping but still facing away. "Two hundred and I'll tell you what I know."

"Fine. Two hundred. Just—please, I need to know everything."

He whips around so fast that I nearly crash into him. "What's it to you? Why do you want to know so badly? I could just take your money and say whatever I feel like. Did you ever think about that?"

"But you won't," I say, surprised at the steadiness in my voice. "You did what she asked. For some reason, she trusted you. And she barely trusted anyone."

He bobs up and down on his heels, then gestures to the other side of the road, where there's a giant fountain surrounded by people. "Follow me. I'll need to see the money before I say a word. But I think it's a waste of two hundred bucks."

When we're seated side by side on the edge of the fountain, I grab the bills from Jasper's wallet and the one from mine and pass them to the guy. Even though it's not very warm out anymore, sweat soaks my upper back. This is stupid, a terrible idea. What if a cop sees us? It looks like I'm paying this guy for drugs, something a lot less valuable than what I'm actually paying for.

"So listen closely," Byron says, dropping his voice. "I seen this girl come over one night, all skinny and kind of desperate and I figured she was strung out. So when she grabbed me and asked if I wanted to walk down the beach, I thought she wanted to do a deal."

The things Trixie did. The ways she used boys and men.

"Relax," he says. "We didn't do nothing. She just told me she needed a favor. I told her favors don't come cheap. But she had the cash to back it up."

Her Cabana Del Shit money. She said she was saving it for school. She was saving it for something else.

"She told me what to say, so I said it. Went over it

with me a million times. Don't think she trusted that I'd remember."

I hear what he's saying but it doesn't sink in, just sits on the surface of my skin while emotions clash inside me. Anger, sadness, and relief that I was right, that I at least knew her well enough to know she's not dead. I'm not crazy. I'm not chasing a ghost, longing for a memory. It actually happened. She paid this guy to tell anyone who would listen that she walked into the water and drowned. *I was right.*

"Did she tell you why? And where did she go?" My words come out in a tumble, clamoring over each other.

His eyes crinkle up in the corners. I wonder if this is why Trixie picked him, because when he smiles, he looks a bit like Toby.

"She didn't tell me any of that. And no way in hell was I gonna ask. We did a trade. That's all it was."

Of course not, I think. That would be leaving a trail. And Trixie wiped the path clean of crumbs.

"So she paid you to tell people she drowned herself," I say. "And she paid you to disappear afterward."

"That last part was my idea. It was time to move on. I seen enough shit down by that beach." He raises a thick eyebrow, making his forehead descend into skinny wrinkles. "Pretty young girl disappears, people care. Nobody gives a shit when I do."

"She told you to cut the pay phone cord," I choke out. "So you couldn't call for help."

He narrows his eyes, looks up. The monkey jumps from his shoulder to his lap. "I didn't cut no pay phone cord. She did that herself." He stands up and glances around, like we're being watched. "Look, we about done here? I've told you all there is."

I touch my face and realize I'm crying. I didn't even feel the tears come out of me but here they are, hot and wet on my cheeks. I don't know what I expected. That he'd magically tell me where she is, that he'd say she left a message for her best friend Fiona, who she knew would come looking for her.

"Hey," the guy says, turning back to face me. "She got a fake ID. Maybe even a passport. From the Preacher. Maybe he knows something." He pauses. "But I doubt it."

"The Preacher," I echo. "I've never even heard of him."

"He wants it that way," he says. "That guy knows how to hide in plain sight."

I close my eyes and clench the cold stone of the fountain with my hands. I count backward from ten. From last summer. From that hot September day.

By the time I open my eyes, he's gone.

55

I DIDN'T FIND out that you quit working at Cabana Del Shit because you told me. I probably never would have known the truth if I hadn't shown up one day to surprise you.

It was pretty dead inside, which was both surprising and not. Every time I went there to meet Trixie, I was one of the only customers. But when I wasn't around, Trixie would text me to complain about how busy it was and how badly she needed a break. That day, there were only two other customers, a couple of guys in their twenties who glanced at me and quickly looked away.

I walked up to the bar. Skylar was perched on a barstool, poring over a magazine. She didn't even bat an eye when I sat down a few stools away. Finally, I asked her if she knew where Trixie was.

She flipped to another page in her magazine before looking up. She rolled her eyes, like she was sick of answering that question. Maybe she had a right to be.

"Trixie?" She started laughing, a slow chuckle, the same kind of sound Mom made when she was exasperated with me. No wonder Trixie hated her.

"Yeah, Trixie," I said, annoyed. "She's a dishwasher. Can you get her for me?"

Skylar rolled her eyes again and stretched her fingers out on the bar. I noticed the rings right away. She had one on each finger, chunky silver with designs and little turquoise stones. Those rings looked too familiar.

"I know who she is," she snapped. "But no, I can't get her for you. Because she doesn't work here anymore."

I fingered the fabric of my skirt and leaned against the bar. My upper arm stuck to its surface.

"What do you mean, she doesn't work here anymore? She was working the lunch shift today. She texted me from here an hour ago."

Skylar shook her head and her bangs fell into her eyes. Her lips twisted into a smile and I could tell she was enjoying this, whatever this was.

"I hate to say it, but your friend must have lied to you. Because she quit a month ago. Gave her two weeks' notice and when her last shift was done, she left without saying goodbye. Just took her last paycheck and walked out. I haven't seen her since."

I didn't say anything else. We sat there, with only the sounds of Skylar flipping magazine pages and the hum of the air conditioner and the low voices of the two guys sitting in a booth.

When I stood up to leave, Skylar stood up too and slunk behind the bar, where she started pouring a beer. That was when I realized why her rings looked familiar.

Because they were Trixie's.

"Did you take those rings?" I almost yelled. "They're exactly like the ones she wears."

Skylar stared at me with that stupid arched eyebrow. "I didn't take them. Trixie gave them to me. She knew I liked them, and on her last day, there they were in my cubby. I guess she didn't want them anymore."

I wondered who the liar was. Maybe Skylar stole them. But then I remembered the week before, when Trixie lugged two garbage bags of her clothes to Goodwill and gave me a bunch of old picture frames with nothing in them.

She called it "decluttering."

But now I call it disappearing.

56

I WAIT UNTIL Jasper finds me at the fountain, until my butt is numb from sitting on the granite.

"What did he say?" Jasper puts his hands on my shoulders, digs his thumbs in. "Did he know anything?"

I wipe a tear off my cheek. I'm mad at myself for even caring. "No. Just what I already knew. That I was right. She paid him to say what she wanted him to say, and he didn't ask questions."

Jasper sits down wordlessly, wraps his arm around me, tucks my head under his chin, like we're boyfriend and girlfriend and this is just another Friday night.

"She might have gotten a fake ID from someone named the Preacher," I say. "Maybe even a passport. She could have left the country, Jasper. Maybe she's across the world. The only way to know is to find this Preacher guy."

"Let's talk about it later," he says, planting a tiny kiss on top of my head. "We at least know she's out there somewhere. That's something."

But he doesn't sound so sure that it's something, and I'm not either. Now that I know, now that what I suspected is the truth, I need to know more. I need to know everything.

I call Mom from the car and tell her I'm fine, that I'm

already in my pajamas, about to go to bed. I know she'll never notice the long-distance charge because our cell phone bills are paid automatically from her credit card each month. "I love you," Mom says, and even though she says it casually, like it's an afterthought, it makes me want to cry all over again.

"I love you too," I say, fighting the urge to tell her everything.

I start to fade on the drive and pinch my knees to stay awake. It feels too hot in the car, almost suffocating. The traffic is heavy and I want to get out of here, but I also don't want to go home and just give up if she could still be here.

"Let's stay here," Jasper suddenly says. "We can look again tomorrow. We barely looked anywhere tonight. We'll stop somewhere and get a room for the night and look around again in the morning. I really feel like she's here."

I don't, I want to say, but I'm too tired to argue so I just nod instead. When we see the neon lights for a shitty motel glowing in the distance, I pull into the parking lot, my eyes burning. My whole body aches and my heart is a deadweight, like it has been wrapped in a wet blanket and is sucking up all the energy I ever had.

We scrounge together enough money in small bills from our collective wallets to pay for the room, but the stern-looking motel owner says he needs to see ID because he doesn't believe we're eighteen. Which we're not, but I didn't think it would matter here, in a city people come to when they want to disappear into somebody else. Then I reach into my purse and dig around at the bottom, where crumbs and change have fallen, and pluck out what I'm looking for, what I tossed in just in case I ever needed it.

"Here you go."

The motel owner raises a bushy white eyebrow and looks from Beth Winchester's face to mine and back again. Finally, he pushes a room key across the desk.

"Enjoy your stay, Miss Winchester," he mumbles, like he can tell something is off but doesn't have the energy to call me on it.

"Miss Winchester?" Jasper whispers when we're walking to the room.

"It's the ID Trixie got for me. I just thought it might come in handy sometime."

I'm relieved when there are two double beds, both with ugly floral covers and pink pillowcases. I kick off my shoes and the carpet under my feet is rough and prickly. I collapse on one of the beds, wanting this day to go away, wanting to sleep forever and wake up when it's over, when this is all a bad dream. I bury my face in one of the musty pillows.

"I'll go get us some food," Jasper says.

I must drift off, because suddenly he's prodding my shoulder and I don't know what day it is or what time it is or what I'm even doing here. I flip onto my back and Jasper pushes the hair off my forehead with a featherlight touch. "I got us dinner," he says. "You have your choice of Sno Balls, Cheez-Its, or Doritos. We can wash it down with delicious tap water."

He's trying to be funny, but all I want to do is cry because it sounds exactly like something Trixie would say. *I couldn't decide, so I got us hot dogs, fries, and one of those giant onion ring things you like so much. Oh, and I never forget your chocolate.*

I bring my arms up to my face to cover my blotchy skin. I'm embarrassed that I'm this close to crying again, ashamed that I can't seem to hold it together anymore. But Jasper

stretches out beside me, presses the length of his b[ ]
takes my hand in his.

"It's okay to be upset," he says. "I think we wer[ ]
ing we'd find her. But we're trying."

"I just don't understand why she did it," I say, my voice coming out scratchy and weak. "Why she needed so badly to get out of her life." *Why she needed so badly to have Beau. Why she needed so badly to ruin everything I used to like about myself.* There's more I could say. More about Toby, about his role in all this. But Beau trusted me with that, and as angry as I am at him, I won't betray him by telling Jasper everything he told me the day my world bottomed out in his kitchen.

Jasper runs his finger down my arm, making little circles. "The way I see it," he whispers in my ear, "if life were that easy, everyone would be in it."

I stiffen because it's either the most bizarre thing I have ever heard, or else the most accurate. Maybe people are right about Jasper. He's strange, it's true. But he's more than that to me, and right now we're sharing something nobody else can possibly be feeling, something that's only ours. I roll over to face him and trace the outline of his jaw, the shell-like shape of his ear, the soft-dry texture of his hair between my fingers. He responds by pressing his thumb into the middle of my bottom lip and kissing me there as gently as the beat of a butterfly wing. He hovers there, not going any further, until I part my lips and let him kiss me harder and his tongue is in my mouth and his hand cups the side of my face.

I keep my eyes shut as he presses me onto my back, as the hand that's not on my face travels to my heart and a finger trails down my stomach, to the fly of my jeans. I feel him hard against me and think how he isn't faking that, how he wants me and he's completely sober and completely *here*, in this moment. I let him wiggle my jeans down even though the denim burns my skin like sandpaper. It would be so easy to reach over and flip off the lamp and be alone in the dark together. So easy for the layers of clothing between us to come off, for us to come together and get rid of our aching loneliness, just for one night, just for one minute.

"Turn off the light," I choke out. He does it without asking why, and I'm not about to tell him. Because the dark makes it all go away.

Jasper's fingers move into my jeans and press against the outside of my underwear, rubbing against the cotton, and I try to hold off my fear long enough for it to feel good. But I can't let it go, not when it's clenched up in every single part of me, trapped like a wild animal in a cage. I pull away abruptly.

"I'm sorry," I say, breathing heavily. "I can't do this."

Jasper presses his forehead against mine and his skin feels hot, charged.

"It's okay," he whispers. "You have nothing to be sorry for."

"I'm just not ready," I say, lying down on my side, a new wave of guilt bubbling up like a rash because if he thinks that's the truth, he might understand. I wait for him to get up and want space, but instead, he curls up around me and doesn't recoil or pull back when I don't fit neatly in his arms.

When he starts snoring lightly, I know he has drifted off. The sound of his snoring comforts me, for some reason, and then I wonder if Trixie ever heard it, if she ever spent a night actually sleeping with Jasper, if she ever got to know that about him. I wonder how she managed to have sex with him when she was so in love with Toby and knew he was still out there somewhere.

That's when I sit up in bed so fast that my head spins.

Trixie started changing right after graduation. I can pinpoint the day she dyed her hair brown. That was when everything became different. And Jasper said he didn't see her all summer. That she blew him off without any real excuse.

That must have been when Toby came back to life, or back to her life.

And when she decided her life as she knew it had to be over.

57

AT FIRST, YOU *and I didn't talk much about the future. I held on to each memory of you like somebody hanging off a cliff and gripping a rope tightly, not letting myself slip down any lower for fear there wouldn't be anything left to cling on to. But the more time we spent together, the more we became a pair.*

"We can share a dorm room," Trixie had said, licking ketchup off her fingers. "You'll major in something to do with fashion and I'll figure out what to do with my life and we'll have our own minibar."

I pictured myself in New York, where nobody would know anything about me. A fresh start, where I wouldn't have to see Jenny and Beau in the halls or hear Mom's unsolicited opinions about my choice of friends. I lusted for freedom just thinking about it.

We talked about New York a lot after that. The plan was that Trixie would do a year of community college first. She would keep working at Cabana Del Shit and make some extra money. That way, we could be freshmen together. We even talked about opening our own boutique eventually. I'd buy and remake clothes and she would balance the books.

"In New York, we'll paint one wall yellow and the other

bright blue," she said. "We'll have a whole closet full of black clothes. And a beret. I want to wear a beret."

It became almost like a game. In New York, we'll do this. In New York, this will happen.

"In New York, I'll fall in love in Central Park," I said a week after her graduation, when we were sprawled on my bed watching *Lost* on my laptop.

It was her turn to say something, but she didn't. She just rolled onto her back and closed her eyes.

I tried again later, when we ordered dinner and she wouldn't stop staring at her phone. She never used to care about her phone when we were together, so it pissed me off that all of a sudden she was glued to it, just like Jenny always was, like I wasn't worth her time.

"In New York, I can intern at a fashion magazine, like in *The Hills*," I said loudly. "And you can start working on a novel or something. We'll meet for long lunches and drink too much wine."

That time, she blew her bangs out of her face. The bangs were new, and I could tell she hated them because she was always pulling them off her forehead with bobby pins.

"Can we talk about something else?" she said. "I mean, who knows what will happen, right?"

It stung like she had slapped me, but I just nodded and finished the last piece of pizza. When I was done with that, I ate the crusts she left.

That was the last time we ever talked about New York. If I had known it would be the last time, I probably would have said what I wanted to say:

What do you think will happen instead?

58

WE SPEND THE next day searching different parts of Tijuana. The Playas de Tijuana beach community and all the way to Plaza Carrousel. We share the streets with millions of people, thousands of possible Trixies. My eyes hurt from darting in every direction, hoping I'll lock eyes with her. My brain hurts from conjuring up what I would possibly say to her. *How could you do that to me? You ruined everything. You were never my sister.*

By the end of the afternoon, I'm red from the sun and more frustrated than I ever thought possible. It's like this whole trip made finding Trixie an even more distant prospect than it was before we left. It's a reminder of how huge everything is and how small she would be in it.

Jasper's hand is on my leg the entire car ride home. It's like after last night, he has decided he's moving on and I'm the one he'll be moving on with. That it's only a matter of time before we fall in love with each other. Terror spikes in my chest at the idea that he's already in love with me, that he has replaced Trixie with me. There's no way I can fill that void. Trixie left an imprint, an empty space with a jagged outline that only her sharp edges could fill.

When I drop him off at his house, he presses his thumb

into my lip again, and I try to corner the thought out of my head that he ever did the same thing to Trixie.

"Sorry we didn't find her," he says. "But at least we can say we tried. We did everything we could." He doesn't mention trying to find the Preacher, so I don't either.

I have the house to myself for another day and I spend most of it in my bed, tossing and turning, spinning out of bad dreams. I open my bottom drawer and shovel a chocolate bar in my mouth, chewing without tasting it, because I know I don't deserve to enjoy it. Then I sit down at my desk and open a file that I had almost forgotten about. My NYU application, which I completed months ago. Now I wish I could answer those long-answer questions differently. *Describe an experience that has impacted who you are as a person. What is special, unique, distinctive, or impressive about you or your life story?*

It's hard to separate anything from Trixie. Her friendship altered me, made me change shape in more ways than I ever knew was possible. Her voice is in my head. She's under my skin, a tattoo nobody else can see.

I wonder if I left a mark on her, or if I was like an article of clothing that got too big and became easy to step out of.

Tell us why you think you're a good candidate for New York University.

Because it's not here I want to write over my actual canned bullshit. Because it's a promise, and I keep my promises. Except the promise I made to myself halfway through the summer: *I promise I'll be skinny when school starts.* I had thrown away all of my chocolate and pulled out my patchwork jeans, picturing how I'd look in them when school started. I'd make clothes again. I'd dress up even if I wasn't leaving the house. I thought I felt good enough to try the jeans on. I only had them around my ankles when I glimpsed myself in the mirror, red-faced and sweaty, and knew I couldn't handle pulling them up any farther. I threw the pants in the garbage and grabbed my keys.

With the car idling in the driveway, I went back up to my room and picked up my sewing machine. Mom had bought it for me for my fifteenth birthday, and I used to love it. But that day, it was a symbol of my failure, a reminder that I'd never be the same again.

I left the sewing machine at Goodwill, drove to the convenience store, and bought chocolate everything.

I'll try again tomorrow, I told myself that night.

It was a promise I still don't know how to keep.

59

I GO AND talk to Dr. Rosenthal two more times, at Mom's insistence. I don't actually dread seeing him as much as I thought I would. It's kind of like looking at myself in a funhouse mirror, except, instead of the reflection being distorted, it doesn't look as bad as I thought it would.

During our last session—two weeks after Jasper and I get back from Tijuana—he says something that sticks. "You might need to get closure from what happened with your friend Trixie before you can mentally move on."

He's only partially right. Of course, he thinks he's talking about how I need to move on from my friend's suicide. He doesn't have any idea that the same friend faked her own death and also had sex with the boy she knew I loved.

I need to move on mentally, but also in other ways. Physically, I've started doing little things to distance myself from who I was with Trixie, like blow-drying my hair instead of letting it air dry how she liked, and wearing generic clothes from the mall, not ones I made that she thought were "totally awesome." I'm in a non-relationship with her not-really-ex, which started as my warped way of getting back at her but might be turning into something else. Changing my mind is the hardest part. In my mind, I still want to find her. Maybe that's the only way I'll find Dr. Rosenthal's hallowed "closure."

The problem is, I have no trail, only a frayed end in the form of the Preacher. But when I tell Jasper I think we should try to find him, he just lets out the world's longest breath.

"We've already been to the beach," he says. "I don't really feel like going back there and asking a bunch of probable drug dealers if they know someone named the Preacher."

He has a point. Maybe it's dangerous and stupid, but it's the one lead we have. He got Trixie her fake ID, her passport. He might remember what name she used, when she left, what she said.

"I know this might sound crazy, but I think it all ties in to Toby Hunter somehow," I say. "What if he came back?"

Jasper doesn't even blink, and that's how I know he'll probably never believe me about Toby. I should drop it because I'm dangerously close to spilling the details Beau trusted me with, but instead I try harder to convince him.

"Just hear me out, okay? He came back. She was writing to someone on her phone, and if it wasn't you, it must have been him. What if he was giving her some sort of directions? Telling her where he was? What if he never actually came back in person?"

Jasper stares at his knuckles. "That's reaching. Trixie was a really visual person. She only believed in something if it was right in front of her face. Once, I told her it was impossible to sneeze without closing your eyes. She made me do it in front of her before she agreed."

"I was thinking it might be a good idea to check her computer. See if she saved anything on there."

Jasper crosses his arms. "We've already established that

she got rid of everything. You told me she dumped all her things at Goodwill, and she deleted her Facebook account ages ago. So I'd be surprised if she left a convenient trail of emails for us."

I fight the urge to shake him, to make him see what I'm seeing. But he just stands there, expressionless.

The bell rings and I start edging down the hall toward Mr. Hanson's classroom. Jasper doesn't even seem to notice. I turn around and walk faster, annoyed that he's this blind. Maybe he was obsessed, and it hurts too much for him to imagine her in love with another guy.

I'm in front of the library doors when he catches up to me and grabs my arm. "Hey," he says. "Hey, I'm sorry. It's just a lot to process."

Before I can protest, I'm letting him pull me into the library, past where Gabby Reynolds is sitting with headphones on, and into the stacks at the back. When we're alone, he lets his back-pack drop to the ground. There's a wildness in his eyes I haven't seen before, something feral. Something scared.

"I want to find her," he says, his words spilling out. "I want to find her more than anything. But if we don't find her, I don't want to lose you."

His hands cup the sides of my face, his palms cold on my skin. His mouth is on mine and it's hungry, desperate, too much. He presses me into the stacks and the blood rushes into my ears, and everything that's pent up inside me comes out as I kiss him back. Love and lust and betrayal and confusion and anger and guilt. My heart beats everywhere, a timer counting down to nothing and everything.

The next day, and the one after that, I let Jasper hold my hand in the hallway, even though it feels wrong, like there's supposed to be someone else by my side, and someone else by his. When we walk past Beau, I manage to look up. It's the first time I have looked at him, actually looked, since that day at his house, the day he reached inside my chest and shredded whatever was left of my heart. His eyes are red and he looks terrible, and it should make me happy that he's suffering but I'm not—I have a boy attached to my hand who wants to kiss me and be seen in public with me, but I'm not happy.

Maybe I can't keep my promises to myself, but I still feel like it's my responsibility to keep the one I made to him at Alison's party, even if I was too drunk to remember it. *I swear I won't let you unravel.*

So instead of waiting for Jasper after school, I pull my car out of the parking lot and follow Beau as he goes partway down the sidewalk, watch him look both ways and pull something out of his backpack. He stares at it and hunches over, and I lean on my horn.

He jumps so fast that the bottle slips and shatters on the pavement. At first, I can tell he's pissed. He throws his hands over his head and punches the air with white-knuckled fists. Then he crouches down on the cement, like he's seeing if anything is left besides broken glass.

I beep my horn again. This time he turns around, so quickly that he's almost thrown to the ground by his own backpack. He squints, like he can't make out that it's me. I consider just driving away so that he doesn't, but then I think about the Beau I met freshman year and won't give up on.

"Hey," I say, hoping I sound more confident than I feel. "Need a ride?"

"I can walk," he says flatly. "You don't need to do me any favors. You hate me."

I want to tell him that maybe I do hate him, and I have good reason to, but I think of something else instead. "Remember when you rode a bike everywhere, and you gave me rides? I just thought it was my turn to drive you somewhere. And there's a place I think we should go."

He hesitates, and something like a smile flickers across his face. He starts moving slowly to the car. "I forgot all about that bike. I think it's rusting away in my dad's shed. But this isn't really a good time. Can it wait?"

I shake my head, try to keep my voice casual. "Come on. I'll have you home in time for dinner."

He glances both ways, then opens my car door and gets in, shoving his backpack on the floor between his feet. He crosses his arms over his chest and exhales deeply.

"Forget dinner," he says. "You know, we used to be all about the family dinner. Not these days. It's like my parents got a divorce and remarried their jobs instead. Those dinners are long gone. I miss walking in and smelling my mom's cooking."

"Her lasagna," I say. When he doesn't respond, I keep talking. "You said your mom made a really good lasagna."

"Yeah, that," he says. "I never thought I'd miss it as much as I do. I never thought I'd give a second thought to those stupid family dinners. 'Home by five, son.'" His voice drops into a steely impersonation of his dad, who I only know from the sidelines of football games. "Like we were the goddamned 'perfect family.' We even had a golden retriever. " He leans his elbow against the window. "The dog died, like weeks after Toby went away. The vet said he died of heart failure."

"But you think it was a broken heart." I put on my blinker and pull onto the street.

* * *

His phone goes off, an annoying chirping ringtone. My heart sinks like a stone because I know it's the ringtone he has for Jenny. He types something back. A lie. It's easy to lie when you're not face-to-face with someone, when they can't even hear your voice.

"Sorry," he says, except I'm not sure who he's apologizing to. Still, I almost smile when he says it, because the Beau I used to know said sorry a lot too. It was like a reflex for him. One time when our group was eating lunch outside, I got stung by a bee, and when I felt the pinch on my arm and said ouch, Beau instinctively said sorry. Which took the sting away and replaced it with something better.

I almost mention that now but stop short because what good would it do, reminding him of who he used to be? It's not like I want to be reminded of who I was, the person I gave up.

We drive past Cabana Del Shit, past the volleyball courts at the beach, past the McDonald's and sushi restaurant in the same shitty little plaza as Dr. Rosenthal's building. I wonder if Alison is in there right now, if she's wrestling with whatever lurks under her perfect façade.

"Do you remember when Colton destroyed the McDonald's bathroom?" Beau says, leaning his forehead against the window. "That time after our game against Blackwood, when he ate like twenty cheeseburgers."

"I remember," I say. "I didn't think it was possible for people to get kicked out of a McDonald's before that."

Beau chuckles, just a couple syllables at first, then it turns into a full-blown laugh. I haven't heard him laugh like that in ages. I had forgotten what his real laugh sounded like. It's funny because it's not what you would expect out of him. It's kind of high-pitched and involves his whole body quaking. I start to laugh too, hard enough that I forget about how I'm paranoid that my stomach jiggles when I do that, or hard enough not to care.

"It used to be fun," Beau says, pressing his fingers into the corners of his mouth. "That day was fun. You were in the PlayPlace throwing plastic balls around with Alison. You had that frilly skirt on, I still remember it. Back then, we had such a good time."

I nod. It was fun back then, when everything felt so easy, when I made cute clothes and friends appeared in front of me and the boy I loved wanted to stare at stars with me. It's not like now, when my friends aren't friends at all and the frilly skirt doesn't fit and nothing feels like a good time.

"Can I ask you something?" he says. "Why'd you really stop hanging out with us? It seemed like you turned into a whole different person. Like, the old group wasn't good enough anymore. Was it only because of her?"

The reality of his words hits me like a pile of rocks. I guess I thought of it the opposite way. That the old group wasn't a group anymore. It was fractured beyond repair and had been too easily rebuilt without me. First Beau broke, then Jenny broke me. And they moved on so quickly that it was like I was never there at all.

"I don't know," I lie. It's not like I can tell him the real reason. *Jenny put a stake in you and claimed you for herself.*

"She's persuasive," Beau says. "I know what she did to you. Same as she did to him. Sucked him into her web like a black widow."

"So what?" I grip the steering wheel tightly. "I'm a stupid fly?"

Beau lets out a long breath. "I didn't mean it like that. It's just, you weren't the only one who got sucked in. That's all." He pauses, and I can tell he's debating his next words, wondering if he wants to let them out. "Most people prey on the weak, but not her. She made everybody her victims."

"Including you," I snap. Maybe it's ridiculous for me to still be this insanely jealous, but it's in my head all day long. Trixie and Beau. Beau and Trixie. What they did, even after she knew how I felt about him. What he did, after I never showed up that night. Maybe I'm that easy to betray.

"I guess so," he says softly. And I want him to keep talking, because as pissed off as I am, it feels good talking about her with someone else who got sucked in. Someone who isn't Jasper, who sometimes likes to pretend she never existed at all.

I make a left at the next set of lights and turn into the parking lot, where a church sits behind a neglected line of hedges, almost like it's hiding there on purpose. Which is why it's the perfect place.

"Why are we stopping here?" Beau says, pushing his hair behind his ears. "Don't tell my mom, but I'm an atheist. Sorry, church isn't happening. It's way too late to pray for my goddamned soul."

I undo my seat belt. "Not church. No religion. Something else."

He follows me across the parking lot, kicking up bits of gravel with his shoes. I can tell he wants to run away, but he doesn't. Until we go down the church stairs and see the sign and he figures out where I have taken him. An Alcoholics Anonymous meeting I looked up online between classes today.

He shakes his head and throws his hands in the air. "No

way. No fucking way. I'm not one of those people." He spins around, turns to leave. I block his way.

"Just stay, even for ten minutes. Give it a chance."

"No," he says, his eyes steel. "Do you even know what my dad would say if he saw me here? He'd never talk to me again. 'The only help you need is the help you give yourself, son.' He thinks all your problems can be fixed if you think hard enough about how to fix them."

"How's that working out for you? You once asked me if I like who I am now. If I ask you the same question, what would you say?"

He leans against the railing. "It doesn't even matter who I am. It just matters who I'm not."

"It matters to me!" I yell, throwing up my hands.

He steps onto the stair in front of me until he's inches away from my face. He's breathing heavily and his nostrils are flaring, and I'm not sure if he's going to kiss me or scream at me. But he does neither.

"Just take me home," he says. "I don't care if you tell everyone what we did at the party. It's better than going in there. Anything's better than that."

I follow him to the car. We drive back to Morrison Beach without saying a word and I can tell that he hates me now, that whatever ground I had made with him has been pulled out from under me.

"Drop me here," he says when we're two streets away from his house. My heart is heavy, like a boulder, like an anchor. He gets out of the car without saying a word, and even though he stops on the sidewalk like he's thinking about turning around, he breaks into a run until he's just a blur.

60

IT TAKES ME another three days to get the courage to go to Trixie's house alone, because I know better than to ask Jasper to come here with me. I know this is a bad idea the second I'm standing at her front door. This time, Mr. Heller is home and I'll have to face him and think of some reason why I need to use Trixie's computer. I still don't know what I'm going to say when he opens the door and I'm face-to-face with him.

He smiles when he sees me. A real smile, like he wants me there. He doesn't know how much hate I have for his daughter, the person he loved most.

"Fiona," he says. He must have just been doing dishes, because his hands are soapy and he's holding a towel, which he slings over his shoulder. He steps onto the porch in bare feet and hugs me anyway, because that's what Mr. Heller does. He's a hugger, and it doesn't matter how long you have known him, whether it's two seconds or ten years. He'll hug everyone like that.

"I'm sorry I haven't been around. I just, you know, got busy."

He pats me on the back. "I'm glad you got busy. You should be busy. Please, come in. Tea or coffee? You'll have to excuse me, the house is a mess."

I accept his offer of tea, even though I don't want him to go out of his way to do anything for me. He owes me nothing, and I owe him an explanation I can't even begin to say out loud.

We make awkward small talk about school and the weather, and I ask him if he has been out surfing. If there was one thing Mr. Heller loved almost as much as he loved Trixie, it was surfing. Anytime I slept over at her house, he was up before the sun to hit the beach, and he'd track sand through the hallway and rave about the "gnarly waves" while Trixie made a face over her cereal bowl.

"No surfing this year," he says. "I'm starting to think it's a young person's sport. My old bones can't take the beating anymore."

I want to think of a thousand ways to talk him out of that, but the words die on my lips. I wish I could make Trixie watch this, watch what she has done to her dad. How could she be so selfish? How could she not realize how badly this would damage him?

"You were a good friend to her," he says out of nowhere, staring into his tea. "She was going through some things, before she met you. I think you were a good influence on her, and I appreciate that more than you'll ever know." His voice is thick and I silently will him not to cry, because if he cries I might just break down and tell him everything.

"What do you mean? What happened?" *I was a good friend, but she wasn't a friend at all.*

Mr. Heller wraps his hands around his mug and sighs, a deflated sound, like air going out of a tire. "I never really knew the answer to that. She just became withdrawn. Didn't want to leave her room. She wouldn't tell me what happened. I tried to get her to talk to someone, but she didn't want to, so I didn't force her. Maybe I should have forced her."

I lift my mug to my lips. The tea is still too hot to drink, but I sip it anyway. *I know why. Because of what happened on eight thirty-one seventeen.*

"It was hard for me," he says. "When I adopted her, the agency didn't know much about her birth parents. I didn't know what ran in the family, what disorders—if there were mental health issues? I wanted to do everything I could for her, but it wasn't enough."

"It was enough," I say, my voice trembling. "She loves you."

He gives me a tight-lipped smile but I know he doesn't believe me, and that makes me feel like the worst person in the world.

"Loved me," he says. "Maybe, but I think there was a lot of resentment that she tried to bury. Growing up and finding out she was adopted was hard on her. I don't think she ever got over the fact that someone abandoned her." He shakes his head. "If I had just done a better job of being around, maybe things would be different."

"You were around. I think she was going to do what she did regardless of who was around."

"I guess we'll never know," he says.

I stare at my mug. It has a picture of an apple and the words *A+ Teacher* on it, which means Mr. Heller must have picked it up at a garage sale. I want to tell Mr. Heller that she was like him, in a lot of ways. Her love of bargains and her peace-sign wave and even the way she hunched forward on her elbows when she concentrated. And I desperately want to tell him how much she loved him, how when she rolled her eyes at his lame jokes, it wasn't because she was embarrassed but because she was proud. She just had a funny way of showing it. She had a funny way of showing a lot of things.

I'm trying to find a way to ask about the laptop when he makes it easy for me.

"You know, I meant to ask you this at the funeral, but it was so overwhelming," he says. "I want you to know that if there's something of hers that you want, you can have it. I know you girls were close, and she didn't leave anything behind for you either."

No, she didn't, I want to scream. Not even a clue. Just secrets that keep opening up to reveal new ones inside them, like those wooden Russian dolls, except they're getting bigger instead of smaller.

"Actually," I say, curling my fingers around the handle of my mug. "I was wondering if I could borrow her laptop. There was this project we were working on together, and I thought she might have kept the notes."

It's a weak excuse, but Mr. Heller just nods. "I don't think you'll find what you're looking for. The police checked it, searched her history, the whole deal. She erased everything. Even all the pictures she used to keep on there." He grips the edge of the table and exhales, a shaky breath. "I think she didn't want any of us to have memories to be sad about."

Or she didn't want to leave a trail, any hint of where she went.

Maybe finding the truth doesn't mean guessing where to look, throwing a dart and following a path to nowhere. Maybe it's knowing what I'm looking for to begin with.

61

I MET YOUR dad by accident. We were eating Popsicles in your backyard, our feet stretching off your deck and onto the grass. Your lips were turning blue, a darker version of the Popsicle you were sucking on. You plucked a daisy that was growing between the deck's wooden boards and rubbed the stem between your fingers.

"If I ever get married, I'm having a crown of these," she said. "None of this glittery tiara bullshit."

"And who are you marrying?" I joked. "Jasper?"

She picked one of the daisy's petals off and blew it into the grass. "Nobody. Forget I said anything." She stuck out her left wrist, the one with the scars on it, which was strange, because she usually hid them. That day, she had no bracelets on, no sleeves pulled down.

"There's something I've never told anybody before," she started. But then the screen door opened behind us and she whipped her head around. A man was standing there and I knew he must be her dad, but he wasn't who I pictured her dad would be. His hair looked like it had never seen a comb, and he was wearing white linen pants and a tie-dyed shirt and sunglasses. His face broke into a huge smile when he saw me sitting there.

"Who's your friend, pumpkin?" he said.

She blew another petal off the palm of her hand. "Fiona," she said. "Dad, Fiona. Fiona, Dad."

"Nice to meet you," I said.

Her dad came and sat down beside us. "So, I finally get to meet one of your friends. Fiona, you're welcome here anytime."

"She already knows that, Dad."

Something swelled inside me. Maybe I did already know that, but it was different hearing her tell someone else.

"How about dinner tonight?" he said. "I'll put some steaks on the barbecue and make some of that guacamole that you love so much."

It sounded perfect. I couldn't remember the last time Mom had cooked a dinner for the two of us that wasn't boring health food. She used to like doing things like that when I was little, trying new recipes from cookbooks she'd find at used bookstores. I would stand on a stool beside the counter and open my mouth and wait for her to ask me to taste this or try that, and I would always tell her it was great even if it tasted like shit.

Those were the first lies I told her. Back then, she couldn't tell when I was lying either.

"We have plans," Trixie said, flicking another petal off her fingertip. "Maybe next time."

"Definitely next time," her dad said. "Fiona, do you like guacamole? Never mind, don't even answer that. Just promise you'll try mine."

"I promise."

"We should probably go." She flicked the last petal into the grass. "Otherwise, we're going to be late."

Late for what? I wanted to ask. We didn't have plans. But then again, she always kept me on my toes.

She was still holding the daisy stem when she stood up, and I watched her tuck it into her pocket.

"Which one was it?" I said. "Loves me, or loves me not?"

She pulled the stem back out and twisted it around her finger. "Doesn't matter," she said, breaking it in half and throwing it on the deck.

Her dad stood on the front porch and waved as we drove away. He waved the same way Trixie did, with his fingers parted in a peace sign.

"Your dad's cool," I said, waving back, my boring regular wave.

"He's such an old hippie." She stared at her fingers. "It's embarrassing."

"What were you going to tell me? Before he showed up."

She shook her head. "Nothing. Just something dumb. Forget I mentioned it."

I didn't forget, though. And now it's too late for me to ever find out what she was going to say, and if it would have changed anything.

62

I BARELY WAIT until I get home to turn on Trixie's laptop. It's bigger than mine, one of the old-school models, too cumbersome to carry around. I hold my breath as the machine boots up and the screen comes to life. And I see what Trixie's dad meant when he said she erased all the memories.

Her desktop background used to be the beach. Now it's nothing. Just the generic charcoal-gray backdrop that came with the computer. I quickly open Word, planning to comb through the files she left behind. Maybe there's a clue buried in one of them. But there's nothing, not a single leftover homework assignment. The only other icon on the desktop is for the internet, and when I click on that, it takes me to Google. Of course, there's no search history, no recently visited pages. What did I expect?

I'm about to shut it down when the Gmail icon in the right-hand corner catches my eye. I click on it and her email address doesn't come up. But it doesn't matter.

Her email address. I know it from sending her emails during class when I was bored. Wickedtrix00. What if wherever she is, she's still using it?

I quickly type in her email address, and in the password box, I type his name. Tobyhunter. *Wrong password. Try again.*

I try again. TobyHunter83117. Nothing. I try every single combination of his name, birthday, and deathday as I possibly can, and none of them work. I slump back in my chair and stare at the ceiling. Maybe this is another dead end, another red herring. Trixie could have picked one of those obscure passwords with numbers and special characters, the kind I wouldn't have a hope in hell of guessing. But everything had some sort of meaning to her.

"I took her computer," I admit to Jasper the next day at school. "There was nothing on it, but now I'm trying to get into her email. If she was going to have a hiding place, maybe that was it."

The bell rings and Jasper stiffens against his locker. "Maybe." He fingers the lock absentmindedly. "But I doubt it. Trixie barely responded to any of my emails. I don't think it was her thing. We could always go back to Tijuana and try again."

"She's not there. I know she's not. What we have to do is find the Preacher. I know you think the people at the beach are a dead end, but if there's a chance of finding him, we need to know for sure."

Jasper blows out a breath. "I don't want you to go by yourself. I'll go with you. Just promise me you'll wait for me to go, okay?"

I promise, but he doesn't bring it up again, and over the next few weeks, I almost forget about it too. Assignments and essays pile up, plus another appointment with Dr. Rosenthal and the inevitable checking of the mail for college acceptances. I think about the places I applied. Florida State. Texas. Princeton. Arizona. Places far away from here. The last application, which I submitted hastily, before I could talk

myself out of it. UCLA, just because I knew tha[
Beau would end up, even though the only thing
staying for a boy is staying for a boy who does
dad's alma mater, and his sloppy, drunken words at the party.
I have to go there. I don't have a choice.

I try not to think about Beau, but he's in my head all of
the time: Why was he at the beach that day and what was he
paying for and what does he know that he isn't telling me? I
picture him as a wet sponge that I thought was already wrung
out, at its limits. But now I know that he's holding in more
that I might never be able to wring out of him. I'm still mad
at him for what he did with Trixie, but maybe he's mad at me
too. I'm the one who didn't show up that night after I told
him I would. I know the food poisoning wasn't my fault, but
it's just another example of the cosmically shitty timing Beau
and I are constantly battling.

Jasper starts showing up everywhere. At my locker after
each class. At my car after school. I can't shake the feeling
that everything he felt for Trixie, all that lust and passion and
maybe even love, is just being transferred onto me because
I'm here and she's not. Like whatever kind of relationship we
have, it's not just the two of us but the four of us. It's a square,
with Trixie and Beau making up two of the corners, even
though they don't know it.

The day before Christmas break, I find a single white
rose tucked under my windshield wiper. It's perfect, with soft
petals and a long stem with no thorns. I reach over to pick it
up and a set of arms loops around my waist.

"I missed you," Jasper says, tipping my head back and kiss-
ing me. There's no hesitation, no gentleness, just a crushing
of his mouth to mine. I'm so surprised by the intensity of it

.hat I keep my eyes open, and over Jasper's shoulder, I see Beau standing there. Watching. The hand dangling at his side clenches into a fist, and as horrible as it sounds, the sight of that sets off fireworks in my stomach.

I close my eyes and kiss Jasper back. It's revenge. Beau gets to pretend I don't exist when it's convenient for him. He doesn't want me, not anymore, so he can't stop someone else from having me.

By the time I open my eyes and Jasper pulls away, Beau and his clenched fist are gone.

"Thank you," I say to Jasper, my cheeks hot. "For the rose. It's beautiful."

The corners of his mouth turn down. "What rose?"

The heat leaves my face, drains from my body. "This one." I gesture to my windshield. He must be joking, because who else would leave me a flower?

"I didn't leave that," he says, taking his hands away from my sides and jamming them in his pockets. "You must have a secret admirer." His voice is flat, monotone, more angry than jealous.

I look over Jasper's shoulder to where Beau was standing. I can't allow myself to hope that Beau left me that flower. That he doesn't hate me after I tried to make him go to AA. That he remembers the rose from that night.

I can't hope for that . . . or can I?

63

THERE WAS A *vase on the counter, pushed to the side to make room for more alcohol bottles. There was a single white rose in it, its head drooping slightly.*

"It needs a drink," I told Beau. "It's dying."

"I need a drink," he said. "I'm dying."

I filled his cup and left the rose, but he remembered.

64

USUALLY, I LOVE Christmas. Not for the presents, but for all the food. Turkey and stuffing and cranberries and mashed potatoes and pumpkin pie. Mom always goes all out, even when Aunt Leslie doesn't visit and it's just the two of us. We unwrap gifts and eat too much and watch Christmas movies on TV all night with a giant bowl of popcorn. But this year is different. Mom is making a Tofurky and her bags are already packed because she's leaving the day after Christmas for a business trip in Portland. I can't really focus on being festive when all I can think about is that I have time off from school and can finally do what I wanted to do weeks ago. Track down the Preacher, if he even exists.

"Are you sure you'll be okay for four whole days?" Mom says on Christmas morning, scrunching up her forehead at the Tofurky, which comes in a box and doesn't even look edible.

"Of course," I say, pasting on a smile. *You left me here all summer,* I want to add, but I don't, because I need to be alone. Jasper and I already have it planned for the day after Christmas. We're going to the beach to see what we find, and if we find nothing, it may be the closure Dr. Rosenthal was talking about, the final dead end in this mission.

Aunt Leslie comes over at noon, with her yappy little dog in tow. She's ten years older than Mom, but lately they look close to the same age. Aunt Leslie seems to age in reverse. Mom once told me Aunt Leslie couldn't hold down a job before she started AA and stopped drinking. Now, Aunt Leslie is all about clean living, to the point where Mom practically idolizes her. Salads and granola and organic juices that look and smell like someone just puked them up.

"Oh my god, look at you!" she says when I open the door. She grips me in a bony hug, then pulls away with her hands on my shoulders. "You look gorgeous. You're all grown up."

The dog pisses on the floor and I'm stuck cleaning it up, because Aunt Leslie is already on her way into the kitchen. I stoop over and mop it up with a wad of toilet paper. I should be happy that Aunt Leslie gave me a compliment, but I know it's not true. I'm not gorgeous and I'm not grown up. I'm a stupid girl who's in over my head, trying to solve a mystery that doesn't want to let me.

Mom and Aunt Leslie and I sit in the living room, and Aunt Leslie talks about a new guy she's dating, someone she thinks might be "the one."

"After everything," she says, sipping ginger ale out of a champagne flute, "I think I might actually get that happy ending."

"You deserve it, Les," Mom says, leaning over to give her a hug. "You've been through so much."

They don't bother to elaborate on what "so much" is. They still think of me as a kid, someone who wouldn't understand. I wonder what Aunt Leslie would say if she knew how much experience I have had with drinking, how it has already changed my life. If I hadn't been drunk at the party, I might have been able to stop Trixie from leaving, or at least followed her to see where she went. If Beau hadn't been drinking—well, his entire life might be different too.

"What a beautiful girl Fiona is turning into, Delores," she says to Mom. "She looks so much like you did at that age." She gives me a wink and a cryptic smile. "How about you, Fiona? Do you have a boyfriend? I bet boys are lined up to ask you out."

I'm about to say no and tell her nobody is fighting over me, even though I think about the white rose on my windshield and hope that maybe I am worth fighting for. But Mom answers for me. "Fiona's focused on school. She's much smarter than I was at her age."

"That's good," Aunt Leslie says. "You'll have plenty of time for boys later."

At dinner, the Tofurky tastes like plastic and has a gummy texture that makes my teeth hurt. Even though I'm starving, the idea of eating it makes me nauseous. I push it around my plate instead.

"You aren't very hungry," Aunt Leslie says, filling her plate with salad and beans.

"I just miss having a real turkey," I say, and immediately regret it because Mom's whole face falls and the table lapses into silence, punctuated by the sound of forks hitting plates. I know she's trying hard to make us better versions of ourselves, healthier and happier, but nothing she does is working.

"Are you still designing clothes, Fiona?" Aunt Leslie asks between mouthfuls of food. "I used to love what you wore. You have such unique ideas."

"I don't really have time for that anymore," I say, really meaning *I hate clothes because they remind me of all the ways*

I failed. I don't meet Mom's eyes, because she was furious with me when she found out I got rid of my sewing machine. That day, I didn't have a lie to tell her that fit.

"Well, how's Sarah?" Aunt Leslie asks. "I hope you're still friends. She was such a nice girl."

"Great," I say, on autopilot. "Still friends."

"I haven't met her yet," Mom says, taking a drink from her wineglass. "Fiona's keeping her a mystery. I couldn't even pick the girl out of a lineup." She says it casually, but I can tell she's getting frustrated that I have a friend she hasn't met. I'm sure she wants to judge Sarah just like she judged Trixie, to make sure I'm not being molded wrong. I almost wish I could tell her they're the exact same person, and I managed to do the wrong things all on my own.

Across the table, Aunt Leslie smiles and moves on to a new topic. Nobody mentions Sarah for the rest of the meal, but Mom's words echo in my head.

I couldn't even pick the girl out of a lineup.

Turns out, neither can I.

65

YOU THOUGHT IT *was strange that I loved snow, that I could feel so strongly about something I had never even seen. You had to see something to fall in love with it.*

It never snows in Morrison Beach. I always knew I should feel lucky to live in a place where it was constantly warm, where I could wear my flip-flops year-round if I wanted to. But I wanted to see real snow, to catch it on my tongue like they did in the romantic comedies Alison loved to watch. I wanted an excuse to wear a scarf and mittens. I wanted to make a snowman.

"I wouldn't hold your breath," Beau said after driving me home on the handlebars of his bike the week before Christmas break sophomore year. "I think there's a better chance of me getting an A in algebra than any snow coming down here."

I fiddled with my backpack straps. I had a gift for Beau, an old poetry book I had found at a used bookstore. It was in my backpack, but I was too nervous to give it to him. It was too intimate, too exposed. He didn't have anything for me, and maybe he would look at the poetry book and laugh and I would know I had gotten it all wrong. So I lost my nerve and said goodbye without giving him anything.

The next morning, there was something on our kitchen table. A tiny little snowman, cool to the touch, with stubby pipe cleaners for arms.

"What is this?" I asked Mom.

"I was going to ask you the same thing. I found it on our porch when I got the paper this morning."

That was when I knew exactly where the snowman came from. Beau found out a way to get me snow.

Of course, it wasn't real snow. It was baking soda and shaving cream, Beau told me when I texted him to say thank you.

One day we'll make sure you see a real one ;) he wrote.

As long as you're there to see it with me, I wrote, but I never hit send. I chickened out again and didn't reply at all.

66

THE DAY AFTER Christmas, Mom leaves early in the morning but Aunt Leslie hangs around. I would normally be glad to be spending time with her—I used to love dragging her into fabric stores and letting her pick patterns for me—but all I can think about is how badly I want her to leave so Jasper and I can go to the beach to try and find the Preacher. Plus, I have no idea what to talk to Aunt Leslie about anymore. She keeps asking me about college and I don't know what to tell her, so I give her generic answers and hope they're good enough.

Then I remember there is something Aunt Leslie might be able to help me with. I don't know how to bring it up, so I casually mention it over breakfast, like I'm asking her to pass the milk.

"How did you know you needed help? You know, before you started going to AA."

She drops the spoon she's using to stir her coffee and her eyes get huge. I put up my hands in protest. "No, not me. It's my sociology class. We're talking about addiction, and trying to understand what makes people seek help." I take a sip of my orange juice, hoping it makes the lie sound sweeter, more ripe.

"Well, if that's the case, I don't think there's a right or

wrong answer." Aunt Leslie pats one of the rollers in her hair. "I think it's different for everyone. The common thread is that a lot of people need to hit rock bottom before they realize they need help. And everyone's rock bottom looks different."

"What did yours look like?" I sit down at the table beside her. I want to know the truth about "everything that happened." I want them to stop treating me like a kid.

"I'm not sure your mother would like us having this conversation." Aunt Leslie grips the edge of the table with fingertips that are turning white. "It's not very appropriate for someone your age to hear."

"I'm almost eighteen. Plus, it'll be our secret. I won't tell her."

Aunt Leslie takes a deep breath. "Okay, but don't go using my name if you put this in your school project. It's called *Anonymous* for a reason." She pauses and I lean into the table.

"I was dating someone who was bad for me, and we were drinking a lot. He had these wild moods. Ups and downs, highs and lows. I guess back then, I thought the highs were worth the lows." She laughs drily. "We had a couple of huge fights, but we always made up after. Then I found out I was pregnant."

Now I regret asking, because I know this must end really badly. Aunt Leslie never married or had kids.

"He reacted pretty well when I told him. But he didn't want to stop drinking. And he didn't want me to stop drinking either. So I didn't." Aunt Leslie reaches for a paper towel to wipe her eyes. "I had a miscarriage, and it was my fault. That's what made me go to my first meeting and get clean."

My mouth feels cotton-dry and tears sting my eyes. I

reach out for Aunt Leslie's hand, fighting the urge to tell her everything.

"What happened to your boyfriend? Did he get clean too?"

Aunt Leslie shakes her head and a roller sags off the end of a drooping curl. "He wasn't ready to try. Eventually, I had to walk away, because he wasn't ready to save himself. Years later, I found out that he died of a heroin overdose." She wipes a tear that has slid onto her cheek. "I didn't want to believe that some people could be lost causes. But they are."

"How can you tell?" I say quickly. "How can you tell someone is a lost cause?"

"You can't. That's the hard part. You can't make someone else your anchor, otherwise they have the power to sink you." She blows her nose into the paper towel and stands up. "I probably said too much. But I hope you can use that for your project. Young people need to realize the whole world is in front of them."

Later, when I'm in the shower, I think about rock bottom and I wonder if Beau has one, if he'll eventually hit the ground and realize he's breakable after all. Or if he's one of those lost causes, the ones who keep falling through layers of the ruin they create.

Maybe it's not my problem and I should walk away like Aunt Leslie did. I don't need an anchor, something rooting me in one spot. I'm heavy enough all on my own.

I get in my car and head to Jasper's an hour after Aunt Leslie drives away, pulling out of the driveway with a honk of her horn and a promise to visit soon. She tells me to say hello to

Sarah and I tell her I will. *If I ever see her again*, I say under my breath when she's gone. *I'm still working on that.*

Jasper is waiting for me on the curb in front of his house, his long legs splayed out. He has earbuds in and his eyes are closed, his fingers tapping his thighs, his mouth moving slightly. It's not until I pull up right in front of him and block his sun that he finally opens his eyes and sees me there.

"Hey." He yanks out his earbuds and stands up, brushing invisible dust off his pants before clambering into the car. I don't know what changed, what shifted so quickly, like a warm breeze that turned into a cold wind. Maybe he's jealous because somebody else gave me a flower. The thought of a guy being jealous over me shouldn't make me excited, but maybe I feel the wrong way about a lot of things.

I tell Jasper about Christmas, about the Tofurky and Aunt Leslie and her dog. He tells me that his parents bought him clothes he'll never wear and a new iPod he'll never use to replace his beat-up MP3 player.

"Why don't you want to upgrade?" I ask, turning onto the street behind the graffiti wall.

"Why fix something that isn't broken?"

I busy myself with finding a parking spot so I have a good reason not to tell him that I hate that saying because it's not true. If you fix something after it cracks but before it breaks, you put it back together before it has a chance to fall apart.

"We're here," I say, putting the car in park. The sun beats down, forming a pool of sunshine in my lap and I'm suddenly terrified, just like I was in Tijuana. Scared of what we won't find. Scared of what we will.

"Did he say anything about what this Preacher person

looks like?" Jasper says when we're out of the car. "Do we have anything to go on?"

"No." I pull my hood over my head and start moving, because he's standing still.

We squeeze through the hole in the wall and shuffle to the sand. They're all there, the same guys as last time, as every time. Or maybe they're different, but they all look the same. Leering eyes and a cloud of pot and sweat and beer. I bite the inside of my cheeks.

I approach one sitting off by himself, leaning with his back against the wall. A cigarette is in his outstretched hand. When he opens his mouth, I can see that he's missing his front teeth.

"You're a long way out," he says, and I don't know what he means, but it makes the hair on the back of my neck stand up.

"I'm looking for someone." I shove my hands in my hoodie pockets. "A guy named the Preacher."

The guy throws his head back and laughs. It's a nasty sound that turns into a nastier-sounding, tobacco-strangled cough.

"Preacher ain't been around for a long time. Went back to the land of the rich. He was never one of us." He blows a smoke ring in the air and taps the end of his cigarette with yellowing fingers.

"Do you know where he went?" I ask. "Did he say anything before he left? About a girl?"

He laughs again, but this time it's more subdued. "We don't get a lot of girls out this way. Not the kind you leave for anyway."

My fingers close around my phone. I take it out of my pocket and scroll to a picture of Trixie, one I took of her school photo on the Dead Students Wall the day before Christmas break. I hold it out in front of the guy's face. "How about her? Do you remember her?"

I watch his eyes. They're dull, the color of seaweed. I watch for a flicker of recognition, of anything. But his face looks blank. "We don't get girls like that out this way." He lets the end of his cigarette drop to the sand and buries the butt with his foot. "You should go home. Kids like you don't belong here."

Jasper's hand grazes my shoulder. "He's right. We should go."

But I won't leave. Not now, not when I was sure there'd be an answer here, even if I have to dig for it.

"What did he look like?" I ask. "The Preacher. Can you describe him?"

The guy closes his eyes. "I didn't exactly take a picture. Young, like you. Blond hair. Good-looking. He didn't look like the rest of us. That's about all I got."

I flip to a different picture on my phone, one I don't even know why I took. "Did he look anything like this?"

The guy stares at the screen, plucks my phone out of my hand. Part of me expects him to run off with it and pawn it. But he just studies it intently, his eyebrows pulled in and a big crease in his forehead.

"Yep," the guy says, handing the phone back to me and going for another cigarette. "That's him. See, good-looking kid. Not one of us."

My legs turn into jelly, into something insubstantial, until I wonder how they're even holding me up.

"That's impossible," I say, even though now the guy is staring past me.

"What?" Jasper pulls on my wrist. "What's impossible?"

I manage a thank-you and let Jasper lead me away, back to the hole we crawled in from. My breath is coming in gasps. "He's been here all along." I thrust my phone into Jasper's hand. "This is our Preacher."

It's another picture from the Dead Students Wall.

A picture of Toby Hunter.

67

YOU NEVER LEFT without saying goodbye, not until you left for real. I wonder if you and Toby had that in common.

The last time I ever saw Toby Hunter, he was waving goodbye to a group of his friends. I was in the parking lot at school with Alison and Jenny, and we all turned to look at Toby, because there was something about him that made people want to be close. Like a fire pit on a cool summer night, when everybody huddled near the flames to get warm.

But now that I think about it, there was something strange about Toby's wave. Two fingers pointed toward the sky, his index and middle. A peace sign, almost. Or maybe he was just too lazy to form an actual wave.

Maybe the people who were really closest to Toby never got warm at all.

68

MY HANDS ARE shaking so badly that I make Jasper drive my car back to my house. I let him follow me upstairs to my room because I don't want to be alone, because then I might be forced to make sense of all this. Of the fact that I not only have some proof that Toby Hunter is still alive, but he could still be here, in Morrison Beach. Which means Trixie could be here too, hiding in plain sight.

"This makes no sense," Jasper says, sitting at my desk chair, pressing his fingers into his temples. "Toby Hunter's dead. There's no way he could have survived. How far out does that pier go, a mile? And how rough is the water? Death would have been imminent."

I flop down on my bed, burying my face in my pillow. "But we don't know that," I say, my voice muffled. "It's like I've been saying, nobody *knows* that for sure. This could all make sense. Trixie thought Toby was dead too, just like everyone else. Then something happened to make it all change. He must have gone to her and convinced her to disappear too."

The more I think about it, the more it makes sense. Trixie changing, morphing into so many different versions of herself that I almost forgot the original. Maybe he was there the whole time, at the beach, watching us on the sand. Or maybe he was on the pier, disguised as a clown juggling balls or a mime with a painted-on smile. He could have crept into Trixie's house when she was asleep, thrown rocks against her bedroom window, whispered in her ear that she had to leave everything and everyone.

It makes perfect sense and no sense at all. Because if the whole point was to disappear, why would Toby Hunter still be in Morrison Beach?

"Well, even if it's true, that guy said the Preacher hasn't been around for a while. So even if he was here, he's probably long gone by now. Which means she's gone too." Jasper tucks his hair behind his ears.

Suddenly, I want to punch a hole through my wall or shred my pillow to pieces. Because if it's true, if Trixie has been here the whole time, she didn't trust me enough to let me know she's alive. I'm just like everyone else to her, someone she could fool, someone who just accepted that she walked into the ocean and drowned herself. She knew I loved Beau and she knew I loved her and she didn't care about me at all.

"Come here," I say to Jasper. He looks up with bleak eyes and just stares at me, like he knows I'm crossing a line. Maybe it's the venom in my voice, the poison inside me that I need to purge. He gets up and walks over slowly, and when he lies down beside me, I roll over so that our lips are touching, then reach for the waistband of his jeans before I can slow down to think about what I'm doing. Jasper makes a little sound, almost like he's hesitating, but he doesn't stop me. When my hand is inside his jeans, he plays with the hem of my hoodie and starts tugging it up.

He kisses me harder, his tongue running over the tips of my teeth, tugging my bottom lip gently. He traces the shape of my face with his finger and it feels like he's drawing a heart. His thumbs are hooked under my jaw and his knuckles graze my cheeks lightly. Then one of his hands slips under my skirt, trailing up the length of my leg, stopping to rest on my thigh.

"Don't stop," I whisper, and my desperation embarrasses me almost as much as my traitor body.

"Are you sure?" He leans over me, his breath hot against my face. "Look, I know you're really upset. I don't want your first time to be like that."

I nod and shake my head at the same time. "Yes." I pull him closer, biting the skin on his neck. "And what makes you so sure it's my first time?"

He doesn't take his hands off me. Sadness floods through me, insecurity. Maybe he feels sorry for me and that's what this will be to him, pity sex. But it doesn't look like pity in his eyes. More like desire, glassy and black.

I make everything else leave my head. Beau and Trixie, *Beau and Trixie* and Toby Hunter and college applications and my discarded sewing machine and the homeless people at the beach. Tijuana and whispers and rumors and fake IDs and peace-sign waves. I tell Jasper to open my nightstand, where there's an unopened box of condoms I got as a joke gift from Jenny and Alison on my sixteenth birthday, and then I squeeze my eyes shut while he's putting one on. I let him tug my underwear down and watch him as he shrugs out of his pants and shirt, his skin so pale it's almost translucent. Only his forearms have any color, a slight pinkish barely any darker than the rest of him. He gets back on the bed and hovers on top of me, grazing his eyelashes against my cheek as he lowers himself inside me.

The relief is instant, immediate. I dig my fingertips into his back and force him deeper and rock back and forth under him, breathing hard in his ear. He kisses my lips, my cheeks, my forehead, my hairline, my neck. The headboard hits the wall over and over, making a thumping sound. I moan into his neck and he cries out and collapses on top of me, his chest damp against me.

I don't know how long we lie there, hearts beating wildly. But when he finally rolls off me and pulls my duvet over us, I start to feel cold, chilled inside. I almost wonder if he's asleep, then I hear him whisper in my ear, so quiet I can barely hear.

I can barely hear, but it sounds an awful lot like I *love you*.

And that's one lie I won't tell him.

Jasper doesn't leave my house until an hour before Mom is supposed to come home. We stay that way, tangled up in my bed, barely moving. I let myself feel wanted, needed. And when we're buried in each other, it's easy to forget about what led us here, who disappeared and brought us together. Who was never here at all.

It's when he leaves that reality comes crashing back, trampling over the good feelings, squashing and shitting all over the tenuous idea that Jasper and I could be something, that the square could flatten into a line with the two of us at either end. When Mom knocks on my door, I feel detached, like a balloon drifting too fast toward the sky.

"How was the rest of your break?" Mom asks.

"Fine. Boring. I just caught up on reading," I tell her.

I'm the first person in astronomy class the next week, the start of second semester. I don't want to risk seeing Beau when I know something that will shatter him. I think about how he told me that when Toby hides, he doesn't want to be found. I don't know how I'm going to tell him what I found at the beach, about the Preacher, that there's a chance Toby is still in Morrison Beach. I can't shake the thought that Beau is hanging on by a thread and might fall apart completely if I tell him a hunch that isn't the truth. So I make a vow to myself that I'll only tell him if I have proof. If I see Toby myself.

Except, I don't know how I'm going to do that. Jasper and I didn't talk about the next step. Maybe there isn't one. The idea of just giving up and moving on is both a huge relief and the heaviest burden of all.

A hand touches my shoulder while I'm staring at my phone and I whip around, my chair making a scraping sound against the floor. And like some kind of omen, Beau is standing behind me.

"You're taking astronomy too," he says. He doesn't sound mad. He kind of sounds normal, actually, and I let myself think that maybe things have changed, maybe he's on his way up from rock bottom. His hand is still on my shoulder and I try to ignore the heat spreading through me just from that one small touch.

"I have all the credits I need," I say. "It's supposed to be a bird course."

He grins. "Plus, you like the stars, right?"

I nod, and before I can stop myself, I say something that bubbles to my lips. "'Between two worlds life hovers like a star.'"

As soon as I say it, I want to unsay it. I didn't even know I remembered that quote but there it was, in my mouth the whole time, waiting to come out. I peek at Beau's face from under my eyelashes.

It's like a light is on under his skin. He huffs out a breath. "Lord Byron. You remembered."

"I remembered." I suck in my lips, suddenly close to crying.

"I never thanked you," he says. "For the whole AA thing. For trying, when nobody else would."

"It was no problem. Whatever."

He shakes his head. His hair has gotten longer since the last time I saw him. It's almost down to his shoulders now and the ends are curly. I think about how it would feel to grasp a handful of it.

"I was an asshole. I'm sorry."

Those two words again, the chorus of Beau's life. I stare at the floor, at the fossilized wad of gum under my desk. "It's okay, and it was nothing."

He sits down at the desk behind me. "It's not okay, and it was everything."

I blink back tears as I face the board. The bell rings five seconds later and everyone else files in, including Alison, who gives me a little smile. I spend the class wondering if Beau is staring at the back of my head, if this hope I'm feeling will last or if it will fall into rock bottom and break like everything else.

Our astronomy teacher, Mr. Sweet, writes a formula on the board that I diligently copy into my notebook, all the while wishing there was a kind of formula that would make sense of the jumble in my head and heart. When the bell rings at the end of class, I bolt out of the room so I don't have to look at Beau and risk seeing a different version of him, the wrecked one. I'm making a beeline for my locker when Alison jogs up beside me, her backpack thumping against her side.

"Hey," she says. "I meant to ask you, did you end up applying to NYU? I know you were talking about it. I just wanted to ask because I applied." She pushes her hair off her face and I notice that she has bangs now.

"I thought you wanted to stay here," I say. "You and Jenny always talked about staying in California." Jenny's name sounds foreign leaving my mouth, rusty and strange, despite how many times it runs through my head every day.

Alison sucks in her lip. "A lot of things have changed this year."

Then the bell rings and she's gone, rushing down the hall with a wave. And I don't have time to find her again and ask about it because Jasper is at my locker after my next class, holding a rose. Except, this one has thorns.

I guess he's my boyfriend now. It doesn't matter to him that the only thing we have in common is a girl who was barely even here to begin with.

"When am I going to meet your mom?" he asks the second week back from break.

"Later," I say, fear unfurling in my stomach and rattling around, the sharpest pieces punching holes.

He hasn't mentioned Trixie or Toby Hunter since that day at the beach when we tried to find the Preacher, and I wonder again if he wants to put the past away, fold it up and store it neatly in a box, find a place for it, just like how everything is organized in his bedroom. Maybe he wants to cover up the stain with a rug and walk all over it with his new life and pretend it's not there. He starts his sentences with *we* and *our* and I haven't stopped him because, as pathetic as it sounds, Jasper is the one person I can count on.

Sometimes I feel like if I want to find the Preacher—Toby Hunter—I'll have to choose between him and Jasper, the boy who is actually here. Jasper thinks we're done searching, and if I keep bringing this up, I might lose him and never find what we were looking for. So what's the point?

He stays over at the end of the month, when Mom goes out of town for another business trip. He says the words again, with his head on my pillow and his mouth against my ear. *I love you.* I still don't say anything back.

The next morning, Jasper presses me onto my back, his fingers in my hair. I let my eyes flutter shut and try to focus on this, the here and now, the kind of moment I never thought I'd have. Then another sound enters my head, and I try not to hear it until I realize what it is.

The garage door opening.

"Shit," I say, sitting up so fast that my forehead knocks into Jasper's. "Shit. You have to get out of here."

I yank on a pair of fleece pajama pants and a hoodie. I shove my feet into slippers and throw my hair into a ponytail, and when I whirl around, Jasper is still in the same position, looking like I just slapped him in the face.

"Seriously. My mom's home. You can't be here when she comes up."

The door downstairs opens and slams shut. The sound of shoes clacking on the tile echoes through the house.

"It's okay," Jasper says. I ball up his shirt and toss it at him, and he finally takes the hint and puts it on, the neckline of his T-shirt drooping down to show his collarbone. I put a self-conscious hand to my own collarbone, invisible under my skin, my breasts straining against the zipper of my hoodie.

"It's not okay," I whisper. "My mom's going to kill me."

I take a deep breath and decide that the best way to play this is to make it seem like Jasper and I were just doing homework. I stretch my duvet over my bed, tugging on each of the four points. I hand Jasper a math textbook. "Sit." I gesture to my desk chair. "We're studying."

Mom calls my name from downstairs, and I yell back at her that I'm in my room. By the time she opens my door, I'm lying across my bed, furiously typing on my laptop.

"Oh," she says when she sees Jasper at my desk. He immediately stands up and shakes her hand, which makes me cringe.

"I'm Jasper," he says. "I'm in Fiona's French class. We're conjugating verbs."

I'm not even taking French. I haven't heard Jasper lie to someone else before, but he's good at it. He makes it sound so much like the truth that I almost believe it.

"Nice to meet you, Jasper," Mom says, but I can tell she's suspicious. "I'll just leave the door open here, if you don't mind." She gives me a kiss on the cheek.

I fight the urge to laugh. She leaves me here all summer, all weekend, all night, but wants my door to stay open while I study. I wonder if those were her mom's rules for her, and if that's what made it so easy for her to get pregnant with me.

When I get back from driving Jasper home, I try to log in to Trixie's email again, even though I feel guilty doing it behind Jasper's back. I don't know where to look for Toby, so I look for Trixie instead, because wherever they are, I'm sure they're together. This time, I try different words. Her street name and birthday and Sarah Brown's name and Jasper's name, and I still get the same error message. *Wrong password. Try again.*

I slump back against my chair. I need to let this go. I need to let her go, but then she wins. Maybe that's why I need to find her so badly. To prove that I can beat her at her own game.

69

YOU HAD A *plan to start community college while you waited for me to graduate, but you never seemed excited about it. I flipped through course catalogs and highlighted the most interesting classes while you nodded with all the emotion of a bobblehead.*

"When are we going to go shopping?" I said.

"We just went shopping," she said. "And might I remind you that you didn't even want to go."

"I don't mean clothes shopping." I hated even having to bring that up again. Nothing about clothes shopping was fun for me. I was too scared to try anything on in case it didn't fit and I'd be forced to confront the reality that I was bigger than I used to be, maybe even a lot bigger. "I mean book shopping. For school. We should go make sure you have the stuff on your list."

Trixie was going to take all kinds of courses, mostly ones I picked for her. Stuff like Introduction to Greek Mythology and Renaissance Literature and even a film class. I was jealous. I wished I were a year older so I could skip the rest of Robson and go there with her. But the first day wasn't far off and she still didn't have her books. I didn't realize why she wasn't jumping at the chance to go to the college bookstore and pick them out. Besides, books were fun to shop for. They always fit.

"Next week," she said. "Next week, I promise."

But we never went. Because when next week came, she was gone. And only then, at her house after the funeral, did her dad tell me that she decided not to go to college after all. That she wanted to work and save up money instead.

"She worked so hard washing dishes at that place," he said, and he sounded so proud of her that I couldn't break his heart.

She told me one lie and her dad the other.

I wondered who got the first lie, or if it mattered. The summer days all blended together, fast food and loud music and sticky wine coolers and bad reality TV and sand stuck to my skin after the beach. Time bled through like a stain, making it impossible to distinguish one day from the next.

Maybe she wanted it that way.

70

IN ASTRONOMY, WE'RE supposed to break into pairs to prepare for a discussion about the rings found around the Jovian planets. Alison starts to turn around, and before she can get out the words to ask me, I turn and put my hands on Beau's desk. I'm not sure what to expect, if he'll be soft like he was the other day or the bottle-smashing version.

"Do you want to be my partner?" I say, because Jenny was right about one thing. I need to be the one to ask him. And I need to find some way to talk to Beau about Toby. If he knows one of his hiding places, maybe that's where the Preacher is now.

"Sure," he mumbles without meeting my gaze. "If you still want me."

He says the last part so quietly I'm not even sure it happened. But if it did happen, that means there's hope, there's some part of him that needs someone to believe in him. And hope might be flimsy, but I've held on to less.

Mr. Sweet says we can move into the hallway or the library to talk somewhere quieter, so Beau and I gather our books and leave the room. I make the mistake of turning around on my way out and see Alison staring at me, her eyebrow raised. My first thought is *She knows*. It happened at her house. The music was loud, and I never would have known if she was standing right there. She's only biding her time until she can expose me to everyone. And what would Beau do then?

We find an alcove in the hall and sit down with our backs to the wall. Beau yawns repeatedly and my heart sinks, because I wonder how I didn't see it already. His red eyes, his sunken cheeks, the sour smell on his breath.

"You've been drinking," I whisper.

"Just a bit. I held up a liquor store before school. The usual." His lips form a slow smile, which disappears when he sees the look on my face. "It's a joke, Fiona. You need to stop worrying about me."

I swallow back everything I want to say, about getting help and getting his life back. If my conversation with Aunt Leslie taught me anything, it's that someone can't be helped until they want to be. So instead of giving him a lecture, instead of tricking him into my car, I open my textbook.

I couldn't save Trixie, because she didn't want to be saved from anything. Maybe I can't save Beau, for the same reason.

"It's probably a bunch of bullshit," he says, craning his neck back to stare at the ceiling. "The stars. There are probably little people looking down on us somewhere up there, laughing at what idiots we are. Judging all the mistakes we make. You know, maybe they even have a way to erase them. Don't you wish you could just go back and redo all the shitty mistakes you've made?"

"No," I say, but I really mean yes. Because if I could, I might have seen all of the little clues Trixie did leave for me. The frayed ends she gave me to grab on to that I was too clumsy and nearsighted to catch.

hen I realize what he means. *Our* mistake. That's the one he would take back. And it doesn't matter, it happened and nothing can take that away, but something still hardens inside me.

"You know what I'd change first?" He takes the pen from my hand and draws a big blue X over the diagram in his textbook. "I would have paid less attention to my asshole brother. That's how this whole thing started. If I wouldn't have been so desperate to find out what he was hiding, I would have been minding my own goddamned business at that party. I wouldn't have ever known about him and Trixie. Maybe he would have dumped Gabby and they could have been out in the open, whatever that would have looked like."

"It wasn't your fault." I'm not even sure I believe myself. "You're his brother. You were worried about him."

He starts to laugh. "I wasn't worried. I was just desperate to find something wrong with King Toby. I wanted to see if there was a human in there."

I don't say anything. I take another pen and write the date on a piece of lined notebook paper and underline it five times, leaving indents on the page.

"I blamed you too," he says. "If you would have been at that party, I wouldn't have been with Toby, because I would have been with you. That would've been our night. I had something for you." He clears his throat. "I never told you about it. I buried it, actually. In my mom's garden. Under her rosebush. And she wondered why it died."

He laughs, softly, but I don't. *You'll be there tonight, right?* But I wasn't. I want to ask so badly what he buried, what he had to get rid of so fast he covered it in layers of dirt. But I force myself not to ask, because I don't want the truth to come out that way. I want him to *want* to tell me. To need me to know.

"My dad wants me to marry Jenny," he says suddenly, pulling a page out of his textbook and shredding it between his fingers. "Can you believe that? He and my mom got married right out of high school. They want us to start popping out kids after college. Carry on the family line. I told him I don't ever want a kid, and he flipped."

I rock back and forth and tuck the corners of my skirt under my knees. The idea of Beau marrying Jenny, being someone else's forever, is enough to suck all the air out of me.

"Don't do it," I hear myself say. "Live your own life."

He shakes his head. "You sound like a goddamn self-help book. Don't turn into one of them. You're the only one who isn't."

Beau's cheeks are turning red. I want to reach out and touch them, to take his face in my hands and press my lips against his and tell him everything will be okay. But I can't say that because even I don't believe it's true.

"I need to ask you a question," I say instead, focusing my eyes on my textbook. "You know it wasn't a coincidence, that both of them disappeared. Did Toby spend a lot of time on his computer? Or his phone? The night of Alison's first party, was he on his phone a lot?"

Beau slouches forward, slumping his head over his lap. "Who knows what the guy did behind closed doors. I wasn't his babysitter. But you need to drop it. I know what you're doing. You're still looking. And all you're doing is following your own shadow." He leans toward me and puts his hand over my textbook. "Listen to me. Don't go digging for a body that isn't there. You'll just get buried too."

"Did he ever mention anything about a preacher?"

Beau shakes his head, but I can tell what I just said has sparked some kind of memory. "No. I have no clue what you're talking about." He says it gently. "Move on, Fiona. I'm telling you, move on."

Our faces are inches apart and I barely breathe. Down the hall, somebody coughs and it's a reminder that there's life outside of me and Beau, that he has a girlfriend and I have a boyfriend and we have nothing in common. We're two people who used to be friends, who made a drunken mistake.

"Promise me you'll stop," he says, but then the bell rings and I'm spared having to make that promise.

71

YOU WEREN'T AROUND to see it, but Beau stopped making sense after he smashed the bottle in Alison's kitchen.

"Orion," he kept saying, pointing at the ceiling. "That's what my mom wanted to call me, but my dad wouldn't let her. Because he controls everything."

Nobody was listening. The party had carried on without him. People were starting to leave, filing out in clumps. I figured Trixie would come and find me soon and pull me away too.

"You remember Orion," he said, but this time he pointed at me. "You saw him too."

I nodded, but I still only saw Beau.

72

I DON'T TELL Jasper, but I start driving around by myself at night, cruising past all the places Trixie and I used to hang out. Anywhere Trixie might be. I even drive to the outskirts of town where there's a trailer park, thinking she and Toby could be living there in a crappy aluminum piece of shit with a leaky roof, the last place anyone would think to look for them. I go back there two nights in a row, watching people come and go, my heart thudding. On the third night, I lean back in my seat, the leather cold, wondering why I even care this much.

My mind wanders to the words I put on my NYU application. *Describe an experience that has impacted who you are as a person.* I wrote about losing my best friend. *She understood me in a way nobody else ever had. She didn't want to change me. We shared everything. She just wanted me to be happy. She always had my best interests at heart. Living without her has made me stronger, because her memory is everywhere.*

But each sentence has a double meaning, a hidden agenda, a secret of its own.

She understood me in a way nobody else ever had. She understood the version of me that listened when she told me to drive away. But that was only one part of me, and she never knew the rest. Or never cared to.

She didn't want to change me. She already had.

We shared everything. I shared secrets and she used them to stab me in the back. Maybe the only real thing we shared was that we both loved a Hunter brother.

She just wanted me to be happy. As long as it was on her terms.

She always had my best interests at heart. She didn't want me and Beau to be together, so she did everything she could to keep me from loving him. Including betraying me in the worst possible way, doing with him what I always wanted to do, just because she could.

Living without her has made me stronger, because her memory is everywhere. This is the part that makes me mad, because it's the part I want to be true. I want to be able to say I'm stronger now, but every day I just feel weaker, like my energy is being sapped with each passing hour.

I jerk upright when I see a guy in a baseball cap holding hands with a girl whose twiggy legs poke out of faded denim shorts. They're walking down the side of the road, kicking up dirt, heading right toward my car. *This is it*, I think, sweat forming under my armpits, sending chills through the rest of me. *I got them.*

But as they get closer to the car, I realize it's not them, not even close. The girl is older, probably in her thirties, with sun-damaged skin and a rattling cough like a lifelong smoker's. The guy is missing teeth and is all wrong for Toby Hunter, too short and too scrawny. His beady eyes pass over me just long enough for me to realize this whole idea is stupid and dangerous and pointless. They might have stuck around Morrison Beach at one point, but they aren't here anymore.

I slump against the steering wheel in frustration. There's something I'm missing here, a giant piece of the puzzle that's right in front of my face, a piece that will lock the other pieces together. All of the clues are floating around in my head rootless, and the harder I try to grab on to one, the farther away the other ones get.

Maybe Beau was right. It's pointless, all of this searching, because somebody who wants to stay hidden that badly won't ever be found. I should just get on with my life. That's what Jasper wants to do, and he wants to do it with me. That's what Dr. Rosenthal thinks I should do, what Mom thinks I'm already doing.

When I get home, Jasper is sitting at the kitchen table with Mom, teaching her a card game. I never invited him but there he is, like he had a place at the table the whole time. He wants to make a good impression on my mom because that's what boyfriends do, which should be sweet, but it just feels wrong. I try to make the painful feeling go away, but it won't lie down on command like I want it to.

And maybe it never will.

73

YOU WANTED TO plant a garden after you graduated. "I'll become a hippie," you said, which made me laugh, because you really were more like your dad than you realized. "We'll always have fresh flowers and vegetables."

It was a hopeless plan. Trixie never ate a single vegetable the whole time we had known each other. The only green things she liked were money and the occasional joint, which she would roll over her bony knee as we sat in the sand on the beach. And she liked my green eyes. She said she wanted eyes that color too, and eventually, she had them, thanks to colored contacts.

I asked her about the garden once, sometime during the summer. I had forgotten all about it. We were sitting in my backyard on a broken lounge chair, flipping through magazines. I looked around and saw our crappy excuse for a garden, the mud and weeds that had taken over.

"What happened to becoming a hippie?" I asked.

She pushed her mouse-brown hair off her face with a plastic headband. "I can't keep anything alive. It was a stupid idea."

It was a flippant comment, no different from so many

others. She probably changed the subject, moved on to something else, and stretched out on her back to tan her flat stomach. But I should have thought about the peace lily on her bedroom windowsill, how lovingly she tended to it. How it had been there for as long as I had known her and probably even longer than that. It always had enough water and sunlight, unlike Mom's plants, which shriveled up and died.

A week before she disappeared, I noticed the peace lily wasn't on her windowsill anymore. When I peeked out her window, I saw a clump of dirt and green leaves on top of the compost heap in her backyard.

"What happened to it?" I asked, pressing my fingertips to the window. It made me unbearably sad, seeing it down there on top of eggshells and other things that had been discarded.

She ran a brush through my hair, yanking my head back, forcing me to look the other way.

"It was dying. I had to get rid of it."

She sounded casual, upbeat, like it was nothing to her. That should have tipped me off. She loved that plant, treated it like a pet. Getting rid of it must have crushed her.

Now I know the real reason why she dumped her peace lily in the compost heap. Because she had to. Because she wasn't going to be there to take care of it. She knew that if she left it on her windowsill, her dad would kill it by mistake. He had good intentions, but he was scatterbrained, forgetful. It would dry up until it was nothing but parched dirt and brittle brown leaves that crumbled at the touch.

She couldn't bear that, so she put it out of its misery.

She killed Trixie Heller too, put her out of her misery.

The question is, who is she now?

74

WHEN I GET home from school the next day, Mom is waiting at the table for me with a stern look on her face. Fear unfurls in my stomach because she must know something she shouldn't. Something about Trixie or the party or Sarah Brown or even what Jasper and I have been doing in my bedroom. But when I ask her what's wrong, her face breaks into a huge smile and she hands me a big manila envelope.

"This looks an awful lot like an acceptance letter." She clasps her hands together. "I have the camera ready. I think you should open it right now."

My hands tremble as I look at the return address stamp. NYU. I tear the letter open and pull out the package inside, staring at the sheet of paper on top.

Dear Ms. Fiona Fontaine,
Hello and greetings from NYU Undergraduate
Admissions! First and foremost—congratulations
on your acceptance to NYU for the fall 2019
semester! We are thrilled to congratulate you on
this achievement.

I skim the rest of the letter as Mom takes pictures of the whole thing and starts to cry. This is probably a bigger moment for her than it is for me. This is an experience she never had, another chapter of life that she's living through me. And even though I should be happy, I feel guilty because I should have given her a better high school experience. I shouldn't have deviated from the course I was on. I'd be ripping open a different acceptance letter, probably a UCLA one, and calling Jenny to jump up and down with her.

"This is a huge deal," Mom says. "We should celebrate. Where do you want to go for dinner? We'll get dressed up and go right now."

I hold the envelope gingerly in my hand, like it could disappear. I don't want to celebrate anything yet, not when I don't even know if this is what I want. Did I ever want New York, or would I have followed Trixie anywhere? *There's a new school opening up on Mars*, I imagine her chirping in my ear. *Want to apply there with me?* I know what my answer would have been.

"Let's wait until I hear back from the other schools," I say. "Then we can celebrate."

"Of course, sweetie," she says, but I can see the disappointment in her eyes. She opens her arms and wraps me in a hug, and after everything, it's the hug that makes me want to cry. Because I remember the way Mom's hugs used to feel. I used to fit perfectly in her embrace, and I just don't anymore.

"Where's Sarah going?" she asks, stroking my hair like she did when I was a little kid. "Did you guys apply at any of the same places?"

I suddenly feel exhausted at the idea of carrying on the charade. I don't tell the truth, but I don't keep lying either. "Sarah and I aren't friends anymore, Mom. It got complicated, and I don't really want to talk about it."

And to my surprise, she doesn't make me.

Over the next two weeks, more big manila envelopes come in the mail. Every school I applied to. Florida State. Princeton. The University of Arizona. The University of Texas. Last of all, UCLA.

I tell Jasper about NYU and all the other schools, but I don't tell him about UCLA. Because he'd want to know why. It's not like I could ever tell him that I applied because that's where Beau is going. Because even though we went nearly a year without saying a word to each other, I can't imagine being separated by several states.

"What are we going to do?" Jasper says when we're eating lunch outside one day.

"You'll go wherever you want to go and I'll go to NYU," I say, hoping I sound more sure than I feel. "We'll see each other on breaks. And we can Skype all the time."

Jasper puts his apple down and grabs my face, presses his lips to mine. He has been doing this more and more lately. Kissing me in public, like he has to stake his claim. Like anyone else would even want me. I'm sure people are staring and the thought embarrasses me. They're probably thinking, *Two freaks in love. How perfect.*

Not perfect. Not even close.

75

WHEN MOM LEAVES for a last-minute conference in San Francisco, I get in my car and start driving and end up at Cabana Del Shit. Normally, when Mom is gone, I stay home and text Jasper and tell him to come over, but tonight I don't want to. Lately, sex with Jasper has been making me feel the guiltiest of all, like we're both cheating on people we never had in the first place.

You can be happy with him, a voice in my head says. *Trixie didn't want him. Beau never wanted you.*

It's the truth, at least on paper. But the paper truth isn't always the one that makes sense.

At Cabana Del Shit, I order a Diet Coke even though I want a chocolate milkshake, and I sit in a booth by the window. I can see the beach from here, the pier Toby jumped from. I picture him secretly swimming back to shore, fighting the undertow and white-capped waves, but even from here, it looks impossible. The pier is too far out, the undertow too strong, the waves too big. He never could have made it.

"You again," Skylar says when she comes by with a menu. "You're alone. Did you break up with that guy? Is he stalking you now?"

"He's not stalking anyone. I just want a cheeseburger to go."

She rolls her eyes and starts walking away. Before I can stop myself, I call out after her. I owe it to Jasper to defend him, since he's the only person who really cares enough to know who I am anymore.

"He wasn't obsessed with her, you know. It wasn't like that."

Skylar turns around, hand on her hip. "I wouldn't be so sure. Seriously, don't make excuses for him. I saw what I saw. Trixie told him she wasn't interested, but he kept showing up here anyway. Like, waiting for her. He tried to say he was her boyfriend, but she said he wasn't. At first I thought it was some kinky game they were playing." She glances down, sticks her hands in the pockets of her server belt. "But it wasn't a game. He was totally stalking her."

The Diet Coke I swallowed churns in my gut. I clutch the glass tightly. "What do you mean?"

"Well, what do you call it when someone keeps showing up where they weren't invited? A couple times, we had to get Max to ask him to leave. Sometimes we'd see him outside this window, like, staring into the ocean. And then she ended up dying in it." Skylar takes a deep breath, rubs her upper arms. She's not wearing Trixie's rings anymore, but a bunch of tacky gold jewelry instead.

I nod. "Thanks." I just want to drink my Diet Coke and get out of here and never come back. But Skylar lingers at the table, places a hand on the edge, near the napkin holder.

"If you're, like, still with him, I'd think twice. Because he'll probably get the same way about you like he did with her. I know from experience, men like that. They never change. They always need somebody to be the center of their world."

I don't want to believe her. Jasper is the one good thing that has happened to me this year, the one person I'm attached to who wants to be attached to me. But I have the sickening sense that maybe some of what she's saying is right. He shows up at my house when I'm not there and waits for me at my locker and makes sure everyone knows I'm his. Maybe I was right in the first place, when I thought he was just replacing her with me. Maybe there's a reason I never came back here to ask Skylar to elaborate about Jasper's obsession. Maybe I didn't want to know, and I still don't.

I stare out the window, at the water. It's nearly black, dark waves licking the graham-cracker shore like tongues. *Trixie*, I say silently, closing my eyes, *where are you?*

When I open my eyes, there's someone outside the window, sauntering down to the beach, hands jammed in hoodie pockets. A familiar lumbering gait, a baseball cap, hunched shoulders.

I slam down a ten-dollar bill on the table, dart out of my booth, and run for the door.

76

I HIDE IN the hole in the wall, sticking my head out to see what's happening. He's standing in the middle of them, pulling his cap off, smoking a cigarette. The ends of his hair stick straight up, almost white in the moonlight. He pulls something out of the back pocket of his jeans and hands it to one of the guys, who gives him something in return. They make the exchange too fast for me to see what it is.

I flatten myself against the wall as he starts to turn around. I can feel my heartbeat in the concrete and I have to know, so I peek back through the opening. I see him, and he sees me. My shock is reflected on his face.

I see who he is. Not Toby Hunter, but Beau.

"Preach," one of the guys calls out behind him. "I'll get you the rest next week."

I cup my hand over my mouth. Preach. The Preacher. The person I have been looking for since Tijuana has been right here the entire time, and I don't know if I should be grateful or mad or sad, so I'm a messy smear of everything.

He turns away and waves at the group, then starts running in the sand toward me. Now I see that he's drunk. His gait is erratic and he's taking bigger steps than he needs to, his arms churning at his sides. It doesn't matter, because I'm not going anywhere.

"How much did you see?" he shouts, slipping through the hole.

"Enough," I say, my throat dry. "You're the Preacher. I thought—I thought it was Toby." I think back to the picture of Toby I showed that guy on the beach and wonder how I didn't figure it out sooner. To him, the Hunter boys were interchangeable.

He puts a finger to my lips, lightly at first, then presses it in deeper. "You know, there are things you remember even though you don't want to. Like, I remember how Toby's running shoes used to stink up the laundry room. And the random places he hid. And this one quote he loved: 'Roll on, thou deep and dark blue Ocean—roll!' Yeah, my brother read Lord Byron too. I do everything he does." I put my hands on his wrists and I'm afraid he's going to push me away, but he just collapses into me, pushing my back into the wall.

I have a million questions for him. *What did you trade? And why are you down here?* But his hands are tangled up in my hair, grabbing fistfuls just hard enough to hurt. His chest is pressed against mine and then he's kissing me, and I'm too surprised that it's happening to even open my mouth. His lips cover mine urgently and a moan escapes his throat. He sucks on my lips, holds them in his teeth. His hands move forward until his fingers are on my cheeks. My face feels small in his hands, like he could crush it between his palms. He pushes me harder against the wall and I finally kiss back, letting my lips encircle his. He tastes like alcohol. He tastes like the night Trixie disappeared.

But as soon as it starts, it's over and he's facing away from me, his hands suddenly stashed behind his back. "Toby used to spout this bullshit," he says. "About how the person you loved was never the one you should love, and that was something you couldn't work hard enough to fix. I never knew what he was talking about, because your whole life you get told that if you put your mind to it, anything is possible. They should just tell kids that's not fucking true."

I bring my fingertips to my cheeks. They're still tingling from where his hands were. Did he just tell me he loves me? I don't ask because maybe it didn't happen at all. The words evaporated into the air, got sucked into the humidity.

"What do they pay you for?" I ask as he walks in circles in front of me. "Is it drugs?"

He starts to laugh, or howl—a terrible, tortured sound. "Fuck, I wish. This is a lot more complicated, but it's the only thing I'm good at."

My legs start to feel weak so I crouch down, my shoes digging into the sandy dirt. "Tell me. You have to tell me."

He shakes his head and makes that noise again, then grabs a wad of money out of his jeans pocket and hurls it at the wall. "That's what I get for doing what I do. I get shit for people. Things they can't get themselves. Fake IDs. Fake passports. Fake high school diplomas. I make it possible for people to become someone else."

The reality of what he's saying sinks into me, soaks into my skin until I'm anchored to the ground, a soggy mass. "You're the one who got Trixie her fake ID. What else did you get her?"

He's on the ground beside me, pulling his hood over his head, suddenly still. "I got her a passport. Months ago. Way before she left. I knew it was because she was going to try and find him, and I told her she was an idiot. That Toby didn't want to see any of us again, so he never would."

My eyes well up with tears and threaten to spill over. I hate Beau all over again for what he had with Trixie, these boulder-sized secrets they somehow kept under their skin. "And you never thought to tell me?"

He presses his fingers into his forehead. "I knew you'd ask questions. Where she went. Why she left. And I don't know the answers, because I stopped asking. Know why I stopped asking? Because she wouldn't have told me anyway. I knew I'd never see her again."

"So you knew she was going to disappear," I say slowly. "And you didn't bother to warn me about it."

He throws up his hands. "I didn't know anything. Nobody could predict what that girl would do. What was I supposed to do, call you up and tell you to watch Trixie like a hawk in case she disappears? We hadn't talked in months. You would have thought I was crazy." His hand grabs mine, and it's hot and sweaty, alive. "I know you think you can find her. But she must have known it was pointless to go after Toby. Maybe she really did end up in the water. You might as well give up and live your own life."

I shake his hand off, white-hot anger surging through me. "What, just like you have? You've done such a great job of moving on. Doing everything you hate just to make other people happy. Drinking yourself into"—I swat at the air— "into this person. You're not moving on at all. You're ruining your own goddamn life to step into his."

I want to take the words back as soon as I say them. I want to open my mouth and suck them back in, chew and digest them and think about the consequences. I shrink in on myself, expecting Beau to explode in rage, to punch his fist against the wall. But when I look over, he's crying. Softly at first, then loudly, like someone in physical pain.

"It's not like that," he says. "You don't know my dad. It's just easier for me to go along with things. Play football and be with Jenny and go to UCLA. Which is why he's going to freak the hell out when I don't."

My stomach erupts, like a fist is squeezing my organs. I smooth my sweatshirt down over my legs, pull the frayed ends as far as they will go without ripping. "What do you mean?"

He tilts his head up to the sky and laughs, tears leaking out the corners of his eyes. "I'm starting over. Everything over. Toby did it, he rolled on, so now it's my turn."

"You're going to disappear." I can barely choke out the words.

"No," he says. "Not like he did. But I'm not living in his shadow forever either. I'm done. Just like I told you at the party. Remember?"

Now he's looking right into my eyes, and I do remember, of course I remember. At the party, when he banged his head against the glass kitchen table and told me to fix him, to fix his whole life. *It doesn't have to be so hard*, I said. *I swear I won't let you unravel.*

I don't even know if I believed the words myself when I said them. They were drunken, not properly formed, spewed out like candy from a dispenser, and it was advice I wasn't even following myself. I didn't know how to live my own life. I had lived Mom's version of it and Jenny's version and Trixie's version, but never my own.

"So what are you going to do?" I whisper.

"I'm going to get clean. And I'm not going to school here next year. I want to be surrounded by buildings on all sides. I don't want to be able to see the ocean, no matter how high up I get. And no more football."

No more Jenny, I wait for him to say, but he doesn't.

"So you're leaving everything behind," I say.

He says nothing. I watch the wind ruffle his hair.

"Not everything. You can never leave everything."

I'm about to ask him something, but then he kisses me, softer, like he always did when it happened in my head, and I don't remember what I could possibly have to say.

77

I WANDERED AROUND *the party. I wanted to call you but I couldn't find my purse, couldn't remember where I left it. The rooms in Alison's house were mostly empty. There were a couple people passed out in the upstairs bedrooms, one on the carpet in her dad's office, mouth wide open, probably drooling. Alison's dad was going to be pissed.*

"Trixie," I kept saying, over and over. "Where are you, Trixie?"

She never answered.

I found him in the kitchen, sitting at the table, trying to pour tequila into a shot glass. He was doing a crappy job of it, sloshing the liquid all over the surface of the glass kitchen table.

"Hey," I said. It was the first time I had struck up a conversation with him in so long. But I wasn't shy anymore. I was bold, fueled by all those drinks Trixie had fed me. "Hey" felt so good that I wanted to say more, wondered why I had waited so long.

He didn't look up, not at first. Not until I sat down beside him and took the bottle out of his hand. Our fingers brushed, just a bit, just enough for an electric current to run through my whole body.

"Let me do that for you," I said. And somehow I managed to pour a perfect shot, which made him smile. I silently thanked Trixie, because after a summer of mixing our own drinks, I finally managed to look cool at just the right time.

He didn't thank me. Just kept grinning like an idiot. He drank that shot and wanted another one, and then I took the shot glass and poured one for myself. It stung my throat on the way down, but he looked at me with admiration, so I poured myself another one. The second time, it didn't sting so badly.

"Usually girls need salt and limes and shit." He leaned onto the table. His elbow, on the glass, was bright red.

I shook my head. My hair was a heavy weight and I hoped it still looked okay, that the curls hadn't fallen flat. "Lemons," I said, passing a shot back to him.

After two, three, (four?) more shots, the chair was too high for me. I was dizzy, weightless, effortless, like I might float away. So I sat down on the kitchen floor. It was cold down there and the tile bit into my legs. I noticed that my dress had ridden up and I was yanked back to reality, the unfair reality where I was bigger than I wanted to be and alone in the house of someone who didn't even want me there.

But I wasn't alone, because he joined me on the floor, rubbed his forehead with his hand and started muttering under his breath, some kind of drunken incantation.

"My friend ditched me," I felt obligated to say, and then I wished I could unsay them because they made me sound like a total loser.

He pulled his hat down over his face and rested his head on his knees and said nothing. I thought he was asleep for a minute, passed out like that guy in Alison's dad's study. But then he nudged my knee with his denim-clad one. "I'm glad your friend ditched you."

Wherever Trixie was, I said another silent thank-you. *Thank you for ditching me. Thank you for disappearing.*

I had no idea what I was really thanking her for.

78

BY THE TIME I get back to Cabana Del Shit to pick up my order, I'm in a daze. I walk up to the bar feeling like I just came out of a dream, or a nightmare. Beau staggered away after he kissed me, but he looked back like he was really seeing me, and it was enough to make me feel like I had seen a ghost— the ghost of the old Beau, the one I knew was still in there. I jump when a hand touches my shoulder, thinking it might be him. But it's not.

"Where were you?" Jasper says, his voice sharp. "I went by your house and you weren't there. I thought we would do something tonight."

"I was here. I-I took a walk," I stammer. "I just went to the beach to get some air. I didn't even think we had plans tonight."

"You're my girlfriend," he says, leaning into the bar. "I didn't know I needed plans to see you."

Skylar raises an eyebrow as she hands me the takeout bag. I notice the look she gives me, the intake of breath and the unspoken *I told you so.* I walk to my car with the bag and Jasper follows me.

"Are you seeing someone else?" He grabs the bag from my hand. "Because you're not acting like yourself."

I put my fingers to my lips and remember the taste of Beau's kiss there, the way his mouth felt on mine. I think of what he just told me, roll the words around. *I'm starting over. I'm done.* Then I remember how easily his promises are broken.

"No," I say. "I'm not seeing anyone else."

Jasper puts the bag on the ground and wraps his arms around me, running his fingers down my back. My shoulder is pressed into his chest and I can feel his heart beating hard and fast, his blood pumping like that for me, because he's afraid of losing me. I wonder if Skylar is watching us from inside the restaurant, if she's rolling her eyes again, if she's genuinely afraid for my safety. I wonder where Beau is now, how he became the Preacher in the first place. I want to tell Jasper because we're in this together, but I don't really think we are anymore, so I don't say a word.

I hug Jasper back, limply, because he's here and because I know he won't leave me. But there's something different in our embrace, something cold. Because I don't know what will happen if I try to leave him, and part of me is scared to find out.

79

DAYS BLUR INTO weeks and I'm a robot going through the motions, taking notes and writing tests and being Jasper's girlfriend. I sit in front of Beau in class every morning, trying to forget about our kiss and that he's the Preacher and that the search for Trixie and Toby has no more leads, no more bread crumbs at all. The path is clean, and everyone wants me to leave it that way.

Alison moved to the back of the classroom in astronomy, and sometimes I feel her eyes on me, like she's watching me and knows what I'm thinking. Maybe she has noticed the elaborate hairstyles I've been trying lately. Braids and low buns and twists, and today there's a fake white rose clip in the middle, just because I thought it might make him remember.

It needs a drink. It's dying.

Today, she finds me after class when I'm shoving my books in my bag and clears her throat, and I'm sure she's about to make some declaration, like *Stay away from my best friend's boyfriend* or *I know what you're up to.* But she just grins and claps her hands.

"I got in," she says. "At NYU. Have you gotten your acceptance letter yet?"

Relief floods through me. I nod. "Yeah, a few weeks ago. Have you decided if you're going?"

She leans against the desk beside me. "I don't know for sure. But I think so. I need a change, you know? My parents want me to stay here and live at home, but I'm not living my life for them. I need to do my own thing."

"What about Jenny?" I say, because I can't help myself. "I figured you guys would be roommates."

Alison crosses her arms. "What about Jenny? We talked about being roommates, doing the whole dorm room thing. Then she decided she was just going to move in with Beau, even though it's a terrible idea. She wants to, like, have his babies and stuff. She wants to save the guy." She blows out a breath and her bangs flop to the side of her face.

I wonder if she's testing me, if she's expecting me to have an opinion. Panic surges through me at the thought of Beau and Jenny in a cute little off-campus apartment. Jenny trying on white dresses. Jenny painting a nursery. That's not going to happen. Not after what Beau told me at the beach, that he's putting an end to all that. But how many times has he said something he didn't mean?

"I'm just leaving the high-school drama behind," Alison says. "You know? I'm over it. Time to move on." She laughs. "I'm taking my shrink's advice. She's actually not as bad as I thought she'd be."

She makes it sound so easy to detach, so simple to step out of everything that used to matter. Then I realize that it's basically what I did last year when I chose Trixie. I detached. I disentangled. But I got myself tangled up in something even stickier, even harder to escape.

"Maybe we'll see each other there," Alison says, nudging

my desk with her foot. "If I end up going. Who knows, maybe we'll be in the same classes. We should grab a coffee or something."

I nod. "We should. That would be fun."

I watch her walk away, her hair swishing against her back, and promise myself that if I end up at NYU, I'll keep that date. Maybe whatever friendship I had with Alison doesn't have to end, but can change shape into something else.

80

"MARCH IS THE worst month when you're a senior," Mom says over breakfast the next week, pushing a bowl of granola toward me. "The end is so close, but yet so far away."

Like you'd even know, I want to say. *You had a baby when you were my age and weren't even in school.*

"Have you made your decision yet?" She cradles her hands around a giant mug of coffee. "You know, whatever you do, don't base your choice on that boyfriend of yours. He's a good kid, but you need to pick the school that's best for you. The rest will fall into place."

It's easy for her to say. She doesn't even go on dates anymore, not since the last guy she met online, who told her he was some big-shot investment banker when he really worked at Foot Locker. Mom's life has been a series of men letting her down, starting with my dad. She doesn't know what it's like to be in love and want the other person to love you back badly enough to believe it'll happen. But then again, that hasn't exactly worked out for me.

"Not yet," I say. "I'm still thinking."

She's right about one thing, though. March is the worst month, because March is Trixie's birthday month. And even though she's not here, by choice, even though I hate her for

Beau and for Jasper and for not saying goodbye, I still miss her like crazy today. March fourth. Last year on Trixie's birthday, we ended up going shopping. We went to the mall and got milkshakes in the food court, and I waited while she tried on clothes, wishing I could join her but being paralyzed by the fear of knowing what size I actually was.

I want to let March fourth pass me by. I want to pretend it's not even happening, treat it just like any other day. But it refuses to pass like any other day. Every time I manage to forget about her, she comes back. She's banging around in my head and doing jumping jacks in my stomach and waving her arms around like *Hey, remember me?*

To make things worse, when I get to school, Jasper completely ignores the fact that March fourth is not like every other day. Maybe he forgets it's her birthday, but somehow I doubt that. The love, or whatever he felt, doesn't just go away or heal up like a wound. Like the heart-shaped mark on my back, still pink after all these months.

"Are you mad at me?" he keeps asking, and I keep telling him no, because the truth is, I don't know who I'm mad at. Maybe him, for being better at moving on than I am. Myself, for lying to everyone. Or her most of all.

When the final bell rings, I drive to the mall instead of going home, wandering aimlessly through stores. I close my eyes for a second and imagine she's beside me, flinging through the racks, grabbing anything and everything, pushing clothes into my arms that I'd never wear in a million years. *This would look great on you, Fi. This would bring out your eyes. You totally have the boobs for this. I wish I would look as good in that dress as you do.* Because that was what Trixie did when I was with her. Made me feel special. Made me feel like a spotlight was shining down on me, even if she was the only one who could see it.

I stumble on the shirt by accident. It's in the window, on a mannequin, accompanied by the same kind of tiny denim cutoffs Trixie lived in all summer.

JERSEY GIRL

If I try hard enough, I can picture her there, her arms poking out of the holes like they did that night. Her nude-colored bra and armful of bracelets covering silvery scars.

I walk into the store and tell the girl behind the counter that I want to buy the shirt off the mannequin. I tell her it has to be that one, that it's a gift for a friend. She eyes me dubiously. I know what she's thinking. *You're too big to wear this.*

When I'm home, I fold up the shirt and put it in my top drawer, on top of all my summer clothes. It seems *fitting*, somehow. A friendship that doesn't fit anymore. A friendship I used to think fit perfectly but was the wrong size the whole time.

81

YOU DIDN'T BOTHER to tell me it was your birthday. I never would have known if it wasn't for your dad, who pulled into the driveway in his station wagon when we were on our way out your front door.

"Shit," she muttered under her breath.

"Where's my birthday girl running off to?" he said, stepping out of the car and reaching back into the open window. He pulled on a shiny piece of ribbon and a comically large balloon came launching up to the front seat. It was almost too big to fit through the window.

I whipped my head to face Trixie. "It's your birthday?"

She stared at the driveway. "I don't like to make a big deal about it. It's stupid. I was hoping to just pass it by this year."

I was pissed off that she kept something like that from me, and mad at myself that I never asked when her birthday was. That seemed like something friends should do. Jenny and Alison and I made a huge deal over each other's birthdays. There was always a cake and plastic tiaras and a gift that cost more than what we said we would spend. And I never got to do any of that for Trixie, because she didn't give me the chance.

"Don't go anywhere, your ice cream cake is melting," her

dad said, passing her the balloon string before lumbering back to the car.

She pinched the string between her fingers, then let it go on purpose. I jumped up in the air to try and catch the tip of the string, but it was too late. The balloon was already floating away, passing the roof of her house and the trees lining her street.

"I hate ice cream cake," she whispered.

I tilted my head back and watched the balloon get smaller and smaller, until I couldn't see it at all.

82

MOM IS GONE for most of March break, so I spend it with Jasper, in our own little world. I try to lose myself in him because it's easy, and because I haven't heard from Beau since that night at the wall. He still walks down the hallway holding hands with Jenny and still plays football and he still slept with Trixie and I have no reason to believe anything he says.

"Do you believe everything happens for a reason?" I say to Jasper. "Like, even the really shitty things?"

His smile fades and his face is unreadable. "Yes. I actually do."

I know what he's probably thinking. Trixie disappeared and we both thought it was the worst thing ever, the worst thing that could happen, and it brought us together. He hugs me tighter, breathing into my hair.

But I'm not thinking the same thing. I'm thinking of something similar, equally selfish. Trixie getting me drunk at the party made me stay, made me talk to Beau, made him talk to me, made him trust me. Made him maybe, despite everything else, despite the fact that I'm not the same girl he looked up at the sky with, feel something for me again. Trixie would have hated that she brought us together when she wanted so badly to keep us apart.

"Where'd you go?" Jasper whispers. "You're somewhere else." His fingers trace a path down my back. I flinch as he puts the pad of his thumb over the heart-shaped mark on my back.

"What's this from?"

"Nothing," I say, pulling on my hoodie, but what I really mean is *everything*.

"Sometimes I feel like you go away," he says, stroking the skin under my sweatshirt hem. "Like you're a million miles away."

My skin erupts in shivers where he touched. "I'm right here. I'm not going anywhere."

"You'd tell me if you didn't want to be with me," he says, his lips grazing my neck lightly. "You wouldn't fake it."

I turn around to face him. "I don't get where this is coming from. We're always together. We're in bed together right now." I force myself to smile, even though it makes my cheeks hurt.

He lets out a shaky breath and looks sad, sad enough that I start feeling sorry for him. Of course he's insecure. He's probably afraid that I'm going to do the same thing to him that Trixie did. Leave.

"Do you believe that it's possible for two people to have no secrets from each other?" he says quietly. "Like, to know all the dark parts of another person and still feel the same way about them?"

I prop myself up on my elbows and think about my dark parts. What I did the night Trixie disappeared. How I kissed Beau at the wall. I try to imagine Jasper forgiving me for that. I'd turn into somebody else in his eyes, the kind of selfish, backstabbing bitch he wouldn't want to know. All of my ugly that he can't see now would bubble to the surface and blot out the good like a stain.

"You can tell me anything," he says, and I almost want to. But I know that he'll never look at me the same way if I do, no matter how much he thinks he will. I'd look different with my secrets in the open, like my skin is inside out.

"You know everything already." I wrap my arms around his shoulders. "I'm a pretty boring person. There's not much to say."

"I somehow doubt that," he says into my neck.

"What about you? What secrets are you keeping from me?"

He pulls away and brushes a piece of hair off my cheek. "Just one." He starts kissing my hairline, my forehead, my nose, then my lips, and I wait for him to tell me what he's hiding from me, but he doesn't say another word.

I must fall asleep after, because when I wake up, Jasper is hovering over my desk, his back to me. His spine juts out and his body is quaking, and I can't tell if he's laughing or crying.

83

"YOU'LL NEVER GUESS *what happened,*" *you said, right before the senior semiformal, a few weeks before graduation.* "*Jasper asked me to the dance.*" *Then you laughed, like it was the most hilarious thing in the world that the boy you were sleeping with wanted to go out with you.*

I wasn't sure what my reaction was supposed to be, but I was jealous. And pissed off. I used to love school dances. I'd always go as part of a group, with Jenny and Alison and Beau and Brad Colton and some of the other cheerleaders and football players. But going with a date—with Beau—was something I wanted. I had this vision of us going to the junior or senior semiformal together, slow dancing in the gym, my cheek on his shoulder.

"I take it you're not going?" I said. Trixie laughed harder.

"It's not even that he asked. It's the way he asked. With a bunch of flowers on my doorstep. Thank god I found them before my dad did. Can you imagine having to explain that?"

"I guess not," I said.

"He doesn't get it. Do I look like a school-dance person? And even if I did, I would never go with him."

"At least he got you flowers. That's pretty nice."

Trixie shook her head. "I hate flowers. And the weird thing about these is that they were half dead already."

Maybe at that point, she was too.

84

A WEEK LATER, Beau keeps his promise. At least, part of it.

I get a text message on April third. *It has to be today, when it ends. If you don't believe me, come and see it for yourself after school.*

So I go and see it. I watch the annual spring scrimmage from the top of the bleachers, as Beau stands in the middle of the field and gets pummeled by one of the giant linebackers from Trenton. I watch as he stays on the ground and doesn't get up, as he grabs his knee. My heart is a hard stone as Jenny sprints onto the field and drops down beside him. Then the medics are coming in with a stretcher and it's all over, the game and Beau's football career as a Robson Renegade.

I realize, after it happens, why it had to be April third. I have that date memorized, from the Dead Students Wall. Toby's birthday. The day Beau stopped living Toby's life and started living his. I know why he thought he had to do it, but it's tragic, somehow, that the only way out was through physical pain. Just like Toby's way out was by diving into the waves.

Almost immediately after, rumors start flying from wall to wall, down hallways, from the floor to the ceiling like a bouncy rubber ball. You can't walk anywhere at Robson without being hit by one.

"He was drunk on the field," I hear someone say. "He could have done something. He just let that guy take him down. I swear, he put up his arms like he wanted it."

"The guy blew it," Brad Colton says to a cluster of freshman girls. "He had a free ride to UCLA. Now he's probably gonna spend the next four years flipping burgers."

Some people are nicer. I hear Clarissa Egan, a wannabe cheerleader who auditions every year but never makes the squad, defending him by the water fountain. "Can you blame him, really? After what happened to his brother?"

Her friend doesn't agree. "That was almost two years ago. He needs to move on."

"He'll come back from this," someone else says. "It's just a minor setback."

"It's a torn ACL," says Jeremy Garner, one of the running backs. "He fucking ruptured it. Might as well be the end of the world."

Jasper and I wade through it, holding hands, even though I'm aching to be wherever Beau is. He doesn't come to school for days after it happens and he doesn't text me, and I wonder where he is, what's happening to him, if he's even coming back. Jasper doesn't seem to hear the chatter in the hallways at all. It ricochets right off him. Either he really doesn't hear it or does a good job of pretending not to.

A full week after the game, Beau hobbles down the halls with crutches and a knee brace, baseball cap pushed down over his head. I will him to look up and feel me there. But he doesn't look up for anyone.

"Where's his girlfriend?" the girl whose locker is beside mine says, watching him pass. "They used to be, like, connected at the hip."

She's talking to her friend, who just shrugs. "I heard he cheated on her."

I slam my locker shut and walk away.

When I walk into the girls' bathroom at lunch, I hear crying in one of the stalls. I turn to leave, but then I see the shoes under the stall door—studded silver ballet flats—and realize it's Jenny. I helped her pick out those shoes. Dialogue from the party runs through my head like music that's cranked too loud.

I thought you were her friend.

I was, past tense. Not anymore.

It was so easy that night to forget Jenny existed, to erase the role she played in my life. It was scarily easy to hate her for everything she had done. But here, in the girls' bathroom, everything comes flooding back. The good memories, the ones I had almost convinced myself never happened. Jenny's smile when she invited me to sit with her at lunch the first week of ninth grade. Her big, blobby tears when she got a terrible haircut the summer before sophomore year. The surprise party the two of us planned for Alison's birthday, the hours we spent making purple construction-paper hearts. The time we borrowed her mom's car and scraped the side in an underground parking lot and covered it up with nail polish.

I buried all of those memories, stored them inside me somewhere the sun would never reach. But maybe it's impossible to keep them buried forever. A sob rises in my throat when I think about Jenny's tearstained face at the party, and I choke it down. I walk over to the door with the studded silver ballet flats and knock gently.

"Jenny? Are you okay?"

Total stillness, like she thinks if she doesn't answer, I might go away.

"Jenny, I know you're in there. Can I help?"

"No," she finally says. "Forget about it."

I can't, I want to say. *I wish I could.*

I linger with my wrist pressed against the cold stall door, then turn to leave. When I spin on my heels, I hear her clear her throat.

"I never should have said yes," she says, so quietly that I have to strain my ears. "When he asked me out. I should have known this was going to happen."

I listen to her cry and blow her nose and can't think of a single thing to say. Maybe I'm expecting an apology, something like *I'm sorry I took the guy you loved.* But an apology never comes. Just more sniffling and the sound of toilet paper unspooling.

I walk over to the sink to wash my hands, and Jenny flushes the toilet and opens the stall door. I meet her red-rimmed eyes in the mirror and feel sorry for her. Mascara pools under her eyelashes and her cheeks are blotchy and her hair sticks to her forehead. She moves over to the sink beside me and sticks her shaking hands under the tap.

"I gave up everything for him, you know," she mutters. "You have no idea what I did for him. What I put up with."

I pull paper towels down and hand her one. On my way out the door, I turn and give her a weak smile. Jenny used to know exactly what I was thinking, almost like she could read my mind. I used to be grateful for it, for having somebody who knew me that well. But today, I'm glad she's not looking hard enough to see my truth.

You have no idea what I did for him.

Neither do you, I want to scream.

85

A FEW WEEKS later, my phone starts vibrating when I'm sprawled on my bed, trying to study for an American history test but making absolutely no progress. There are too many images, awful pictures I wish I could blot out. Trixie hopping on a plane, a train, a boat. Disappearing into thin air. Grabbing Beau's hand, leading him up the stairs to her bedroom. Kissing Jasper. Leaving huge marks everywhere she went and wiping them clean like they were never there. I try to ignore the phone, but it keeps buzzing and finally I pick it up.

Meet me, the first message says. *On the field. He's out again tonight, the Hunter.*

The next message is just as cryptic. *It's me, I promise, the real me.*

I pull on a sweatshirt and grab my car keys and drive to Robson with shaky hands, afraid of what I'll find. Afraid of what he's talking about. The Hunter. What Hunter? What real me?

I don't even see him at first. It's almost pitch-black out and the lights that illuminate the football field during games are shut off, leaving nothing but darkness. I park in my usual spot and walk over, practically tiptoeing, hoping he hasn't done something stupid.

I walk onto the field. The grass is wet and cold and licks my ankles. That's when I see him, sprawled on the twenty-yard line, arms and legs outstretched like a starfish, crutches strewn beside him. I start running because I think he must have hurt himself.

But when I get to him, he just smiles and reaches out his hand. "Hi. Come here."

I sink to the ground slowly and wrap my knees into my sweatshirt. "What are you doing out here?"

"This is the best place to see him," he says, stretching an arm behind his head. "You know when I told you my brother was the best hider? Well, sometimes I think that's where he went." He points his other arm straight up to the sky. "And if he's all the way up there, no wonder he doesn't want to come back down."

I suck in a sharp breath and hold it there, along with everything else I'm holding in that I wish I could say. *I don't think he's up there. I think he was here. I think maybe he still is.*

"Why the name Preacher?" I ask him instead. "You're not even religious. I figured the Preacher would be some ranting Bible-thumper."

He half smiles. "Exactly. Nobody would think a preacher has any demons to hide." He tilts his head back. "Do you see them? They're out again tonight and you're not even looking."

I let go of my knees and lean back. "What, your demons?"

He shakes his head. "No, the stars. Can you see Orion? The hunter? He was out the first night I ever met you." He reaches out for my hand, even though he's not looking at me. "Orion. He was a messed-up guy. And his problems started happening when he got wasted."

I take his hand and squeeze it. I stare at the sky and try to see what he's seeing, but I still don't see the constellation, just a random smattering of stars.

"You remember the night we met," I say. "If you felt that strongly about me the whole time, if you felt it too, why didn't you ever ask me out? Why did you ask Jenny out instead of me?"

He drops my hand and tilts his face to mine. "You scared me. I never knew what to say, and I felt like there were never words good enough. And after Toby, you weren't there, and Jenny was. Maybe I asked her because I was mad at you. Because you weren't there. Then all of a sudden she was drawing pink hearts beside my name and showing up all the time, and it's not like anyone else was fighting for me. I thought maybe it was in my head. You and me."

"It wasn't," I say. "And you always had the right words. I loved that about you."

It's the closest I've come to saying *I love you*.

"The rose," I say slowly. "You left it for me that day. Why did you do that?"

He pinches the skin between his eyebrows and closes his eyes. "Because I remembered. Drinking makes me forget. That's why I started, because Toby made it sound like the magic cure for too many thoughts in my head. But I didn't forget anything about that night, and maybe there's a reason."

We're both quiet and I touch his hand again, tentatively, daring myself to believe that everything will be okay, saying a silent prayer to whoever is listening that this is all I want.

"What happened to Orion?" I say, putting my other hand on my stomach. "Did he get the girl?"

Beau purses his lips and shakes his head. "He went blind. Then he got destroyed by the goddess who loved him and placed into the sky."

I make one last effort, one last plea. "We could find him, you know. If we work together. We can figure out where he is and bring him back."

Beau pulls on the ends of his hair. "No, we can't. I can't. If I don't start moving on, I'm going to be stuck here forever."

We're both quiet, and Beau lifts his head up to stare at the stars again. I do the same and I squint as hard as I can, hoping the sky will give me some kind of answer. But there's nothing up there. Beau might see the hunter and maybe he sees himself, scarring the dark, but all I see are burning balls of gas.

86

EVERY TIME MY *eyes fluttered shut, I felt like I was going to spin off the face of the earth. I thought about everything you had taught me about drinking. Have water every so often, so that you don't feel hungover in the morning. Take a Tylenol before you go to bed. Don't mix liquors.*

It was too late for all of that.

Besides, I didn't want to stop drinking. Beau was on another bottle, an expensive-looking one he found hidden below the pots and pans in one of Alison's kitchen cabinets.

"They're probably saving that for a special occasion," I said.

He pulled the top off and took a long drink, and when he passed me the bottle, he was smiling.

"This is a special occasion," he said.

"What's the occasion?" I stared at him.

"Us," he said slowly, and I wanted that word to last forever.

87

THE NEXT MORNING, I knock softly on Mom's office door. Music is coming from inside, some sort of opera. Mom always listens to opera when she's stressed out, because she says it relaxes her. "I can't understand a single thing they're saying," she once told me. "And there's something peaceful about not having the chance to interpret anything." Now I get what she meant.

"Come in," she says. When I open the door, she's not even looking at me. She's sorting through a thick stack of papers on her desk, her hair in a messy knot on top of her head.

"I wanted to talk to you about something," I say. I want to collapse in a pile on her office floor and spill out everything I have ever kept from her. I want to see if she would still love me, even after all the lies I told.

"What's wrong, honey?" She pushes her glasses up like a headband.

"Nothing's wrong," I lie. "I just have this huge decision to make and I don't know what to do."

Mom gestures to the loveseat in the corner and I perch on a cushion, feeling out of place. I used to come in here when I was younger and stare at the framed world map on the wall, closing my eyes and circling my finger over the glass and deciding I'd visit wherever it landed. Maybe it wasn't such a bad way to make choices.

"Talk to me," she says.

I take a deep breath. "It's between NYU and UCLA. They're my top choices, and I'm so torn. What do you think?"

Mom folds her hands over her papers and beams. That's the only word for it. She looks proud, so proud that I'm going to university somewhere. And I know that should make me feel good, but it just makes me feel rotten inside.

"It's not up to me. This is a huge accomplishment, Fiona. You've earned the right to make this decision for yourself." She leans back in her chair. "You know, when I was your age, I would have been so happy to go to school anywhere. It was so hard for me, watching my friends go off and come back on Christmas break with stories about the classes they were taking and the boys they were dating. You have your whole life in front of you. My only advice is to make the choice for you, not for anyone else."

"I feel like I'm being pulled in two different directions." It's the complete truth. What I don't say is that it's worse than that, like I'm being split in half, that if I don't pick a side, I'm going to be ripped apart and never be whole again.

"That's normal." She stands up and comes over to sit on the loveseat beside me. "What you're feeling, it's normal. You're seventeen, and where you go to school is one of the biggest decisions you'll have to make. Just remember that there's no right and wrong, not really. There are two different paths, and they'll both throw up rights and wrongs along the way."

I lean into her shoulder. "I just feel like one wrong move will screw everything up."

"It won't. You're so much smarter than I ever was," Mom says. "Smarter and better, so sensible and good. If only I had been more like you." She pauses. "You know, I was worried about you last year. Not because you and Trixie got close. I know you think I didn't like her, but that's not true. I guess I was worried that you'd change yourself to become what someone else wanted from you and lose who you were in the process. And who you are is pretty great."

I hang my head and avoid meeting her eyes. She's all wrong. Who I am isn't great, and I did change myself to become what someone else wanted. I've been doing it my whole life.

"I know this has been a rough year, losing Trixie. But I'm so proud of how you've come out of this even stronger."

I haven't, I want to scream. *I can barely stand up on my own.*

"You can talk to me about anything, you know," she says. "I was such a follower in high school. I did whatever my friends were doing, even if it felt wrong for me. But you . . . you've made your own path."

It's a compliment I don't deserve. The only path I've created this year is a trail full of dead ends to a girl I never knew in the first place.

The phone on Mom's desk starts ringing, and she pecks me on the cheek before springing up to answer it, and then she's all business again. She gives me a wink and a wave as I leave her office and shut the door behind me.

She's right about one thing. I know both paths will sprout their own roots for me to trip over, and neither will be straight and simple. Then I remember what Jasper said at the motel after our search in Tijuana. *If life were that easy, everyone would be in it.*

Later, when I'm in my room, Mom knocks on my door. "I'm going to Denver tomorrow, sweetie. I'll probably be gone a full week, or at least five days. But when I get back, I want to take you out to celebrate whatever choice you make." She kisses me on the forehead, like she used to when I was a little kid. "Because I have faith that whatever you pick will be the right decision for you."

I only wish I believed her.

88

YOU CAN'T PLAY *spin the bottle with only two people. It kind of defeats the purpose of the game. Unless your game has a totally different purpose.*

"It's supposed to be a wine bottle," he said, but he was grinning and his face was shiny and I had never seen anyone look that happy, not ever.

I stared at the label on the bottle I was holding. My vision was blurry and the words were swimming together, but there was a picture of fruit on it. Peaches. I put the bottle to my lips and took a long swig until there was nothing left but a sticky-sweet smell.

"This'll work," I said.

I spun the bottle first. The funny thing was, it didn't even land on Beau. It pointed in the other direction, toward the laundry room.

It didn't matter.

He pressed me onto my back, his lips landing hungrily on mine. His breath was hot and smelled like tequila and his hands were sloppy and everywhere. I felt a pinch in my back but ignored it because it didn't matter. Maybe I was in a dream, the kind where you pinched yourself to see if it was real.

I fumbled with his belt buckle. I didn't know what I was doing and half of me expected him to stop me. That same half waited for the guilt to creep in. *I'm kissing Jenny's boyfriend. Jenny's boyfriend is on top of me. Jenny's boyfriend has my breast in his hand.*

It didn't happen like I thought it would. It's not like I had spent that much energy imagining my first time, but I thought it would at least be in a bed, maybe with soft music playing. Not on a floor, with the bass from the party still reverberating when I pressed my ear to the tile. I didn't ask what would happen after because I knew that whatever answer I got would only be for tonight and would dissolve before tomorrow morning.

I expected it to hurt. When Alison lost her virginity to Brad Colton, she told me and Jenny with big serious eyes and a stern tone about how painful it was. But Beau nudged my legs apart and I pulled him down so that his heart was directly over mine, our ragged breathing in sync, and it didn't hurt at all. Later, I wondered how we could be so careless about not using protection, and I promised myself next time would be different. If there was a next time.

When I sat up afterward and pulled the top of my dress back up, I saw the blood on the floor and realized that's what the pinch in my back was from. I had cut myself open on a piece of amber-colored glass from the bottle Beau smashed. I pushed my index finger against the cut but it kept bleeding profusely.

Beau barely had his pants back on before he started to panic. "No," he said, tripping over the bottom of his jeans and hitting a wall. "This isn't how we were supposed to happen. This isn't right."

I wanted to cling on to what just happened, cleave to the Beau I just shared everything with. But that Beau unraveled. He started smacking his cheeks with his hands, gently at first, like he just wanted to wake up, then harder, so hard that he left red marks on his cheekbones.

I used my dress to wipe the blood off the floor. It was red anyway. "Nothing from tonight will matter ever again," I consoled him. "This never happened."

Then I made myself smile, even though I suddenly wanted to cry.

89

THE NEXT DAY, I wave at Mom through the window as she leaves, even though I woke up feeling nauseous and just wanted to stay in bed. This used to be my favorite month of the year. May, when everything is lush and the end of the school year is almost here. But this time it feels like everything is happening too fast and there's no beginning or end, like the farther into the year we get, the more Trixie seems like she never existed at all. Her gestures, her mannerisms, her voice, everything that I used to hear so loudly is more like a whisper. *Come back*, I want to shout with my hands cupped around my mouth. *Don't leave me. Give me the chance to leave you.*

The doorbell rings a few minutes later, when I'm on my way back upstairs, and I roll my eyes, thinking Mom forgot something as usual. Her wallet or her briefcase or the shoes she wanted to wear to her business dinner. But when I open the door, I'm face-to-face with Beau, standing on my porch with his crutches.

"Hi," I say awkwardly, hating the fact that I'm wearing a huge pair of sweatpants and a ratty pajama top that says MEOW in big pink letters.

"We need to talk," he says, hopping on his good leg. "Well, I need to talk. I'm just asking for you to listen."

I nod and open the door wider. He eases himself in and sits right at the bottom of the staircase. I realize he has never been here before, and maybe it should be strange, having him in my foyer, but it's not.

"You're getting around okay on those things," I say, sticking my slippered foot toward one of his crutches. A dull pain manifests in my abdomen, throbbing steadily, but I ignore it.

"Yeah," he says with a laugh. "I could get used to this. Guys on crutches get special treatment."

I sit down on the stairs beside him and he turns toward me, his face suddenly serious. "I can't just let this happen anymore. You know, they were right. All those people in AA. I'm killing myself. And I think I wanted to die, because of how guilty I felt. Because it was all my fault."

I suck in a breath. "You went to an AA meeting?"

He stares at the ground. "I wanted to ask you to come with me, but it's not your battle. It's not your demon."

"I would have."

"I know." He reaches into the pocket of his hoodie and pulls something out, a little square-shaped blob in a Ziploc bag. "I did something for you. I unburied it. Turns out, you can do that."

I hold out my hand. It's a book. The one he buried when I didn't show up that night. The cover is brown and I can't read the title and there aren't pages, just crumbling mush. It's barely a book at all anymore.

"It's Lord Byron," he says. "I know you read the one I asked you to hold onto that day, so I got you your own copy."

I force myself to look up at him even though it's the most

scarily intimate thing, him seeing this much emotion on my face, even scarier than seeing my body without clothes on. But then I see that he's blushing too. "How do you know I read it?"

"I watched you," he says. "You stood at your locker and read it, and I stood there like some kind of creep. That's when I really knew." He pauses before I can ask him what he really knew. "Anyway, since it's been underground for more than a year, it's pretty much just mulch. I'll buy you a real copy. I just needed you to know that this one existed."

I press my back into the stair behind me. I want to tell him that it wasn't his fault, that Toby would have run away no matter what. I want to tell him I forgive him for what he did with Trixie. I want to tell him that everything will be okay. But I don't know that anything will be okay.

"I'm doing what you told me to do," he says. "But after graduation, you're not going to see me for a while. I'm sick of being this person. I'm sick of screwing everything up." He hangs his head and pulls on the brim of his baseball cap. "I'm doing the actual rehab thing. You know, my dad thinks if you put your mind to it, you can fix anything by yourself. And maybe he can, but I can't. I need help."

I stretch my legs out. There's a rip in the knee of my sweatpants and I fixate on the skin underneath. "That's good." I swallow a lump in my throat that feels like a rock and fold forward over my stomach, willing the ache to go away. "I know you'll get better."

He balls up his hands. "You know something? I've been drinking every single day since Toby left. Sometimes a little, sometimes a lot. And it's made me so numb. And everyone just let it happen, except you. And I need to know why." He stares up at me with watery blue eyes.

Because you know me. Because you care. Because you brought snow to Southern California. Because you can do the impossible.

"Because I let my best friend disappear," I say. "And I couldn't let you disappear too."

He shifts over, planting his hands on the wall behind me, our faces almost touching. "I'm kind of excited, in this weird way. And I haven't felt like that in a really long time. It's like I'm seeing that light at the end of the tunnel that people always talk about." He pauses. "I don't know what's going to happen, after rehab. Who I'll be. It freaks me out, you know? Like, I won't know the guy who comes out of there."

"It'll be good for you. You'll still be you."

"But I don't want to be me," he says sharply. "Not this version of me. Which is why nothing's going to carry over. From this life. It's all a reminder of the mess I made."

I nod, feeling small and far away, like a speck of dust. I'm part of the mess he made and he doesn't want me to carry over. You can't have a fresh start when there's a big stain soaking in on the surface.

"Except for you," he practically whispers. "I don't know what it is, why I feel like this around you."

"Like what?"

"Like you don't want me to be anyone but me. Like I can be myself without trying to be Toby too. It's like, everyone's adding weights around my ankles and you've got the key to cut them off."

"So what are you trying to tell me?" I say, my voice shaking. "What are you saying?"

He stares up at the ceiling and I follow his gaze. I smile because there's pink spray up there, and I realize it must be from last summer, when Trixie's cream soda exploded everywhere. I'm glad I didn't do a good job of cleaning up that mess, because now it's a memory that doesn't make me hate her.

"That first night we looked at the stars," Beau says. "I knew you felt what I was feeling. But I didn't know what to do with those feelings. You know?"

My heart pounds out an erratic rhythm. I do know.

"Well, that was the last time I ever felt totally peaceful. Like, everything had stopped and it was just you and me and those stars and that moment. That was the last time the world stood still." He traces the shape of my face with his finger. "I wonder if we could go back to that."

"But what happened at the party—what happened that night. You were so afraid of Jenny finding out. You said your life would be over."

He moves his hand to my lips, his fingertips brushing them lightly. "I think my life *was* over after I cheated on her with you. I fucked it all up and let everyone down. Especially you. But it wasn't over in the way I thought. I don't know. I guess I'm different now than I was then. What I used to think was important somehow doesn't matter at all. And everything I wasn't looking for that I need is right in front of me." He blinks repeatedly. "That sounds totally lame. But it's true."

"So how do I fit into all this? What do you want me to do?"

"I want a fresh start," he says. "I want to do everything right. I just want it to be us looking at the sky, like none of the shit between then and now happened at all. And I know you're seeing that other guy and I have no right to ask you not to see him, but I'm asking anyway."

Tears sting my eyes. It's everything I always wanted to

hear, but now that it's actually happening, it feels different, better and worse, more sticky and complicated than I ever thought was possible. "Why? Why me? I'm not who I used to be. I'm not the same girl."

"You're not who you used to be," he says, twirling a piece of my hair around his finger. "Trixie changed you, just like she changed Toby. And me." He pauses. "We're not the same anymore, but I still feel the same about you."

I don't know how long we sit like that, staring at each other. "I'll call you," he eventually says. "I promise. If this works, if I make it out in one piece. And if you want to talk to me, you'll answer. If you don't want me in your life, I won't bother you again."

He's saying everything I've always wanted to hear, but I'm not ready to hear it, to attach myself to the idea of Beau all over again. After a long pause, I tell him not what I think he wants to hear, but the truth.

"I need some time too. You put me through a lot. I need to figure out who I actually am, not who I am with another person. I think you understand."

He nods. He does understand. He has been Beau the brother and Beau the boyfriend and Beau the football star, but never just Beau Hunter. I've been me with Jenny and Alison and me with Trixie, and now I need to find out who I am when I stand alone.

After I help him up and we say goodbye, I watch him walk down my driveway, pulling his hood up over his head. "I love you," I say, even though he can't hear me. Or maybe because he can't hear me. And when I can't see him anymore, when he's fully out of sight, what he said hits me. *And everything I wasn't looking for that I need is right in front of me.*

I run upstairs as fast as I can, pain shooting through the right side of my stomach. I open my dresser drawer with trembling hands and pull out the tank top I bought at the store.

JERSEY GIRL

I rummage around on my desk for my NYU acceptance letter. Underneath it, buried in the pile, is my letter from Princeton, folded up and stuck back in its manila envelope. I stare at the return address. New Jersey.

The tank top she wore to the party, the one the police found folded on top of her flip-flops on the beach. It was too big for her and I wondered why she chose it that night. She didn't wear that shirt by accident. She didn't leave a suicide note. She left a two-word map, a clue I failed to see, even though it was there the entire time, begging to be discovered. She left me a bread crumb after all.

I open my laptop and pull up Trixie's email, my fingers hovering over the keys, terrified to hit the letters in case I'm wrong and this isn't her password. Or in case I'm right, because the truth is, I'm scared of whatever there is to find.

j-e-r-s-e-y-g-i-r-l

The two seconds it takes for her inbox to open are agonizing. Then I see them, all of the messages.

I start from the beginning.

90

EMAILS FLOOD THE screen. Hundreds of them, all from Toby Hunter, all the same email thread with the same completely benign subject line: *hey*.

I didn't think I would be surprised. This is what I have been looking for the whole time, everything I suspected was under the surface. But the shock is still crippling. It still sends waves through my body, a flurry of invisible knives slicing up my gut. I scroll down to the very bottom, dated January 18, 2017, and read the conversation between them.

> the_toby_hunter@gmail.com
> *Sorry you got stuck with me for a lab partner, I know I suck. But hey, I'm great at orals.*

> wickedtrix00@gmail.com
> *Fuck you.*

> the_toby_hunter@gmail.com
> *I meant oral presentations. What did you think I meant? Look, sorry I bailed on the last assignment. Football crap got in the way. Let me make it up to you?*

wickedtrix00@gmail.com
And how do you plan on doing that, exactly?

the_toby_hunter@gmail.com
Meet me in the library after school. I'll bring the coffee, you bring the textbooks and that wizard brain of yours. (Just kidding, I'll bring my own textbook. But you should still bring that wizard brain, because mine's, well, kind of crappy. Too many hits on the field, you see.)

wickedtrix00@gmail.com
More like too many beers.

I scroll farther up the chain, heart pounding, landing on March fourth. Trixie's birthday.

the_toby_hunter@gmail.com
Happy birthday, Wizard. Did you like my present?

wickedtrix00@gmail.com
That was from you? And stop calling me that.

the_toby_hunter@gmail.com
You told me you it was your favorite, remember? Or did I get it wrong? I thought you said peace lily. You told me you liked plants, not flowers, because flowers are already dying.

wickedtrix00@gmail.com
I barely remember that. How do you?

the_toby_hunter@gmail.com
Because it was important.

When I reach April, my chest constricts and I can barely breathe. The pain in my stomach amplifies, an excruciating crescendo.

the_toby_hunter@gmail.com .
I'm sorry, but I can't do what I said I was going to do. I can't pretend it was a one-time mistake, because I don't want it to be. I want it to happen again.

wickedtrix00@gmail.com
Look, we were both upset and going through stuff. I was pissed off at Jasper and you were mad at your girlfriend and we both agreed that it didn't happen, because too many people would get hurt. I'm seeing someone too, you know. This was a bad fucking idea. Anyone could have seen. God, it was stupid.

the_toby_hunter@gmail.com
Fuck, don't make me feel needy here, Wizard. I know we both felt that. Kind of like in class, that whole laws of attraction thing.

wickedtrix00@gmail.com
And that just goes to show how much you don't pay attention in class.

I skip past a bunch of one-line arguments to June, just after junior prom.

wickedtrix00@gmail.com

> *You bastard. You completely suck, you know?*
> *You made me go and fall in love with you and*
> *then you take her to that stupid dance and*
> *probably fucked her after. I wasn't kidding,*
> *this is so over. In fact, this never happened.*
> *I'm deleting you. Click.*

the_toby_hunter@gmail.com

> *Wizard, it was just for show. I told you, I'm*
> *breaking up with her. We just had to do the*
> *stupid prom thing because my dad was on*
> *my back about it. He rented the limo and*
> *already got a fucking corsage and everything.*

wickedtrix00@gmail.com

> *Yeah, because your daddy runs your life. I'm*
> *sick of hearing your sob story. God, just get*
> *over yourself. I'm not waiting around for you.*
> *In fact, there's another guy who loves me*
> *more than you do. He's better for me. It's*
> *better that we go our separate ways.*

the_toby_hunter@gmail.com

> *But you don't love him.*

wickedtrix00@gmail.com

> *So? You can learn to love someone, it's not*
> *that hard.*

I keep scrolling until August twenty-ninth, two days before Toby disappeared.

wickedtrix00@gmail.com
> *You sure you want to do this? You're going to blow the lid off your whole perfect little life. You can't go back.*

the_toby_hunter@gmail.com
> *My life's not perfect. Not sneaking around like this. I'm over it. Plus, I think Beau suspects something. I already told you, he knows something is up. I'm getting bad at covering my tracks. Maybe because I just don't want to anymore.*

wickedtrix00@gmail.com
> *What are you going to tell your dad? About the ring and stuff?*

the_toby_hunter@gmail.com
> *I don't know. He's going to kill me. You know, he had it in his head that I was going to marry Gabby, ever since I was fifteen years old.*

wickedtrix00@gmail.com
> *Maybe we should just go away somewhere. Drive away and not tell anyone where we're going.*

My breath catches in my throat and I press my knee into my chest. This is it, I think. This is where they planned it. This is where I'll find what I have been looking for.

the_toby_hunter@gmail.com
> *We're not going anywhere.*

Then the messages stop. I blink at the screen in confusion and grimace as my stomach flips in on itself. Then I see the date for the next message.

July 1, 2018.

A week after Trixie's graduation.

The same week she dyed her hair brown.

the_toby_hunter@gmail.com
> *Wizard, it's me. Please, be there.*

wickedtrix00@gmail.com
> *If this is someone's idea of a sick joke, it's not funny. Leave me alone or I'll call the cops.*

the_toby_hunter@gmail.com
> *It's me. I did it. I went away, just like you wanted us to. I made a whole life out here. And now I'm ready for you to join me. Wizard, you have to believe me. How can I prove it to you?*

wickedtrix00@gmail.com
> *Show up at my door. Pick up the phone and call me. No? Okay, I'm calling the cops.*

the_toby_hunter@gmail.com
> *I can't do that, Wizard, because it's not safe. They're watching me.*

wickedtrix00@gmail.com
> *Who's watching you? Who are you? Come on, this is really freaking me out.*

the_toby_hunter@gmail.com

> *You have a tattoo of a rosebud on the very top of your inner thigh. You only let me come over when your dad wasn't around, because that's not how you wanted him to meet me. You used to flash me a peace sign every time I drove away and when I asked, you said it was because you didn't want it to be good-bye. We first had sex in the back seat of my car in the school parking lot, when it was pouring rain. Your back was pressed against the window and after it was over, you stormed into the rain and ran away. I started calling you Wizard when we were partners because that's what you were to me, a wizard.*

wickedtrix00@gmail.com

> *Oh my God oh my God oh my God. Toby, where are you? You realize everyone thinks you're dead? Including me, until ten seconds ago? Why did you put me through that? It doesn't even matter, I'll do anything to see you again, please, please come back to me.*

the_toby_hunter@gmail.com

> *I'll explain everything, I promise. But I need you to come to me. I'm somewhere we can finally be together with nobody else getting in our way.*

I click open each email frantically, the back-and-forth banter, the plans being made. I don't realize I'm crying until

I feel tears hit the neckline of my shirt. It just hurts so badly, all of this. All the time Trixie spent on her phone, the time she snapped at me when I came up behind her and she was on the computer. This is why. He was on the other side, messaging back.

the_toby_hunter@gmail.com
> *I'm in New Jersey. I have a place here, a job.*
> *A whole new life. It's everything we always*
> *talked about.*

wickedtrix00@gmail.com
> *Why New Jersey?*

the_toby_hunter@gmail.com
> *Why not?*

And a day later, another message.

wickedtrix00@gmail.com
> *There's a lot of stuff you don't know. Stuff*
> *I did after you left. Things got bad. I thought*
> *you were dead, and I wanted to die too.*
> *I even tried to cut my wrists, but I couldn't go*
> *deep enough. Maybe I knew you were still*
> *alive the whole time. But some of the things*
> *I did, I'm not sure you can forgive.*

the_toby_hunter@gmail.com
> *Whatever you did, it's okay. I love you. We're*
> *going to be okay.*

wickedtrix00@gmail.com
> *I'm coming, Toby. But not yet. I can't do that*

*to them, to Fiona and my dad. I don't know
how to tell them. Fiona and I were supposed
to go to New York together. She's going to be
devastated.*

She had doubts. I read them, the words stabbing into me like daggers, my own name a deadly weapon. I wasn't nothing to her. We were real. New York was real.

wickedtrix00@gmail.com
*I don't know if I can do this. I'm freaking out,
Toby. I never even ran away as a kid, you
know? My dad will blame himself.*

the_toby_hunter@gmail.com
*I love you so much. And it won't always be
this hard, once we're together. I'm sorry that
it has to be like this. But if life were that easy,
everyone would be in it.*

I read as the whole plan gets hatched. Her trip to New Jersey, how she'd take the bus and hitch rides the rest of the way and use her fake ID if she had to stay anywhere. They covered every single possible scenario, every bump in the road. Except for one.

wickedtrix00@gmail.com
*I'm not leaving anything behind, Toby.
I'm never coming back.*

I double over in pain. I imagine Trixie at the beach, kicking off her flip-flops and pulling the JERSEY GIRL shirt over her head. She had to leave something behind. Her version of a suicide note. She was scared, too afraid to cut all ties. So she left one right in plain sight, but I didn't catch on until it was too late.

But then I get to a message that makes my blood run cold. A day after Alison's party.

wickedtrix00@gmail.com
You said you'd be here. Where are you?

the_toby_hunter@gmail.com
I had to move. Someone was onto me. Just wait, lie low. I'll let you know where I am.
I love you.

wickedtrix00@gmail.com
Toby, I'm freaking out. God, where are you?

the_toby_hunter@gmail.com
There's a bridge we can meet at. Here are the directions to get there. Tonight, midnight.
I'll be waiting.

Then the messages stop abruptly, on both sides. My fingertips are numb, my heart racing so fast I'm sure it's going to choose now to give out. I pinch my arms and legs because this must be some awful nightmare that I'm going to wake up from soon. And just when I think it can't possibly get any worse, that my shoulders are going to break if another ounce of pain is added to them, I scroll back and not just read but actually see the words that permanently flip my whole world upside down.

But if life were that easy, everyone would be in it.

I scream out, punch my desk. I'm back in the motel with Jasper. My voice, thick with tears. *I just don't understand why she did it. Why she needed so badly to get out of her life.*

Jasper, trailing little circles down my arm. *If life were that easy, everyone would be in it.*

There's a ringing sound coming from far away, maybe the phone, maybe the doorbell. Or maybe it's the ringing in my ears. I curl up in a ball on my carpet, wanting to make it all go away, wanting to rub out the past year, wishing I didn't know any of this. I should have been like everyone else and accepted that she was in some watery grave. I could have gotten over that, but not this.

A pair of shoes appears before my eyes. Clunky black boots, the kind Jasper wears. *I never locked the door.* He crouches down in front of me and tries to touch me but I swat him away.

"It was you," I sob. "It was you the whole time. You made her leave." More pain coming from somewhere inside me, like my stomach is being torn apart, ripped open at the seams. My scream rattles my own eardrums.

"Fiona, what are you talking about?" he says as I roll away from him.

"The emails," I yell. "I found them. I know it was you. I'm calling the police and telling them everything."

"Wait, please," he says, crouching down beside me and prying my face out of my hands. "Wait, please, look at me. You don't know what you're saying. Can we please talk about this? What emails are you talking about?"

I try to sit up but it hurts too much. I look at the walls, the boxed-up Barbies I didn't have the heart to get rid of, the spot where my sewing machine used to be. I don't look at him. I'm alone with him and he did this and he could hurt me, shut me up. I want to cry out for Beau to come back, but he's gone and nobody can help me.

"It was you. If life were that easy, everyone would be in it? You were him. You—you—"

"No," he says, gripping my wrists. "I can explain everything. Will you let me explain?" His eyes are wide and unblinking and his voice is getting faster, higher, more panicked, and that's the scariest thing of all, Jasper coming apart in front of me. I pull away from him and he starts moving his mouth, gaping like a fish, but no sound is coming out. Maybe that's what happens. Maybe everyone gets a quota of lies and he has used all of his.

"How," I say, pushing my back against my desk. "How could you do that to her? How could you—pretend to be him? Don't you know what you did?" I start to cry, huge tears that make my whole body convulse.

"Fiona," Jasper says, his eyes bulging, but this time it's like he's underwater. Except, the more I kick my feet, the closer he gets. His hands are on my shoulders now. I know his secret. He knows I know. *What is he going to do to me?*

"I didn't mean to hurt her," he says, but so quietly that I can almost convince myself I never heard anything.

"What did you do to her?" I wiggle away from him. *What is he capable of?*

"It just happened. I didn't mean it. Please. I'll tell you, I swear I'll tell you the truth. But there's something wrong."

"Everything's wrong," I say, my breath coming in ragged gasps. "It's all wrong. Every second of the whole time I have known you was wrong."

I stand up too fast and almost immediately I'm on my knees again, grabbing at the carpet. This pain is coming from inside me, inside my body, not from the words Jasper is saying. He's right—something is wrong. I must be dying, eaten alive by everybody's secrets, and this one won't fit inside me. There are too many lies cloistered in there already, jostling for space.

"You need to go to the hospital," Jasper says, his face ghost-white, except I don't know what his panic is for, because I'm dying or because he's afraid I'll tell. Maybe he wants me to die, because his secret dies with me.

"No," I say, but the stabbing in my right side is more intense than ever and I know there's something very wrong with me. There are too many secrets and they all want out. Something is ruptured. Some vital organ. Maybe my heart, if it's even still beating.

I don't have a choice, so I let Jasper lead me to my car and strap me into the passenger seat. I don't remember much about the ride except his hand on the back of my neck. At first I recoil from his touch, thinking he's trying to strangle me. What would he do to keep me quiet?

"Where is she?" I mutter under my breath. "Where is she now?"

"I'm going to make it all right," he says, but when he touches me again, I flinch.

Even in the hospital parking lot, I don't want to go inside. I just want to stay in the car and wait to wake up from the nightmare. But Jasper drags me in by the hand, his eyes wild.

"I don't know what's wrong with her," Jasper says once we're in a too-bright emergency room. "She's sick."

Usually, you have to wait in the emergency room. I waited for hours the time I cut my finger open on a knife while I was cutting fruit. Mom wrapped it in a tea towel and drove me to this very hospital, perfectly calm, even as my blood soaked through the towel.

Today, I don't have to wait. Questions are shot at me like bullets. *Are you on drugs? Have you been drinking? Did you ingest anything toxic? Do you have a history of thyroid problems?*

I want to tell them everything. All of my secrets and especially what Jasper did, whatever it was, because I know it was his fault. He did something to her and she's never coming back.

But before I can say it, everything goes dark.

91

THE PURPOSE OF an appendix has long been debated. Apparently, it was seen as useless for years, but now doctors believe it stores good bacteria and is involved in immune functions. If that's true, mine didn't do its job. Mine decided to betray me, just like the people I let into my life.

"The surgery went great," the doctor told me when I woke up afterward. "No complications. We had to perform an emergency appendectomy. We managed to get it out before it ruptured. You were lucky."

I nodded, feeling groggy and numb and not lucky at all. He kept going on about how if left untreated, an inflamed appendix will burst and spill into your abdomen. That part can kill you. Something that's supposed to help protect your body from bad things can be what blows you up.

"You're lucky he brought you in when he did," the doctor says now, gesturing to the door. "Your friend. He made the right call."

"My friend," I mouth, my lips cotton-dry. There's that word again, *lucky*. I'm not. *I didn't mean to hurt her.* Even though it feels like my brain is wrapped in something fuzzy, like gauze, I need to know the truth.

"He has been waiting to see you, but if you'd rather not

have visitors, I'll tell him to head on home. We also called your mother. She's on her way here."

I don't want to see Jasper. I don't want to see Jasper ever again but I need to see him, because otherwise I'll never know.

"Did he save my life?"

The doctor gives me a smile like he feels sorry for me, like I'm asking the wrong questions. "If you hadn't come to the hospital when you did, things might have been a lot worse. But I promise, you're in the clear now. You won't even miss that appendix."

He's trying to make a joke but I know what's under his words. He thinks Jasper is a good person, someone who cares, someone who made the right call. Someone who helps, not hurts. He's wrong.

Jasper walks in, staring at the floor, and folds into a chair beside my bed like he's purposely trying not to take up too much space. "How are—" he starts, but I don't let him finish.

"You did something to her." My voice is small and far away and I'm weirdly detached from my emotions. Maybe some of those went out with the appendix. The useless ones, like caring. "You hurt her. Where is she, Jasper?"

His eyes dart around, like he's trying to make sure we're alone. I almost wish we weren't. Hospitals are supposed to be safe, but he could still hurt me like he hurt her. He could make it look like an accident.

"You made her think he was still alive," I say when he doesn't respond, my voice almost a whisper. "Is she still alive?"

He sighs and then I realize he's crying, his head hanging down like it's too heavy for his neck. I stare at his blond roots, at who he really is. "It was never supposed to go that far. It just started out because I wanted to know the truth. That she was seeing someone else. I didn't know it was him, but I knew her well enough to know she was covering something up. And finally, I saw her with him, running through the rain together to his car. I was going to surprise her with flowers, but I just stood outside and watched them together." He clenches his hands.

"The next day in the lab, she acted like he didn't exist, same as always. But something had changed. I gave her the chance to tell me herself. I asked her point-blank if she was seeing someone else, and she said no. So I hacked into her email and found their messages. Then he was gone, and for a while, I thought she could be happy with me. But I could never make her happy. I was so mad, Fiona. Mad at her and mad at myself and mad at Toby. So I hacked into his email and played a really stupid joke. They made it easy. Their passwords were each other's first and last names." He pauses. "Then it all got so out of control."

Her password. j-e-r-s-e-y-g-i-r-l. She must have changed it before she left, a lifeline tossed out for someone who knew her well enough to go looking.

"You drove her away," I say. "What happened after that?"

"I went," he says. "To New Jersey. This town called Lambertville on the Delaware River. I was going to be there and she was going to see that I was the one who cared. The guy who was always there for her. And we were going to come back home together."

I thought about Trixie's funeral, about how Jasper wasn't there. Now I know where he was. I tried to picture Trixie seeing him instead of Toby, the way disappointment and shock would sharpen her features.

"But what happened? She wouldn't come back with you?"

Jasper looks around again. I'm very aware that the door to my room is closed. The doctor said I could press the button on my bed if I needed help, but maybe help won't get here fast enough. My hand hovers over the button.

"It was an accident," he practically whispers. "She was standing on this bridge, where I told her to meet Toby. To meet me. I came up behind her and put my hands over her eyes. She turned around and smiled, then she saw it was me and freaked out." His voice catches. "She pushed me into the railing. I told her it was me the whole time, that Toby wasn't coming back. I said we were meant to be together. But she just kept shoving me and trying to punch me. I grabbed her to make her quiet down, and she wouldn't. She started to scream and that's when I . . ." He trails off.

"That's when you what?" I feel like I'm going to throw up. I ball my hands into weak fists, knowing I can't do anything with them.

"I shoved her. She was shoving me, and I just shoved back, and I didn't mean to shove so hard—but she lost her balance and went over. She was wearing that backpack and she just disappeared under the water. I was going to jump in after her but the current was so strong, and I couldn't even see her anymore. I ran down to the banks, figuring she'd wash up onshore and I could save her. But she never did. I walked back and forth for hours. And the next day I checked the news, and the day after that, and I'm still doing it every single day, because her body must be out there somewhere and it's going to wash up and somebody's going to find it."

He starts to cry in earnest. Obviously, this is the first time he's telling this story, maybe even the first time he's admitting to himself what he did. I shared most of this year with a monster. I started kissing Jasper as a way to get revenge on Trixie, but the whole time I was playing house with her killer.

Killer.

Trixie is dead. She really did drown with that backpack on. She really is in a watery grave. Except, she didn't walk into the water. She was pushed into it. I try to imagine what her last moments were like, the panic that must have spread over her body like fire and ice, the helplessness she felt when the river dragged her under. I wonder if she looked up at Jasper and knew he would be the last person she ever saw. I wonder if she thought about Toby. I wonder if she believed in an afterlife where she would get to be with him.

I can keep wondering forever but what I want to do is go back in the past, to a stupid-hot September day when I was walking to cheerleading practice with Jenny. All I want to do is go to that practice and not run back to my car.

"I'm going to call the police and tell them everything." The coldness in my voice surprises me. I don't care about Jasper anymore. Whatever part of me ever cared about him is gone, weighted to the bottom of a river in New Jersey. He once mentioned that Byron St. James remembered all the details because he saw Trixie die and you don't forget watching a person die. But he was talking about himself the whole time. I wonder how many times a day he sees her face, hears the splash she made when she landed in the water.

"Don't." Jasper wipes his face, clears his throat. "Don't call them. I'll do it myself. If that's what you want."

I almost press the button, but the doctor's words echo in my ear. *You were lucky. Your friend. He made the right call.*

"This whole year was one giant lie," I say. "You knew she wasn't in Tijuana. You just didn't want me to get close to figuring it out. You just wanted to keep me in the dark. *That's* why you got close to me."

"No," Jasper says, reaching for one of my hands. "Tijuana was so you'd see she was gone. I wanted us to move on together. I love you."

I pull my hands away. "Just like you loved her."

"We could be together, you know," he says, hushed. "Keeping this from you almost killed me. Now that you know the truth, and that it was an accident, you know all the dark parts of me. You know I'm not a bad person. I just made a mistake."

It's crazy, but for a second, I think about what that would look like, us being together. Nobody would ever know the truth except me and Jasper. I don't owe Trixie anything. She never cared about me, and Jasper does. He pushed her, but he didn't mean to kill her. Or at least, that's what he wants me to believe, and what he wants to believe. Maybe he meant it.

Or maybe he picked that bridge in the first place because he knew it was easy for a person to go over the railing. Maybe he smiled when he heard the splash. Maybe he laughed as he wrote those emails, picturing Trixie's face when she opened them.

"I swear, Fiona. It was an accident. I messed up so badly, and I have to live with that. But you don't have to throw away what we have."

I don't know what version of Jasper to believe. The one who loved Trixie or the one who says he loves me, the one who killed her or the one who saved my life when he could have left me to die in my bedroom with a burst appendix. I can go to the police and tell them everything, or I can keep it all inside me, stretched under my skin. But for once in my life, I know what I have to do. That's the thing about choices: When you put them on either side of a scale, they never weigh the same.

One is bound to be heavier.

92

SHE'S NOT COMING back. And I'm not sure I would even want her to. Because I don't think she would ever forgive me, and I don't know if I can forgive her either.

I still see her a hundred times a day, in a hundred different girls I pass on the street, in the mall, everywhere. She's every girl with short blond hair and a lip ring. She's every girl with long brown hair and a collarbone that juts out. She's every girl with a cigarette, every girl in denim cutoff shorts. She's every laughing girl, every crying girl, every girl standing by herself, every girl in a hurry with her head down. She's everywhere and nowhere, just like she was the whole time I knew her.

Maybe I made the wrong choice, because I still think about the other way my life could have gone. I think a lot about choices these days. Not just the huge, colossal ones that plant themselves like boulders in front of you. Those start to crash down, even when you push your whole weight against them. Those, inevitably, will crush you.

But so will the pebbles, the little bits of plaster that crumble down. You don't think about those at the time. They're so small, so insignificant. You wipe off the dust and forget about them. You shouldn't. Because being buried alive really does happen.

I chose to blow off cheerleading that day, and I chose to drive with her away from Robson. I chose Trixie, and she chose me. I thought I knew her, but everything was the opposite. Her happy was sad. Her sad was jealous. Her jealous was angry. She wore her emotions like clothes, and none of them fit right.

Sometimes I think of me and Trixie as people in one of Alison's favorite rom-com movies, except without the happy ending. She picked me for a reason, because she wanted to break Beau for the way he wrecked her life. She didn't care about what it would do to me, not at first. But it became about a lot more than revenge to her. It turned into friendship and sisterhood, and when she left to find Toby, I like to think it was hard for her to leave me.

I could be wrong. But I don't think anyone can lie that well.

EPILOGUE

Six months later

WINTER IS EVERYTHING I thought it would be. Big
coats and fuzzy hats and mittens and boots. Snow, actual
snow, not just shaving cream and baking soda. Sometimes,
when I'm all bundled up and trudging across campus, I feel
tiny, like I could disappear going from my dorm room to the
lecture hall and nobody would even notice.

I have disappeared, but only from the broken versions
of myself, and reappeared as someone I want to be. I cut my
hair short and used my graduation money from Mom to
buy a new sewing machine, a big one that sits in the corner
of my dorm room and takes up too much space. I haven't done
anything with it yet, but I will. I don't talk to Dr. Rosenthal
anymore, but I'm seeing someone here. Little by little, I'm trying to be nicer to myself, to not feel like such a prisoner in my
own body. Maybe one day I'll even like who I see when I look
in the mirror.

I'm starting to understand Trixie more and more, why
she got so deep into becoming somebody else. It's easier than
I thought it would be to shed my old skin. Nobody here
knows anything about me or Trixie or any of last year. I make

myself talk to everybody. I go to the bar with my fake ID and drink frothy beers out of huge pint glasses. I study in the drafty library with hot chocolate. I have a group of friends, including Alison—who is in two of my classes. We're not like we used to be, but we might be able to get there again. Right now, I don't let anyone get too close. Trixie left a space that is not only too big, but too oddly shaped for me to ever fill, no matter how many people I try to stuff into it.

Sometimes I think I'm just a repeat of the women in my life who made huge mistakes. I'm my mom, a teenager dealing with things so much bigger than she is. I'm Jenny, whose heart got broken in a million pieces. I'm Trixie, a girl who loved the wrong boy and lied to protect that love. But mostly I'm just me, a girl who figured out who she was the hard way.

Today, I can't pay attention because this lecture room has windows and all I want to do is watch the snow falling outside, big fat flakes and little flurries. Everything is white. Blanked out. A fresh slate. At least, that's what I tell myself.

He's waiting for me after class, standing in the stairwell outside Intro to Fashion Design. He's put on weight since last year. His jawline isn't as sharp and his ribs don't jut out and his arms are meaty where they used to be wiry. I like feeling smaller than him, I like how his body curves around mine in my little dorm room bed.

He wraps me in a one-armed hug and kisses my cheek. He's holding out a coffee. I smile and take it, and now that both his hands are free, he puts one on each of my cheeks. One is hot and the other is ice-cold. He has stubble on his cheeks and chin, and it's coarse against my skin as he gently places his lips on mine.

"'The heart will break, yet brokenly live on,'" he whispers so quietly the wind almost carries away his words.

"Lord Byron," I say. He bought me a real book, just like he said he would, but I kept the disintegrated one too, because it's a reminder that you can dig up the past and, sometimes, you can fix what was wrong with it.

We walk across Washington Square Park holding hands. We're together now. Boyfriend and girlfriend, out in the open. He doesn't go to school, but now that he's clean, now that he goes to AA meetings every day, he's thinking about starting next year, maybe studying poetry. Or astronomy. He rides his bike everywhere, and sometimes I ride on it with him, gripping the handlebars tightly. We can't go back to the people we were, but the people we are feel something like okay.

"I love you," Beau says, spinning me around to kiss me in the snow. After everything, all the times I wanted to say it to his face, he was the one to say it first.

It was always Beau. He was always the choice that weighed the most. I didn't report Jasper to the police, because after I told him I would, he went and turned himself in. He's spending the next several years at a psychiatric hospital in Chula Vista. Maybe I'll visit him one day, but probably not. We wrote emails to each other for a while, which is morbid in itself, considering emails were the trail that led Trixie out of her life and onto that bridge. Sometimes I wish I could fully hate him, cut off all communication with him and pretend he doesn't exist. But the truth is, he's the last link I have to Trixie, and he might have saved my life. That bond is something I wish could cave in on itself, but it never will.

I got an envelope in the mail from him yesterday, a picture

of me and Trixie. The one that used to be in our locker, the one that disappeared from the frame. Just the picture—no note, no explanation.

Maybe we have both said all we could possibly say.

I think about what his jealousy drove him to do and I can't breathe, because I used to be jealous too. Jealous of Trixie, jealous of Jenny, jealous of people who had what I didn't. Jealousy is on the inside like a bad appendix, something you don't need that can burst and destroy you. Maybe I was closer than I think to letting it ruin me.

I still have the list, the one I made with *REASONS WHY TRIXIE DISAPPEARED* written at the top of the page. There's still only one name under it: Jasper Hart. Turns out, I was right the entire time, from the very beginning.

"What are you thinking about?" Beau asks as we descend a hill, our boots crunching the snow underfoot.

I kiss him again. He asks me that a lot. *What are you thinking about?* I never tell him the truth. We don't talk about Jasper. We don't talk about what happened between Toby and Trixie. I know that Beau likes to pretend they're out there together, that they both found their way to the surface and met up somewhere in the world. He likes the lie—points out that no bodies were ever found to prove otherwise.

I don't tell him I'm thinking about them. I never do. We're supposed to have moved on. So in a way, I guess I'm still lying, and I always will be.

"I'm thinking," I say, "that I want us to build a snowman. A real one."

So right there, halfway between the lecture hall and my dorm room, somewhere between my old life and this new place, we do.

ACKNOWLEDGMENTS

I STARTED WRITING what would become *Last Girl Lied To* while flying to Costa Rica for my honeymoon. Looking out the airplane window, I considered the vastness of the world, and how easy it would be for a person to disappear into it. From there, I wondered what would make someone want to vanish entirely, and Trixie Heller was born. (I promise, the rest of my honeymoon was not morbid.)

I'm incredibly fortunate to have worked with an amazing team to make *Last Girl Lied To* come to life. Thank you to my agent, Kathleen Rushall, for believing in this book and helping it find the perfect home. To my editor, Erin Stein, whose brilliant insights made the story both darker and more incisive. To Nicole Otto, for your editing prowess. To Natalie Sousa, Connie Gabbert, and Jessica Chung, for creating a cover that perfectly encapsulates the pages within. To Dawn Ryan and Kerry Johnson, for whipping this story into shape with their copyediting magic. (Apparently I'll never know how to properly use further/farther.) Thanks also to production manager Raymond Ernesto Colón, and everyone at Imprint who helped *Last Girl Lied To* become a book.

I'm not sure where I would be without my critique partner and writer friends. Endless hugs to Emily Martin for years of support and friendship, and the many hours you have devoted to reading my work (and my long, rambling emails). You understand my books so well and your suggestions always make them better.

Move to Canada so we can hang out more in person! Panda love to Samantha Joyce, who always lends an ear and champions my writing (and makes the coolest book-cover cupcakes you've ever seen). Wine and cheese to Marci Lyn Curtis for the hilarious DM chats, book love, and Jax Teller GIFs. (Keep sending those, please!) To all of my Sweet Sixteen and Sixteen to Read friends—I'm honored to still be on this crazy roller coaster with you years after we debuted, and I'm excited for our careers to keep evolving. Thank you for encouraging mine.

My biggest supporters have always nurtured my unruly imagination, starting with the two people who knew I was meant to be a writer: my parents, Denis and Lucy Burns. Thank you for literally everything—for cheering on every crazy dream I've had to sending me home with leftovers aplenty because you know I have no time to cook. I hope to raise my daughter to be fearless and bold, just as you raised me. I love you both more than I could ever say.

To my sister/BFF, Erin Shakes—you'll always be my partner in crime, no matter how old we get. Thanks for all the chips and dip nights, shopping trips, and many (many) shared bottles of wine. I'm so glad we both have little girls (hi, Fiona!) who can grow up to be as close as we are. To my brother-in-law Jermaine Shakes, thanks for your energy and positivity, and for recommending my books to all your family and friends.

Thank you to the entire Flynn clan for your bottomless support. To the best in-laws, Jim and Doreen, and a special shout-out to Suzanne for telling literally everybody about my debut. To my many girlfriends—you know who you are, and I consider myself lucky to be surrounded by so many inspiring women. To the ladies of the RBF row for never failing to make me laugh (often at myself). To my extended family, especially Aunt Linda, Uncle Tom, and Aunt Pat, for being here for all of my milestones.

And to my guardian angels Grandma Gibb and Grandma Burns, who I know are looking out for me from somewhere right now.

A thousand butterfly kisses for my daughter, Astrid, for being the sunshine in every single day and my forever muse. I want to write strong, complicated girls that you can someday read about. (Just not quite yet.) Undying love for my husband, Steve, for indulging my writerly whims and giving me the time and space I need to create characters and their stories. Thanks for bouncing ideas around, walking miles in the woods, hugging me when I need it (always!), and loving me even when I'm in my own little world (also, most always). I couldn't imagine building a life with anyone else but you.

Abby the Chihuahua—we've been together for over thirteen years, and you've seen it all. I firmly believe you bring me good luck. And yes, Hans, you're pretty cool, too.

Last, but certainly not least, thank you to all of the book bloggers, booksellers, librarians, teachers, and readers for your passion, enthusiasm, and adoration of books. I'm so grateful to be part of this community. This story belongs to you now—I hope you enjoy it.